FICTION   Campbell, Ramsey.
           The face that must die / Ramsey Campbell. --
           c1983.

           ISBN: $12.95.

           I. Title.

THE FACE
THAT MUST
DIE

SCREAM/PRESS

SANTA CRUZ,
CALIFORNIA
1983

RAMSEY CAMPBELL

Illustrated by J.K. Potter

CONTENTS

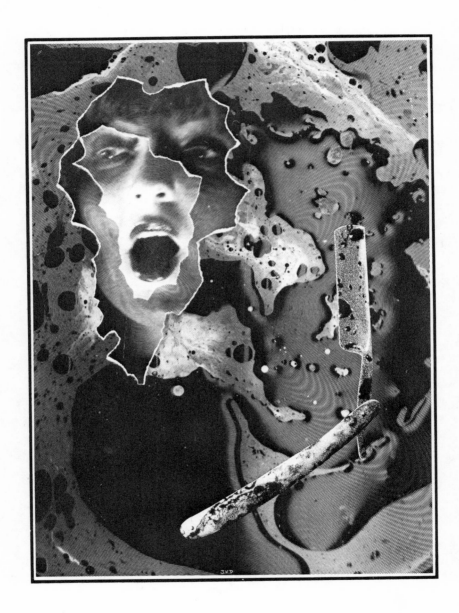

TEXT ILLUSTRATIONS

Foreword

When I met Ramsey Campbell the first thing I noticed about him was his grin.

Having read his work, I more or less expected to see it, and I wasn't disappointed. The grin was there because almost all of them seem to have it—Stephen King, Peter Straub, Richard Matheson, Ray Bradbury, and a half-dozen others. It comes with the territory, and with such grins on their faces I can hardly wait to see their skulls.

At any rate (as my agent so frequently says) Ramsey Campbell's grin is especially broad, even for a writer of horror fiction, and there's ample reason for it to be emblazoned on his face. I sometimes suspect that many of us who work in this genre tend to cultivate grins in order to disarm those who might feel that we resemble the characters we write about. The broad smile indicates just how harmless and lovable we really are, and as such it's about as convincing as a not-guilty plea from Jack the Ripper.

But Campbell's grin has a different reason for being; it is a grin of satisfaction, even triumph—satisfaction in doing what he does best, and triumph in the knowledge that he does it better than most of his contemporaries. There's nothing smug or complacent about the grin; what it indicates is fulfillment. I don't pretend to know what impelled Ramsey Campbell to devote his life to scaring the living hell out of people, but he has certainly succeeded in his endeavors—and in so doing, transcended triteness and transformed the technique of inducing terror into true art.

Perhaps I have a special affinity for Campbell because, in a way, his career parallels my own. I too started, as he did, writing under the influence of H.P. Lovecraft's style and subject matter—though I can't lay claim to having produced anything as effective as his first collection *The Inhabitant of the Lake*.

And again, like Campbell, I gradually developed a style of my own and shifted my attention from Lovecraftian monsters to those one encounters in daily life around us. Once more Campbell has proven his superior mastery in novels like *The Doll Who Ate His Mother* and the book which you—lucky you!—are now holding in your hand.

He has evolved a gritty, utterly and convincingly realistic style reminiscent of the early Graham Greene—The Greene of *Brighton Rock*—but has added an extra dimension of dread. And that, I assure you, is not an easy achievement. Only a few writers can lay claim to such a level of consummate craftsmanship.

But the most gratifying phenomenon attendant upon Ramsey Campbell's work is the constant, unremitting improvement he displays in each successive effort. I can think of no higher accolade to bestow upon *The Face That Must Die* than to say it's arguably his best book thus far. Long may he grin—and I can hardly wait to read his next!

—*Robert Bloch*
April, 1983

At the Back of My Mind:
A Guided Tour

I want to talk honestly at last about why I write what I write. This Introduction Supersedes All Others. In particular I want to suggest why I wrote this book, which of all my stories seems the one most prone to provoke unease or worse. For example, not long ago I was sorting through the horror titles in a second-hand bookstore (split spines, wilting corners, ballpoint scrawls, unidentifiable stains) when the shop woman told me she liked horror too: King, Herbert, but not that Guy N. Smith — rubbish, him. I was opening my mouth when she corrected herself: not Guy N. Smith — who was that writer who set his stories in Liverpool? Ramsey Campbell, that's right — that *Face That Must Die*.

She wouldn't have encountered much disagreement from most of the editors I was published by when I wrote the book. For a while it seemed it would never be published, and the eventual British edition was edited without my knowledge (taking out most of the paranoid puns, which still seem to me to ring truer than almost anything else in the book). The edition you have in front of you is definitive, including a complete restored chapter, but more of that later.

There's no doubt the book is very dark. I had reasons at the time: the first edition of *The Doll Who Ate His Mother* had sold, as Barbara Norville of Bobbs-Merrill put it over Black Russians at Thursday's, "dreadfully"; I'd suffered the aftermath of some psychedelic experiences, had spent a night trying not to see things such as my face becoming mouthless in the bathroom mirror, and was terrified of a recurrence, which led eventually (terror, recurrence, or both) to a writer's block on the first day of chapter X, when I saw the words I was penning begin to writhe on the page. Of all my novels, this is the one that strays least from its original plot, improvised hardly at all once I'd settled on the title, having played with *Knife-Edge* and *The Man Who Killed A Face* and *The Face That Called For Killing*. Under all the circumstances, presumably I was scared to take risks. Really, though, I think the book is so dark (not least in its well-nigh complete identification with Horridge) because its sources in my experience were.

Describing them is a risk in itself. Steve King tells how one Janet Jeppson claimed that he'd been writing about a macabre incident in his childhood "ever since," and I sympathize with his resentment, not least because it's a very small step from "ah, so *that's* what your fiction is about" to "that's *all* your fiction is about." All the same, I think that in interviews I've been too concerned with presenting myself as a genial everyday guy who just happens to write horror stories. Steve King to the contrary, I don't believe there's any such animal. As Steve himself points out, it's pretty strange to write fiction for a living at all, and there are cases besides mine in which the reasons are stranger: Robert Aickman (who wrote, "My father remains the oddest man I have ever known"), and Lovecraft, and two writers with whom I feel a particular affinity, whose family lives gave them an obsession with madness that the conventions of their genre were sometimes unable to contain— Cornell Woolrich and John Franklin Bardin. I have to hope now that knowledge of a writer's life can enrich, rather than diminish, one's reading of his work.

Last year, while reading to a student audience in New York, I had the disconcerting experience of realizing what I had "really" been writing about in several stories: *The Chimney*, and *Mackintosh Willy* (the old man whose face you never see) and *Again*. It seems I had to write about my deepest nightmares before I could remember what they were. The process of overcoming my fears as best I could, which I take to have been the process of gaining confidence as a writer and performer, somehow involved forgetting them while acquiring whatever was necessary—technique, distance, trusting to imaginative instinct— to write about them. It has often been disconcerting to realize that I could have forgotten, or at any rate filed away in the dustiest rooms of my mind, so much.

Though I lived in the same small house (three bedrooms, a bathroom, two rooms downstairs) as my parents, I didn't see my father face to face for nearly twenty years, and that was when he was dying. My first memory of him—of anything, I believe—dates from when I was three years old. He used to take me out on Sundays, and that day he'd walked across the line at the end of a railway platform with me instead of using the pedestrian bridge. He told my mother this, to her horror. They had a hearty argument above my head which ended, as I recall, with my mother ordering him out of the house.

The front door contained nine small panes of glass, reaching from chest level to the top of the door. My father blocked the door from outside as my mother tried to close it: presumably they were struggling for the last word in the argument. My mother's hand went through one of the panes, bloodily.

I remember my mother dripping bright red blood and crying out that he'd deliberately closed the door on her hand. The sight of blood except for my own has distressed me ever since. A neighbor looked after me while her husband took my mother to hospital. I suppose they humored her to calm her down, but they seemed to me to be accepting her version of what had happened. Since my father had fled, I tried to set the record straight. What did I know about it? I was only three years old.

I don't recall the aftermath, but my mother told me years later that she had subsequently asked me in front of my father if I wanted to go out with him again. How could I have said yes when it might have led to another such scene? It feels as if that was the last I saw of my father, though it may not have been. Certainly relations between my parents grew steadily worse, until soon they met hardly at all. One reason must have been that my father (who was in his late forties, my mother having been thirty-six when I was born) felt robbed of his only son.

Divorce wasn't easy in those days, not least because my mother was a Catholic. I accompanied her as she trudged from lawyer to lawyer in a futile quest for legal aid to help her make a case for a divorce on the grounds of mental cruelty. Soon the refusals convinced her that the lawyers were conspiring to thwart her, perhaps on instructions from the police, since my father was a policeman; many people in Liverpool (which she hated) were in on the secret too. Recently I found the notes for a novel she was planning at the time, in which her neighbors were given fictitious names and classed according to their attitudes to her— "snoopers," "kind but afraid for themselves," "were nice but obviously worked on," "passer-on" (of gossip about her, presumably). By now she hated the house for its smallness, and frequently told me how much better her home in Huddersfield had been. She insisted that my father had tricked her into living there by promising it would be temporary, though in fact she had written to him shortly before they were married that she would live there always. They kept each other's letters, and I found them after my mother died.

For most of my childhood, then, my father was heard but not seen. My mother told me things about him (she referred to him solely as "him," in a tone of loathing): though he was a policeman he dressed like a tramp, he spoke several languages but made no use of them, he wrote letters in my name and hers to the Christian Science Monitor (religion therefore being one of their early conflicts, and his use of Americanisms to me another), he'd got her lost on a fell in the Lake District during their honeymoon (an incident which she grew to believe meant he'd tried to kill her), he came downstairs in the mornings and damaged the already dilapidated furniture, he blew his nose with his fingers in the bathroom sink (for years she would go in the bathroom every night as soon as his bedroom door closed and I would hear her ritual cry of disgust), he'd thrown a toy of mine in the fire, she'd given up the love of her life for him. . . . He left her housekeeping money on Fridays, and she cooked his breakfast last thing each night and left it on the table. Now I imagine him coming downstairs in the mornings to be faced by congealed fried egg and bacon seven hours old in the cold kitchen with its flagged floor (hardly surprising if sometimes he went and kicked the furniture), but then his unseen presence was infinitely more powerful than anything I might be told about him.

I used to hear his footsteps on the stairs as I lay in bed, terrified that he would come into my room. Sometimes I heard arguments downstairs as my mother waylaid him when he came home, her voice shrill and clear, his blurred and utterly incomprehensible, hardly a voice, which filled me with a terror I couldn't define. (Being a spectator to arguments has made me deeply nervous ever since.) If he was still in the kitchen when it was time for her to make my breakfast she would drive him out of the house—presumably it was unthinkable that I should share the table with him. Once I found I'd broken a lens of my glasses as I'd put them down by the bed the previous night, and was convinced by my mother that my father had come into the room while I was asleep to break them. In my teens I sometimes came home, from work or from the cinema, at the same time as my father, who would hold the front door closed from inside to make sure we never came face to face. Very occasionally, when it was necessary for him to get in touch, he would leave me a note, in French. (He'd lived in Glasgow, his birthplace, until his family moved to Liverpool.) Worst of all was Christmas, when my mother would send me to knock on his bedroom door and invite him down, as a mark of seasonal goodwill, for Christmas dinner. I would go upstairs in a panic, but there was never any response.

My mother did her best to make up for his absence, though perhaps she never realized that his presence was the problem. We drew pictures together, played word games and board games and cards and ball games, the last of which must have been a trial for her, since she'd suffered a prolapsed womb at my birth. She encouraged me to write and to finish what I wrote. She saved up to take me on holiday to Grange over Sands, where she'd stayed on her honeymoon, or Southport, where her widowed mother lived until she came to stay with us; sometimes we stayed with her sister and brother-in-law in Yorkshire. As I went to films more often in my teens, so did she with me: she liked the Hammer horrors and Tourneur's *Night of the Demon*, William Castle's films and Hitchcock's with the exception of *Psycho, Last Year in Marienbad* and *Muriel* and *8½* and (apart from the rape scene) *The Virgin Spring*, Vincent Price's films except for those he made with Corman, for premature burial was one of her nightmares. Her favorite film, to which I accompanied her dutifully on each reissue, was *Gone with the Wind*. At home we listened to radio shows together — plays and serials and comedies, though she never liked Spike Milligan's "Goon Show," with its gleeful explosion of taboos — or simply sat by the fire and read (sometimes the same authors: Highsmith, Ray Bradbury, Cornelia Otis Skinner). I was always enthralled when she told me her memories, of Father Young, the Catholic priest who used to scuttle after her and her sister in Lon Chaney's latest role, of working at Rushworth's department store in Huddersfield where eventually she became a buyer and where her assistants used to confide all their problems to her, of her years at the Ministry of War Transport and the Christmas Day she had been working there alone while a man prowled outside in the deserted street, her chaste love affairs which she always terminated, her pet dogs (one of which had been kicked to death), the plots in great detail of films she'd admired: *The Barretts of Wimpole Street*, the Mamoulian *Dr Jekyll and Mr Hyde*, the Claude Rains *Phantom of the Opera*. . . . More than once she told me her most terrible memory, of the morning (five days before her birthday, I realized many years later) she found her father burned to death, having had a stroke and fallen on the fire. Recently I found she had shared many of these memories in her several years of correspondence with my father. It was her way of sharing herself, which she did with only a very few people—too few.

I'm reminded by her letters, heartbreaking though I find them, how skillfully she could tell an anecdote. She had published short stories in a Yorkshire journal before the Second World War, and during the war she wrote her first, largely autobiographical, novel. It was encouraged by my father, whom I gather she met through an advertisement she'd placed under a false name (possibly in a writers' journal) for pen friends. As their marriage deteriorated and divorce prooved unavailable, she set her hopes on writing novels, mainly thrillers, to make enough money to bring me up on her own. My impression is that they were technically skillful but already dated. She used numerology to work out which titles ought to bring her good luck. In my early teens she listened to "The Archers," a nightly radio soap opera, and grew convinced that the names and actions of the characters represented messages of hope for her. When her manuscripts were rejected yet again, she concluded that the messages had been deliberate lies, meant to break her down. I think it was then I became fully aware that all was not well with my mother.

I don't think my grandmother was living with us then, but I believe I was only a few years old when she gave up her flat in Southport and divided her time between her two daughters. I don't know why I remember her only in glimpses—her singing "Just a Song at Twilight" to me in a high sweet voice, her groaning loudly on the toilet, her praying ("Through my fault, through my fault, through my most grievous fault") and beating her breast so loudly that I could hear it in my room. I say "my" room, but during my adolescence I shared it and its single bed with my mother. It may be that the reason why she didn't share her mother's room was that she refused to accept there could be anything wrong with her sleeping with me: it must have been about then she began to fulminate Freud and his dirty mind.

My grandmother died of gangrene when I was fifteen. Later my mother told me that she'd found one of her mother's toes in the bed. I was in my room when I heard the doctor pronounce her dead, and I began sobbing uncontrollably. Yet that night, as I lay on the ramshackle couch downstairs because I didn't want to sleep upstairs where the corpse was, I read nearly the whole of a John Dickson Carr novel. Sometime after midnight my mother woke in the chair in which she'd dozed off and told me angrily to go to sleep. Once we returned from the funeral I had my own room at last, and lay in the dark praying hysterically that some undefined terror would stay away from me, now that I no longer had the night light my mother had always kept burning, whether in case she had to go to her mother in the night or in case my father came into the room. Some months later she saw her mother at the top of the stairs, wearing a nightgown which, she claimed, crumpled emptily to the stair and was still there when she went up. Now and then she would feel the ghost of her father tap her meaningfully on the shoulder.

(One more thing I've only now remembered about my grandmother: during her final illness I once had to help lift her onto the bedpan, and this was my first glimpse of a female pubis. It appalled me, and made me think for some reason of a spider.)

It must have been soon after the funeral that we began to have our differences. I was the only one left there in whom she had invested her affection, and I suppose it seemed a betrayal when I turned into a drinking cursing adolescent who read dirty books (Henry Miller and William Burroughs whose banned books I had sent to me from abroad, Nabokov, Lawrence Durrell). I took a wicked delight in quoting her some of the naughty bits and, I admit, in being generally disagreeable. (My correspondents of the time will confirm this: sorry, Alan Dodd, David Johnstone, John Derry . . .) I became involved in science fiction and fantasy fandom, which she viewed with deep suspicion: half the writers were probably homosexual and lying in wait for me. Later I discovered she'd been opening my letters and had written to one correspondent telling him to moderate his language. With very few exceptions she refused to let me invite friends home, since she was ashamed of where she was living. Soon we no longer laughed together, perhaps because I'd grown too pompous to.

All the same, I needed to build my self-confidence somehow. On top of all I've recounted, I spent my adolescence at a Catholic school, much of the time in terror of being beaten for getting answers wrong. In my experience, this is not conducive to learning, and I did rather badly until my last year there, when I was taught by several excellent teachers. (Corporal punishment is a British institution, of course, especially in our pornography, where the use of school settings points up to the Sadean isolation of schools from outside intervention; clearly it appeals to something in the British.) I went into the Civil Service when I was sixteen, and floundered about for several years, trying to relate to people. Several characters in my stories show how I was: Vic and Kirk (both ironically named) in "The Cellars" and "Concussion," Lindsay Rice in "The Scar," Peter in "Napier Court" — Peter being how I became as I put myself together to my own satisfaction, if to nobody else's. You can see what a loudmouth I was from my pontification in the fanzines.

I was twenty when my mother decided I could be left alone while she went into hospital for the operation she should have had twenty years earlier, on her prolapsed womb. A neighbor of about her age, Miss Holme, took in my laundry, much to my embarrassment and resentment. Resentment and impatience and indifference were all I felt at the sight of my mother in a hospital bed, a well-nigh psychotic reaction I have never understood. I remember leaving one Sunday before visiting was over so as not to miss the pre-credit sequence of *Modesty Blaise*; I remember telling my mother that I'd allowed a friend who was giving me a lift to come into the house while I put on my coat. She never forgave me or him for that, and took me to task for it for years.

Her operation led to complications, and she was moved to a different hospital for further treatment. She believed she'd been misled about the operation and its aftermath, and refused to undergo a further operation to repair the damage. She left hospital as soon as she could, and tried to sue the surgeon, but couldn't find a lawyer to take the case.

When I suggested that the lawyers weren't necessarily in league with the surgeon, she felt I had turned against her — that someone had got to me. I don't know if that was the first time I tried to persuade her that things weren't always as they seemed to her: that Liverpool wasn't full of people conspiring against her, that radio programs weren't about her under an imperfectly disguised name. My denials seemed like betrayals to her, and she tried to find reasons why I was changing: I'd turned gay, I was taking drugs (which I wasn't and hadn't been), my friends were turning me against her. Sometimes I tried to argue her out of her paranoia, but it was fruitless: she would accuse me of trying to drive her into a hospital or a home, and make me swear never to have her put away. Increasingly, perhaps defensively, I accepted that this was simply the way she was and that I could do nothing.

The house seemed much smaller. I went to the cinema a great deal by myself. Just as my mother avoided many local shops because she disliked the people there, so she ceased going to church on Sundays, but insisted I continue attending. I strolled to a church a couple of miles away, then turned round and came back, reading a book all the while.

My fiction was becoming steadily more autobiographical. My invented town of Brichester, originally intended as the Severn Valley equivalent of Lovecraft's Arkham, was Liverpool by now in all but name. I believe I was still avoiding using Liverpool itself because my mother had half-convinced me that offended Liverpudlians would hinder publication of anything they thought detrimental to the town. Writing "The Cellars" cured me of that nonsense — it was too good a setting to waste.

I met Jenny Chandler at Eastercon in Oxford, in 1969, after we'd met briefly at the previous year's Eastercon in Buxton. In 1970 we bought a flat in Liverpool, and I moved away from home at last. That year my mother's dog Wag, her pet for most of two decades, died. Soon Miss Holme brought her a dog which both women insisted was the same dog, having escaped the vet who'd pretended to put it down only to take it away for vivisection. I tried to point out that it didn't even look much like Wag, but soon gave up.

Jenny and I had a belated honeymoon in the Lake District in the summer of the following year. I think it was actually on the first day we were away that my father fell (or, according to my mother, was pushed) downstairs at the fireplace manufacturers where he now worked as a clerk, having retired from the police. My mother called me long distance to demand I go back to see him in hospital, but I told her she had to be kidding. Even when we returned to Liverpool a week later, I let a couple of days pass before I made myself go, and then I couldn't find the hospital; my mother had told me it was behind a department store when in fact it was several streets away from the front of the store. I wandered about until visiting time was over. I wasn't trying very hard to find the hospital.

I did find it the next day, and my father. He looked old and feeble and unfamiliar; he wore bandages on his skull and a tube up his penis. Only his blurred murmur, which he must have been unable to control, seemed familiar from all those overheard arguments. I couldn't touch him or understand what he was saying, only feel repelled by my mother's belated concern for him. I left as soon as I could, and a few days later he died.

I attended his funeral in the pouring rain. His sister peered into the open grave and cried "Where's mother?" Subsequently my mother claimed that policemen at the inquest had told her they weren't satisfied that my father had died of natural causes, but I heard no more of this.

The sense of relief I'd felt on leaving home didn't last long, for my wife and my mother disliked each other profoundly. The spectacle of their mutual politeness made me increasingly tense, not least because I felt as if I were somehow in the middle of all this. Besides, her front room seemed unbearably small to me with both of them in it. On the other hand, my mother disliked visiting us when she would have to take a taxi home, for she suspected the drivers of wanting to rape her. Soon I was finding excuses to visit my mother by myself, but this only made her even more suspicious of my wife. She frequently accused me of discussing her with Jenny, though I wasn't; over the years she'd managed to inhibit me against discussing her with anyone.

Perhaps all this had something to do with how I was developing. I'd grown very much like Peter in the present novel. I deleted chapter XX from the first edition but now, for the sake of autobiographical honesty, I've put it back in. That was how I was when I wrote "I Am It And It Is I" (a title which Lovecraftians may recognize). It was to be one of a collection of tales called "Marihuana Marvels," a project which, thank heaven, got no further. All the same, I find I quite like the story, one of my funnier pieces, and I'm glad to see it into print at last as a complement to the novel.

Eventually I roused myself from my apathy. Jenny and I bought a house and I went back into production. I was in libraries now, but growing frustrated. In 1973 I went after jobs in journalism and in the Civil Service but, luckily, was unsuccessful. Instead I went full-time as a writer and began to live on the edge of my nerves. I'd had a couple of curious mental experiences when I was younger—I'd spent most of my eighteenth year unable to perform the mechanical task of reading, spending so long on each phrase that I lost the sense of the context (though I had this trouble only with fiction), and I think it was earlier in my teens when I was intrigued to notice that the pattern on the seat opposite me in a railway carriage had turned into lines of print in an unknown language—but being compelled to write, even if by the pressure of untold stories rather than the need to make a living, feels much crazier. My story "The Change" pretty well conveys how I often felt until I learned to relax, largely by being aware that one can always rewrite.

Of course the situation with my mother could only get worse, though gradually enough to let me believe she was just the way she had always been. She became convinced that the neighbors were circulating a petition to have her put out of her house because she was only a tenant whereas they owned their homes, but a few of her neighbors were on her side and refused to sign. Miss Holme began to accuse people of stealing items from her house, which was infested with demons, and my mother called in Miss Holme's nephew to help, but after Miss Holme's death some years later she denied that she had ever said anything was wrong with her friend. By then, however, my mother was on the same path.

I suppose I realized this soon after my wife and daughter and I moved house to the far side of the river from Liverpool. We invited my mother for dinner on her birthday that October, and I arranged to meet her at our local station. She never arrived. I waited several hours, phoning her home between trains, and eventually went home to a phone call accusing me of having played a trick on her. She'd been waiting for me at the station in Liverpool, where, she insisted, people had taken her for a prostitute.

After that things quickly grew worse. Airplanes were being used to spy on her, though perhaps one of the pilots was protecting her. When we gave her a photograph of herself holding our daughter, she refused to believe she was the woman in the photograph. Her next-door neighbors had bought her house from her landlord and were trying to take over one of the rooms for their daughter's use. Her neighbors on the other side were social workers who wanted her to take care of a mad old woman during the day. She would phone me in a panic, saying that the room was full of people who were staring at her, or that she was in the house that looked like hers but which was miles away from hers. Sometimes she felt she was being drugged to cause her to hallucinate. When I tried to persuade her these things weren't happening she would accuse me of conspiring against her, trying to drive her mad.

Even I couldn't pretend nothing was wrong now, but more than thirty years of not discussing her at her insistence made me incapable of seeking medical advice on her behalf. I felt helpless and increasingly desperate whenever I thought of her. Usually on my visits I had to try and disentangle the truth from her account of something that had happened, or that she claimed had happened, since my last visit; often we had violent arguments over nothing at all—sometimes we came to blows. More than once I grew so frustrated that I ran at a wall of the room head first. I wasn't always sane myself. Eventually, on the theory that living near me in a house she knew I owned would make her feel more secure, I managed to obtain a mortgage for one from the bank.

Perhaps this seemed the perfect solution because I was at my wits' end, or because it was so close to the ambition she'd nursed throughout my childhood of owning her own home. I couldn't see (though my wife tried to make me see) that it was too late and might very well make the situation worse. It wasn't long before we found a house my mother was delighted with, a few minutes' walk away from me.

The negotiations for buying it took months, as they will. Meanwhile my son was born and my mother kept calling to say that heads were looking at her out of vases or to plead with me to take her home from the house someone had left her in. She slept downstairs on the couch, because people came into her bedroom and pushed her out of bed. By now I left the phone off the hook when I went to bed, but more than once I woke in the dead of night convinced I'd heard its ringing.

Shortly after the contracts of sale had been signed, my mother decided she didn't want to move house after all: she felt at home where she was, she had friends among the neighbors. I managed intermittently to persuade her, sometimes by making wild promises, and spent the week before the move in packing her belongings, since she was either incapable or unwilling. Spending so much time in that house reminded me of my childhood. Remembering how she'd looked after me made me realize how unrecognizable she was now, and how little was left of our relationship. In the garden I burst into tears.

At first she seemed happy in her new house and finding out where the shops were, two minutes' walk away. She bought a television, which she'd wanted for many years. I imagined her settling in, making friends, taking strolls along the promenade to which steps led at the bottom of her street. I was as trapped in a fantasy as she was.

It took me a while to notice she was no longer changing her clothes. People had stolen all the rest and replaced it with inferior stuff which she refused to wear, instead tying it in bundles which she hid around the house. I was visiting her every day, and now that I'd learned to drive I took her touring the nearby countryside. None of this helped: it simply let me believe intermittently that it was a partial solution. Of course I knew it was nothing of the kind.

By now she often called me several times a day to go round and tell the people to leave her alone—the children, my sister, the man who looked like the devil. Often she told me I was there with her, or someone who was pretending to be me, who looked extremely ill and who had her worried sick. Occasionally I persuaded her that she'd just woken from dreaming. Sometimes I rushed to her house to prove her wrong, but either she denied having called me or the people had just gone: this lady in the corner and the people in the curtains would confirm she was telling the truth, or were they afraid to speak? She knew they weren't really people in the curtains but photographs of people that someone kept putting in the room—hadn't I heard of talking pictures? That was as far as I could argue her back toward reality. What was I trying to do, drive her mad so I and that woman could have her house? Oh no, of course, it wasn't *her* house, though I'd said it would be. I'd shown her three houses and this was her least favorite, she hadn't really wanted it at all. . . . She refused absolutely to believe that anything was wrong with her or that she needed help.

I did. For the first time in my life I considered seeking help on her behalf, considered it and was too desperate to behave as she had programmed me to. Even so, I spent months trying to persuade her to enroll with our family doctor, until one day I drove her there and dumped her in the waiting room. She told the doctor I was her husband who had left her for another woman. The doctor agreed with me that something had to be done.

Nothing could be, since my mother refused help. The doctor referred me to the social services, who ran luncheon clubs and day care centers for the elderly. The case worker made two visits to my mother, at the second of which I was present and saw her fail to explain what services she was offering (presumably assuming, quite unjustifiably, that my mother was capable of remembering what she had been told the first time). She left after five minutes and put the case away among the dormant files. The few times I went to the social services after that she was usually on holiday, or not back from holiday when she was expected, or off sick. Once she told me that perhaps my mother's hallucinations were company for her. Her colleagues praised her professional competence.

So began the worst year of my life. I realized that my mother never went out of the house by herself, though she was convinced she did. Her calls became more frequent and more terrified, and all I could do was grow used to them, respond indifferently, tell her I'd be round later. I still visited her every day, though by now we loathed each other: either we had violent arguments in which she clung to the idea that nothing was wrong with her, or hardly spoke. I was becoming everything she feared and hated. Sometimes when I took her for a drive I was tempted to leave her miles from anywhere; sometimes I thought of killing her, reaching across her on a deserted stretch of motorway and opening the passenger door. Perhaps she would leave the gas fire on unlit or finally wander down into the river.

The doctor could see how I was, and called in the community health officer to visit my mother. He was sympathetic, and more skillful than the social worker at the job she ought to have been doing, but all he could do was visit my mother regularly in the hope of establishing a rapport. Meanwhile my behavior toward my wife and children grew steadily worse. When we took a fortnight's holiday in the summer of 1982, I made sure the social services knew I was away, but I was hoping that my mother would either have to go out shopping by herself or starve to death.

When I came back her house smelled worse and was swarming with flies, but otherwise nothing had changed: the same arguments, the same helpless mutual loathing. She had clearly not been out of the house. She accused me of having stolen her key, and when I showed her she had several copies in her purse, insisted that they didn't fit the lock. She went to the front door to demonstrate, and I watched her trying to turn the lock with a box of matches.

Either I was able to see clearly at last that she needed constant supervision, or two weeks' respite had made me even less able to cope. I called the community health officer, who had concluded independently that part of his problem in establishing a rapport was that my mother felt (however bitterly) she could always rely on me. I told her that I wouldn't be visiting her for three weeks; if she needed anything she would have to call on the services available, whose phone numbers I had posted on the wall above the phone. Surely this would break down her obduracy.

She called me a couple of days later to ask if we were still friends. Those were just about her last words to me. Nearly two weeks later I heard from the community health officer. He'd visited my mother's house two days running but had received no answer. I hurried round and let myself in.

The kitchen and most of the hall were flooded by a tap that had been left full on. My mother lay on the sofa, breathing but past waking. She looked twenty years older. The kitchen drawers were full of liquescent sliced bread, months old. The television was turned over on its screen; a mirror lay smashed in the hall. From the cuts on her hand it seemed she must have punched her reflection in the face.

I called the community health officer and drove to the social services. The case worker was off sick, and the officer I spoke to complained that it was nearly her lunch hour. She tried to make me feel guilty enough about my mother to go away, until I began to scream at her. I should not like to have to rely on most of the Wallasey social workers I met, and perhaps after all it was to the good that my mother never had.

Our doctor and the community health officer had her admitted to hospital that afternoon. She'd regained consciousness, and was pitifully grateful both to see me and to go into hospital. I hoped this would be the first step toward her going into care, but every time I visited the hospital she seemed worse. Soon she didn't recognize me. Sometimes she lay with her eyes moving back and forth, very fast, like a metronome. I fed her water from a toddler's lidded cup, managing a cupful an hour if she didn't spit it out. Less than two weeks after she had been admitted, the ward sister called to say she had died during the night. I feel she died of my neglect and of my having destroyed her memories.

You may feel that all this has strayed rather far from the source of *The Face That Must Die* and of my fiction generally, but I wouldn't have known where to stop. I think it reads coldly, but I can't justify rewriting to protect my own image, though perhaps that is just my trying to display how honest I think I am.

My mother was cremated, and I took the ashes to the family grave in Huddersfield one weekend, only to find that there was nobody to tell me where the grave (which I'd seen once, twenty years before) was. I set out to look for it, but found after an hour that I'd examined perhaps a tenth of the headstones. I gave up then, planning to come back on a weekday when someone would be in attendance, and wandered aimlessly through the graveyard until suddenly I halted, turned, and found myself looking straight at the family headstone. I had walked to it by the shortest possible route. I should like to think that my mother had managed at last to take me where she wanted to be.

—Ramsey Campbell
Merseyside, England

I Am It And It Is I

There can't have been much stuff in that cake. Or else it must have been all seeds. I must have had the best of it last night.

I don't want to think about last night. Maybe I should listen to some sounds.

So why shouldn't I think about last night? I'm not going to be stoned on this stuff. There were some nice sounds going, and I was listening to them, and that must have been when everyone went out for a walk. Sylvia went to crash with Den and Heather. She'll be back. It was just a temporary thing. I wish I could remember exactly what happened. She wanted to turn the sounds down, that's right, because the gays upstairs were banging on the floor, and we had an argument. I forget what I said. I know I told her to fuck off, and she went out crying with Den and Heather. They're not on the phone, or I could tell her I'm sorry. I mean, I am, but it was weird because at the time I felt bad about it yet something told me I had to be on my own for a while. Weird.

I can't suss why I'm not stoned now. It's nearly two hours since I ate that cake. It was the last piece, right enough, and I know it was full of seeds because we didn't spread them out properly. But last night, I mean, wow, that was cake. Den had brought along some Debussy. I said shit when I saw it, but they were really some sounds when he put it on. That's right, I had my eyes shut, and I was sailing down out of space through the clouds into this ruined temple, and just as the sounds were really freaking out there was light, brighter and brighter. Had Sylvia gone by then? No, she couldn't have, because Den didn't leave the sounds. I can't remember.

But that was good dope. A friend of Den's was growing it in Sefton

Park, right in the middle of all those streets. I mean, all those straights in the streets never knew, that was the incredible part. Just beautiful. And he was making it to Amsterdam, so he sold his plot. Plot of pot. Wow, must remember that. He sold it, half to Den and half to me. Last night was the first crop. Said he scored the seeds in some little village with a ruined temple in the background. It sounds like William Burroughs, I know, he said.

It sounds like William Burroughs, I know he said.

My God, I'm slowing down. It's coming on.

Right. I'm going to listen to some sounds. See if it's as fantastic as last night.

This room's too purple. Look at those velvet curtains. It's like your spit thickens when you're sick, they're thickening the sunlight. So are those cars in Lodge Lane. Grinding away and throbbing and rattling — they're interfering with the sunlight. No, they can't be. Who said that? Come on, come out wherever you are.

I'm going to hear some sounds.

Look where the records are. I'll never get over there. It'll be a miracle if I can stand up. Jesus, look at that! My purple shadow! It's turning to look at me! You're turning to look at yourself, you mean. Who's saying these things?

Oh Christ, there's Sylvia. I just flashed her. In the doorway with tears running down her face. Trembling like she wants to shake herself to pieces and never be put together again. Oh I'm sorry, love. I didn't want you to go. It was the shit talking. I never wanted you to go.

— Why do they call it shit?

— Who's there? Oh Jesus, it's not Sylvia who came apart, it's me. My mind's splitting down the middle like a cleaver's gone through it.

— Of course. There's a calm side and a paranoid side. You're on the paranoid side now, man.

— I've had this before. Like my mind's a battleground between the strong and the weak. Vietnam in the head. Like that book by someone, Aldiss, Barry was reading us last week. All right, I can play it. What did you say back there?

— What? What did I say? Oh, I was wondering why they call dope shit.

— Weird question. The color, maybe, I don't know. Listen, however many of me there are, we're famished. Let's make it to the kitchen. You take this leg and I'll get the other.

— Go on! You can do it! Listen, you aren't turned on to this scene at all. You've got to become me, man, you've got to become the strong calm side of this mind we've got, then there'll be no more paranoia, no more weakness. Merge, man, merge.

— Maybe, but how long have we been walking toward that door? The purple's pulling us back. We aren't going to make it. Anyway, listen, we don't even know what's on the other side of the door. Let's just lie down and maybe hear some sounds.

— You crawling cowardly bastard. I could show you things that'd make your experiences look like shit, if you had the courage.

— All right. All right! We're out. Don't ask me how I got through that shadow. Felt like cobwebs. My God, is that the bedroom over there? All that way? Oh wow, that orange door is my scene, though. This whole hall, it's like those comics Barry had last night, what were they, Marvel Comics.

— We aren't going over there. Just in the kitchen. There, you made it. Fantastic.

— Look at those pans hanging up. What are they, mouths? Mouths on sticks! Sylvia used to feed those mouths. She loved having her own kitchen.

— Forget that. Forage, man. What's this? Duck paté. A duck made into paste. Don't know how you could think of eating that, even if you weren't stoned. Sylvia bought it, don't forget. She bought it and you were supposed to eat it.

— Don't you say that. I used to walk around the block sometimes when I was stoned and think of coming home to Sylvia when we were old and we could just sit together.

— She stuffed a crushed duck down your throat. She didn't care.

— Don't you put her down, you fucker! I want to see her! I want to tell her I'm sorry!

— All right. There's nothing good here, anyway. Let's take a walk.

— See Sylvia?

— If you want.

— Just so you know who's running things here. Clump. That door sounded satisfied. It wanted me to come out for a walk. There you are,

Croxteth Grove. That means all these trees and look, on that wall, that cat sitting like a gargoyle. All its fur with the sun running off like water. Summer is to sit with Sylvia, like that kids' book I was reading.

— Maybe so, but look: Lodge Lane. Main roads aren't good for the summer.

— For once I think you're right. There's something bad about those cars. It's like the cars are using people for parts, you know, cogs or valves. My God, look at all those cars sitting at the side of the road waiting to catch someone! That's right, they draw off energy somehow and drive about on it.

— But what about all these people walking around?

— Well, what about them? Look, look at them jerking about! There's that guy tapping his umbrella, there's a woman brushing her hair back from her face, look, she's doing it again, there's some kids kicking a can. "Yes, that's right, they've been thrown out by the cars because they've got too much excess energy. But the cars will get them again. Am I walking along Lodge Lane talking to myself?"

— "Yes, I think you probably are. We are."

— "I thought that guy with the umbrella was looking at us weird. Fuck off, cog! Listen" — listen, the cars won't get us on the way to Sylvia, will they?

— Those cars waiting at the lights look pretty bad. If we run we can make it across the lights and into Sefton Park.

— "But we're going away from Sylvia."

— "That's true. Well, it's your scene, but I can tell you I don't like those cars. Half an hour in the park and I'll take anything, but not right now. And remember this, man: you need me."

— "Fair enough, I suppose. Run!"

— We're across. Don't slow down. Did you see that car straining to get at us past the lights, those eyes? Blind but they could see us.

— Right, but I like these trees. The leaves are talking about summer. Listen, we won't get too far away from Sylvia, will we? I can feel my mind stretching. I don't want it to snap. Christ, that would be painful, all my thoughts snapping back together.

— Don't hassle. We want to get away from those tenements on Lodge Lane. You can feel everyone weighing on everyone else. Think of having twenty floors on top of you. All that sweat and flesh.

— Bad scene. But this going in the park to get it together seems like a kind of a return to the womb thing.

— Feel all the life growing around us, the grass and the flowers and the trees. Taking their own time.

— Beautiful. But let's not forget Sylvia. She's beautiful too, and we hurt her.

— Nobody's forgetting. Now just feel your foot crossing over from the pavement into the park. Feel the grass accept you.

— Fantastic. It kind of breathes in so I don't hurt it.

— It's more than that. It's welcoming you.

— This is incredible. There's nobody about except the grass and the trees. Where are we going, down to the lake to see the ducks?

— I shouldn't think you'd feel too good about ducks right now. Let's go and see where your dope is planted.

— That's a great idea. Maybe it'll talk to us. Like those trees aren't moving but they're talking about the sun.

— They're talking about life. You aren't there yet, though — the dope has been talking to you since you came on.

— I'm with you. Look how the shadows of the trees are lying down on the path to be in the shade. But they are the shade.

— Identity is a weird thing.

— Right. Those shrubberies, I mean, the sunlight just lies there like honey. I could eat it. But what I meant to say was, the dope is just behind them.

— That's where I have to go.

— We don't have to anything, man. We're free. We can just let the sunlight splash over us.

— We have to go there. Don't you want to visit it? Aren't you grateful for what it's giving you?

— Shit, you're right, I am ungrateful. Come on, I'm going to thank it. The shrubberies are caressing us. Like —

— There are shoots there if you look. They're quiet now, but when they grow someone's going to eat them or smoke them. Then they'll tell him everything.

— Right. Shoots, thank you, you're beautiful. But I was going to say, those shrubberies were caressing us like Sylvia. I was just wondering if she's still at Den and Heather's. She might have come back to ours.

I mean, if someone told me to fuck off while I was stoned I mightn't be able to get it together either. But I do love her. She knows that.

— I can feel the shoots growing. Birth, that's what life is for.

— Right. You know, Sylvia wants a baby, I can tell. Maybe we weren't into getting married before, you know, the whole straight scene. But if she wants it, it's my scene. "If this is you telling me this, shoots of dope, we'll both come and thank you."

— I could be reborn.

— That's fantastic, man. How?

— Just think how a seed must feel.

— Don't stop! I mean, too much!

— Thrusting down through the earth, feeling the soil hug you, the trees meditating.

— Digging in the earth?

— That's right.

— Like this?

— Right, but stay cool. Not so fast. No need to break your nails. Time's stopped.

— Look at all these stones, been down there nobody knows how long without anything to hassle them. That worm's going to fuck the earth. Think of all the straights living round this scene and never knowing. Sylvia would love this. We ought to show her.

— We will, but don't worry about time. She'll come to see you. You can talk to her then.

— Man, this hole is deep. I'd never have thought I could do it.

— Don't stop now. Don't think about it.

— If we're going any deeper I'll have to stand in it.

— Stand in it. I mean, straights wouldn't even think about it, never mind do it.

— I ought to get a job in the country if I can dig like this. Jesus, I can't even see over the top of the hole. I never realized earth was so warm. Protective, kind of. Feels familiar.

— This is where I was born.

— Come *on*, man.

— This is only the beginning. Wait till you feel yourself pouring through someone, touching their being and speaking to it. It might be Sylvia.

— That's amazing. Just imagine. I'd like her to feel—Christ! I can feel something growing up from my stomach like a shoot!

— You know who that is.

— Shit, man, it isn't you!

— Yes, but now I'm you as well.

— What's that? Rain? Look, the soil's raining on us.

— It's giving itself to us. Stand still. Let me feel it for you. It'll be easier.

— Clods of earth! Christ, it's hailing!

— Pull your hands in now. Think of what you'll have to tell Sylvia.

* * * * *

J.K. Potter

THE FACE THAT MUST DIE
by Ramsey Campbell

Illustrations
by J.K. Potter

Also by the Author

NOVELS

THE DOLL WHO ATE HIS MOTHER
THE PARASITE
THE NAMELESS
INCARNATE

SHORT STORIES

"The Inhabitant of the Lake"
"Demons by Daylight"
"The Height of the Scream"
"Dark Companions"

ANTHOLOGIES

SUPERHORRORS (THE FAR REACHES OF FEAR)
NEW TERRORS
NEW TALES OF THE CTHULHU MYTHOS

Also by the Artist

TALES OF THE WEREWOLF CLAN Vol. I
(H. Warner Munn; Grant, 1979)
TALES OF THE WEREWOLF CLAN Vol. II
(H. Warner Munn; Grant, 1980)
WRITING FOR THE TWILIGHT ZONE
(George Clayton Johnson; Outré House, 1980)
THE DARK COUNTRY
(Dennis Etchison; Scream/Press, 1982)
DELUSIONS OF A POPULAR MIND
(Martha McFerren; New Orleans Poetry Journal Press, 1983)
AUTUMN ROSES
(G. Sutton Breiding; Silver Scarab Press, 1983)
WHO MADE STEVIE CRYE?
(Michael Bishop; Arkham House, 1984)

for Dave and Moy Griffiths

ACKNOWLEDGMENTS

I seem to have written this one more or less on my own. The Social Security people were remarkably loath to tell me what benefits John Horridge would receive, while the Planning Department wanted only to convince me that nobody was transported to a housing estate such as Cantril Farm against his/her will. I suppose I may be the only person to thank the planners responsible for building Cantril Farm and sending people there; at least they helped me write this book. Since writing it I've heard that Cantril Farm claims an abnormally high number of fatal heart attacks among young men.

I hope that my good friend George Cranfield, manager of the Odeon London Road, will forgive the liberties my character takes with his cinema. Incidentally, some readers may like to know that Peter Sellers appeared in both *Murder by Death* and the Inspector Clouseau films.

Lastly, I'm especially grateful to Piers Dudgeon for encouraging this book.

CHAPTER I

Perhaps he should stay on the bus, and avoid the tail end of Christmas.

In Lodge Lane, shops had broken out in fairy lights. Tiny colored bulbs spelt MERRY CHRISTMAS. The shoppers on the narrow pavements looked as though they all had hangovers. The window of a wine store glided by, glittering with an oval of frost false as a carol singer's smile.

If he stayed on the bus he would reach the park more quickly — but he wanted his sweets. He'd loved them ever since he was a child: boiled sweets which bulged his cheeks, hard as fruity stones, while he sucked and sucked until it seemed they would never crack and yield up their sticky secret. Why should he deny himself? He hadn't had much in his life.

Ambushed by wind from the side streets, the bus shuddered. The brakes squealed as a bus stop flagged it down. If there were too many people upstairs, might the bus topple over? Horridge felt unsafe, for the lurches of the bus had set everyone nodding, as though agreeing with a whisper which he'd failed to hear.

The bus had stopped. He limped rapidly to reach the doors before they closed. His hip bumped something. "That's my hat!" a woman protested like an outraged parrot, patting the furry pink cap back into place. "That's my hat!"

"I'm very sorry," he said sweetly, cursing her for drawing attention to him, to his limp.

He gripped the rusty bus stop for a few moments, like a crutch. People trudged by, greeting one another, laden with bags of anything but turkey. Nobody looked up beyond the shops, to the windows blank with dust, the jagged holes admitting weather to the deserted flats. Above a supermarket, bared nails spelt out the unreadable ghost of its name. Didn't these people realize that all this could be used as an excuse to herd them into concrete prisons miles outside the city? So long as they had their pubs and betting shops, they didn't care.

He made for the sweet shop, slowly enough to conceal his limp. The shopkeeper was serving a customer: a packet of razor blades lay between them on the spread of newspapers. Cupboards and racks made the shop even smaller. Magazines were pegged like printed towels hung up to dry. Framed by romances and toilet rolls, glossy women exposed huge chests.

As he turned to the jars the shopkeeper said, "They'd rather not work these days. They're too well off."

Was she referring to him? He wasn't one of the layabouts who drove new cars to collect their dole. Dole! Fortune, more like. It wasn't for him; he was only partially incapacitated, the Social Security had decided after cross-questioning him like a common criminal. All they needed to live up to their initials were jackboots.

"I couldn't agree more," the other woman said.

Oh, surely she could if she really tried. These days nobody could think for themselves.

"All these men walking the streets. I've never seen anything like it."

He wasn't a streetwalker, and he never would be. Just let her watch whom she was calling abnormal! He rapped a lid with his knuckles. "A quarter of these, please," he said, to shut her up.

As he started forward to grab the bag — a sweet was poking over its lip, ready to fall if she helped it a little — his leg gave way. His hand splayed a stack of newspapers across the counter, spreading headlines — NEW MURDER SHOCK — and razor blades. A dozen repetitions of the identikit drawing stared up at him, an unnatural family — as though the man had infected a dozen victims until they looked like him. Horridge snatched his hand away. "Bloody leg," he muttered.

The customer stared at him as he groped for his wallet. Her hair was full of plastic burrs, her eyes were sunk in mascara. "He's got a lot in his pockets," she said. "Been robbing a bank, have you?"

Let her mind her own business. He thrust his documents deeper into his pocket: disability benefit order book, medical card, birth certificate.

She stared at his overcoat as though it was an insult flung into a jumble sale. Yes, the pockets were discolored with bulging. Let her try to live on the pittance they gave him!

Once out of the shop he made for the park. He felt shabby. He could have turned his coat, which was a reversible — but he was no turncoat, and besides, the tartan was too bright; he preferred the unobtrusive gray.

The sweet which he popped into his mouth tasted soapy. His hand was stigmatized by the newspapers. If the blur of ink was a word, it was indecipherable. He rubbed his skin clean with the sweet bag, but his hand still felt smeared.

A twinge counted his steps as he quickened his pace. Street signs were obscured by incomprehensible graffiti, as though invaded by a foreign language. The villas of Sefton Park Road were spacious and grand, with deep porches. Trees, promises of the park, grew in the large gardens.

On Aigburth Drive, which curved round the park, two men stood talking outside a house. The house looked discolored and blurred, like something left in an attic; its three storeys of pairs of bay windows gleamed sullenly. It must have been dignified once.

Now it had fallen into bad company. Two men? They weren't what he would call men. One was a thin pale youth with long black ratty hair and a paler tuft of beard. Was he pretending to be a man or a goat? His eyes were nervous yet blank. All these students tripping on their drugs — sooner or later they'd trip themselves up.

But the other was worse. He looked stiff, as though he was ashamed of his movements — as well he might be, for he was gesturing like a parody of a woman. In his dark heavy overcoat he was a blot on the landscape. He was hefty; the youth had no chance against him. Had he built up his body to convince people he was a man? Everything about him was a lie. When he turned to stare at Horridge the too-small face looked like a petulant mask, swollen with flesh.

Horridge glared; then, feeling queasy, he hurried between the granite columns into the park. As he limped past the obelisk, wind tugged at his coat, trying to expose the tartan. Huge warty swellings grew on some of the trees which bordered the walk. Shouldn't those trees be cut down before they infected their neighbors?

The sweet cracked open. Within was nothing but a disappointing hollow. Horridge crunched it and sucked a red one, which tasted vaguely of strawberry. Pain plucked at his teeth like a dentist's hooks. Once his father had made him visit the dentist. "Don't be a baby. Look how you're upsetting your mother. Be a man." He had never felt so terrified as then, lying helpless in the air with his mouth forced open, awaiting more pain. Since then he had visited the surgery only in nightmares.

At the end of the walk, near an ice cream café, a statue of Eros posed with a bow. He'd used to enjoy that, until he'd seen a man loitering beneath it, ogling children. Was nothing left unspoiled?

At least the park was deserted, apart from distant childish shouts. Years ago, when he'd lived nearby in Boaler Street, he'd learned to come here in the afternoons. People spoiled his peace.

A small bridge led him across a narrow of the lake. Beyond it the concrete path sloped toward the first calm pool. His aching leg ceased to bother him. The descent always reminded him of climbing down into the quarry.

When he reached the place opposite the bandstand, he halted. The desertion of the bandstand seemed to orchestrate the quiet of the artificial valley. Everything was vividly precise: the austere trees, the bushes with their glossy pelt of leaves, the grassy slope above him refreshed by the morning's rain, the sky blue as a summer lake fading subtly toward the horizon. Everything felt clean as the quarry.

The wind had fallen. The inverted bandstand and trees lay perfectly still in the pool, their reflections glazed by the water. He stood tasting the slow explosion of strawberry.

Ducks glided by, feet waving like submerged orange fronds. Their ripples passed through the reflections; the bandstand wriggled a little, branches flowed and quivered gently. He watched zigzags undulate along each separate twig, as though the sound of lapping had been translated into sight. The ducks returned, the ripples overlapped. Though the patterns were intricate, every detail was clear to him.

Soon the ducks left him for a man who was throwing bread. Their flight shattered the reflections. He trudged away, past a statue of a man who gazed across the lake, trying to ignore the graffiti on his pedestal.

· Beyond stepping stones enclosed by railings, the lake widened. Fishermen glanced up like watchdogs. He crossed on the stones and followed a path to Lark Lane. Though the lane resembled a village street, it soon led to the dual carriageway. Beyond the petrol fumes and headlong metal stood a Bingo hall, the Mecca. Wasn't that what foreigners thought of as heaven?

But here was the mock-Tudor library. The ceiling was supported by high white beams; briefly he thought of a church. Beneath them hung faded paper festoons, and an iron gallery clung to the wall, so that the staff could look down on people. He remembered the first time he'd climbed his father's ladder.

As he reached a table, he cursed himself. This library took no newspapers; he couldn't read the murder report. He'd visit another library on his way home, or buy a newspaper. At least the place was quiet. He tried to think of the pool or the quarry.

The blonde girl serving at the counter wore no shoes. You wouldn't think it would be allowed. And she wore trousers, which was unnatural. A lady in tweeds was asking her about books. "Will the titles be in the index, yonder?"

"Yes, I should think so. Shall I show you?"

"I can look after myself perfectly well."

The girl grinned secretly at her colleagues. She ought to look out for her own speech instead of mocking people who could speak properly. Her trace of the catarrhal Liverpool accent made her sound common, however glossy she kept her long hair.

The junior wing grew noisy. Schoolboys gazed at the girl's breasts, tittering. Tittering—yes, he knew what the word sounded like, no need to think it. He hated people who corrupted the young. She must know what her right sweater was doing.

He watched her until she went home. She tucked her hair beneath a black wool cap, as though she didn't want to look like a woman. There wouldn't be so much unemployment if they stopped all these women working. No chance of that: it wouldn't please the herd.

The noise of children drove him out into the dark. Passers-by were carrying plastic trays of curry, as though English food weren't good enough for them. On the road that encircled the park, lamps lit trees from beneath. Was that the blonde girl ahead, or a man? Horridge plunged his hands deep among his documents, to try to warm his fingers. Before he could overtake the figure, it disappeared.

He knew when he reached the house where he'd seen the two men, for he'd observed the number; nobody could say his vision wasn't sharp. Besides, the van which he had vaguely noticed was outside: a battered vehicle painted with large cartoonish flowers. Whoever was responsible had no idea what real flowers looked like. No doubt that was the fault of all their drugs.

He was staring at the parody of a flower when light reached out from the house toward him, and displayed a face.

The light came from curtains parting: no reason for his fists to clench. But the face which the window displayed as though it was something to admire was the face of the hefty effeminate man. It looked even more masklike now. It turned as if searching the dark road, then faced Horridge.

Suddenly he realized how he looked, standing beneath the lamp as though waiting to be seen, while the sly corrupt mask hunted eagerly. Shivering, his face frozen by rage and the night into an expression which he could not read, he limped violently away.

The lights of Sefton Park Road dazzled him, but could not clear his mind. The face at the window clung to his memory; it lay on his thoughts, close and heavy. His skin felt prickly, nervous. He had seen that face earlier, outside the house. But where — his thoughts struggled vainly, as though in a dream — had he seen it before?

CHAPTER II

Before Cathy was halfway upstairs she was running. Somewhere in her pocket, amid the clumsy bundle of iced sticks that were her fingers, was the key. She poked the time-switch outside the flat and aimed the key; it was like trying to thread a needle while wearing gloves. The god of frozen fingers was on her side, for she managed to turn the key before the light clicked off.

She nudged the door shut with her shoulder, which felt like a huge lump, as though she were Quasimodo made of ice. A tiny Charles Laughton went swinging away in her mind, shouting "Sanctuary, sanctuary." She ran to light the fire and squatted before it on the floorboards. Sanctuary much. God, her puns were getting worse.

The flames rose in their cage. As the bars turned orange, her body thawed and grew familiar; she wasn't Quasimodo with fat unwieldy fingers, after all. Christmas cards had fallen from the kite's-tail display on the dangling tapes over the mantelpiece; she stuck them into place. She drew the curtains and began to tidy the room.

She picked up Peter's sweater, which was lolling on the bed. He must have come home and gone out again. She collected the sprawl of his comic books from the round Scandinavian table and stacked them on top of the storage units. Books and a Tangerine Dream record occupied the chairs, as though keeping all his places. She put them away, sighing. It would be nice if he occasionally did more than empty ashtrays.

Today was macrobiotic day. This week she was going to make a vegetable curry. She hoped it would work. She cooked, adding more or less what the recipe indicated, tasting constantly.

Somewhere beyond the kitchen window a man was croaking. At last she made out that the word was "Rags, rags." He sounded like a throaty old night-bird. But wasn't it late for a rag-and-bone man to be calling? Perhaps he was searching for a lost dog.

Footsteps clumped upstairs. She heard Peter opening the door. "What's for dinner?" he called.

"Vegetable curry."

Silence. A little encouragement would do her no harm. "Are you home?" she called.

More silence. Redundant questions made him irritable. But he might have been going out again, for all she knew.

"The old arse-bandit was after me today," he said loudly as he closed the door.

"Peter!" Why must he be so eager to shock? Mr. Craig might have heard him. Perhaps Peter had wanted him to hear, or perhaps he didn't care.

"He can't get enough, that guy. He'll end up leaving boys tied up in cupboards."

"You shouldn't joke about that sort of thing."

"Who's joking?" He strolled into the kitchen, pulling off his black wool cap. Dark straggly hair flopped over his shoulders. She must trim it soon, despite his protests. "He'll be keeping them in his wardrobe soon," he said. "Maybe he already is."

He often trapped himself in his own jokes—carried on until they ceased to be funny, if they ever had been. It was as though he couldn't find his way out, and it annoyed both of them. "Were you really speaking to Mr. Craig?" she said, to help.

"You mean the arse-bandit? Right on. We had a really intimate conversation."

"What about?"

"What do you think? Can I please turn down that nasty rock and roll? I play it *so* late, and it's *so* noisy. Not nice music like Beethoven."

"He didn't really say all that," Cathy said, half-convinced by the gist if not the wording.

"He wanted me to turn the fucking records down."

For a moment she felt as though his unexpected violence were directed at her. "You ought to buy some headphones," she suggested. "Save up for them instead of buying comics."

"No way. Comics are an investment. I just got a new *Swamp Thing* and a whole stack of *Fantastic Fours* by Jack Kirby." Perhaps he was fleeing that subject when he added, "I'll tell you what was weird — there was some weirdo watching me and Craig."

That was all he seemed interested in telling her. "There was a man watching me in the library," she said, mocking the hint of mystery in her words.

"Yeah?" He sounded indifferent, restless.

"The man with the limp. He came in the week you were working there. The one who limps. You know."

"No, I don't. That's why you're telling me."

He knew she couldn't describe people, the pig. "There was a rag-and-bone man out there before," she said: that seemed a better anecdote. "This little voice calling 'Rags, rags.' Or maybe he was calling his dog." But Peter looked bored. She was glad when someone knocked at the door.

"Ben and Celia have split up," Peter said.

But they'd been married less than a year. News like that disturbed her, yet he'd announced it as though it were the weather forecast. Before she could begin the struggle of questioning him, he'd let in Anne and Sue.

"Can we borrow your phone?" Anne said. "There's supposed to be some good dope around."

They must have heard him coming home: they wouldn't have asked Cathy. Of course it was silly to be nervous — the phone wasn't tapped.

Sue wandered into the kitchen, smoking a joint. "Oh, hello," she said as if she couldn't quite place Cathy. Eventually she doled out a question. "Been to the library today?"

No, she'd been pouring boiling oil on people's heads. "Yes," she said curtly. She disliked intruders in her kitchen. She refused the joint and said, "Will you ask Peter to empty the bin?"

When Peter appeared, he plainly resented being asked in front of the girls. But he grabbed the bin, and shouted to Anne, "Ask if there's any acid."

Cathy hoped there wasn't. Grass she didn't mind so much, but LSD dismayed her. In the park Peter had cried, "For Christ's sake don't leave me," gazing at a crippled decayed branch; his pupils had been swollen and flickering. She wouldn't take acid; the idea of losing control frightened her. Besides, she'd never seen anyone made more pleasant by a trip, nor any couple grow closer.

Peter returned. "I emptied it in Harty's bin," he told the girls. "Old bugger thinks he owns the place." He displayed the empty kitchen bin to Cathy, like a hunter's prize.

"Jim says he can get some good Canadian acid," Anne told him. "Purple Pyramid — it takes you right out of your head."

"Great. I can keep a tab for summer."

Sue dawdled in, coughing as she smoked the joint down to the cardboard tip and lit another from it. "I hope you know how lucky you are, leaving the libraries," she told Peter. "We couldn't get through the day without a joint."

Cathy grimaced, sharing her thoughts with the stove. The only time she'd worked with them, the girls had sat stoned and giggling at the desk for most of the afternoon. When the flat across the landing had fallen vacant Peter had told them at once, though Cathy had wanted it for Ben and Celia. Would her friends have split up if she'd been close enough to mediate?

"Craig was after me to turn the records down. Christ, his flat isn't even under ours."

"It couldn't have been our records," Sue said. "We were out last night."

"He complained to us once, though. Isn't he oily?" Anne squirmed and grinned, as though at a disgusting joke. "And the way he tries to be sort of stiff, as though if he lets go he'll flop all over the floor. We told him to piss off."

"I don't mind him," Cathy said.

All of them stared at her. "Sure, he's a very warm and wonderful human being," Peter remarked in a spurious American accent.

That joke had become a cliché in itself. If she heard it just once more — They were wandering more slowly and aimlessly; they made her kitchen feel crowded and untidy. The girls gazed at the wall-charts of recipes; they might have been in an art gallery. "Pass me the garam masala, please," Cathy said.

Sue stared as if she were talking a foreign language; Anne turned to the spice rack, but stood looking bewildered. Peter began laughing.

"Never mind," Cathy said irritably. "All of you go in the other room."

As they did so, someone else knocked at the door. Bloody hell! She made for the door; she wouldn't put it past them to answer it while smoking. But Peter was already there. It was Fanny from downstairs.

"Hello, Peter. Oh, there you are, Cathy." She advanced, stretching out her hands, which were multicolored as a palette. "I'm sorry to come pillaging. Could you spare any sugar? Oh buttocksbumanarse, I forgot to bring a cup."

"I might have half a grain to spare." Cathy filled a mug from the tin. "What are you painting?"

"I've just finished. Come and see." When Cathy hesitated, she added wistfully, "You can tell me if it's any good."

Fanny's flat looked as though a living room, a bedroom, a newspaper cutting service, and a studio were battling to occupy the room. An easel stood on a wad of paper thick as a carpet; a drawing-board was folded behind the couch, which at night spread its arms and became a bed. Faces clipped from publications gathered everywhere; a mug of coffee defended its island on the crowded table. The walls brandished spotlights. "That's it," Fanny said with an uneasy laugh, and gestured at the easel.

The painting teemed with babies. Some sat in prams, some lay in cartons, on yellowed newspapers, on earth. They laughed, cried, dreamed, played with the air or with themselves, look bewildered, delighted, abandoned. They were many colors. Some were vivid yet false as photographs in a housewives' magazine, others were drawn in crayon or marker pen and had a child's truth about them. Some were fat as tires, some were skeletally thin. A few were bruised or worse.

"Yes, it's good," Cathy said. "It's really good. You've put a lot into it." Her words seemed inadequate. She wondered what features a baby of hers would have: Peter's teeny leftover of a nose, her eyebrows that met in the middle like a Hollywood werewolf's, Peter's beard?

"And here's my masterpiece." Fanny showed her a notice painted in the style of her signature, elaborate as New York subway graffiti: PLEASE KEEP THIS DOOR CLOSED. "Commissioned by Mr. Harty, my first patron. I keep forgetting to put it up," she said. "Come and hold the tacks while I remember."

On her way to the door, Cathy noticed a metal bird. It was rough as chipped flint, yet gracefully slim. "Are you going in for sculpture now?"

"Someone gave that to me." Did her tone imply a new relationship or a treasured memory? "I want to try working in clay sometime," she said.

At the bottom of the stairs she tapped on Mr. Harty's door. His dressing-gowned shoulder emerged, and then his bald head; two tufts of gray hair perched above his ears like packing, as though he'd just been removed from his box. "That's right, Miss Adamson," he said to Fanny. "Too many people have been wandering about. We don't want just anyone coming in. There are enough criminals, without putting temptation in their way." He withdrew like a jack-in-the-box; his lid clicked shut.

Fanny pointed at the other ground-floor flat. "I forgot to tell you," she whispered, "I saw Mr. Nameless Bell at work the other day."

His was the only doorbell that lacked a name. "You've found out where he works?" Cathy hissed. "Is he a spy?"

Fanny thumbed tacks into place. "No," she said mournfully. Her words threatened to collapse with laughter. "He works in Woolworth's."

"Oh dear." Cathy couldn't control her voice, which broke into a jumpy shout. "I thought he must be at least a detective."

They fled upstairs, giggling. The last of the babies were drying. "When's your exhibition?" Cathy said.

"Next week. They've given me the whole of the Bluecoat Gallery."

"That's good." Fanny's grimace made her ask, "Don't you think so?"

"I don't know. I hope so. I just don't know if it'll reach the people I want to reach." She sounded embarrassed and self-deprecating as she added, "Come and see it if you want to."

"Thanks, Fanny. We will." The smell of curry drifted downstairs, mixed with a hint of cannabis. "I must go and give himself his dinner," she said.

She'd reached the top landing when Fanny called, "Cathy!" She looked down unwarily. The fall plunged away beneath her; the walls shifted, the stairwell gaped like a throat.

"I'm awfully sorry, I forgot to ask if you had any raisins. This exhibition has me all jumbled up."

The moment had passed, and Cathy felt better for having survived it. "I'll send Peter down with them," she said.

The girls and Peter were reading his comics. They glanced up to see who Cathy was. She felt like an intruder. Sometimes, in unguarded moments, she wondered if Peter preferred them to her. This year she'd cooked her first full Christmas dinner — but he'd seemed more interested in going next door to smoke.

Grumpily he undertook to deliver the raisins. "And then your dinner will be ready," she said.

The girls looked up, in case that included them. At last they wandered out, saying, "See you later, Peter."

Not here, if Cathy could help it. They cluttered the flat. They weren't worth resenting: Sue had a big bum that flopped from side to side as she walked, Anne's hair was like a thatched crash helmet. But she could stand seeing less of them. Were they trying to turn the top floor into a commune? It annoyed her to have to ask persistently for things which they'd borrowed. On Christmas Day her mother had come for dinner; on Boxing Day she'd invited her father. Even on Christmas Day, when Peter's parents had come too, he'd kept sneaking next door.

When he returned from Fanny's she said, "When are we going to see the Halliwells?"

"Yes."

She hadn't time to be infuriated. "I want to see them on New Year's Eve. We'll go out for a meal, just the four of us."

"It'll have to be somewhere cheap."

She was looking forward to seeing her friends, and didn't feel like arguing. "Did you like Fanny's painting?"

"It was all right."

"She wants us to go to her exhibition."

"Oh Christ, you didn't say yes, did you? They're all a con, those exhibitions. Full of posers pretending they know what they're talking about."

But it was Fanny's. Her look of reproof must have reached him, for to break her silence he said, "Anything interesting happen today?"

Interesting? She was no longer sure. She'd meant to tell him how the park had looked that morning, grass and bushes painted with light and rain — everything had glowed, and the tears it brought to her eyes had made the landscape crystalline — but he seemed to resent her ability to see these things without drugs.

"Nothing special," she said, hoarding the memory. "Come and help carry the plates."

When she brought the rice from the kitchen he was peering through a crack in the curtains, like someone made wary by loneliness. Before she could join him, he let the crack fall closed. "Just some guy watching the house," he said. "Probably one of Craig's boyfriends. I thought he might be fuzz. He's gone now." Perhaps he was reassuring himself as he said, "Nothing to worry about."

CHAPTER III

Lime Street Station was thick with queues, sluggishly advancing on the ticket windows while trying to avoid the rain that dripped through the roof. Horridge edged toward the bookstall. "Excuse me. Excuse me. Excuse me." Sometimes he had to shout. He felt absurd and irritable, as though caught in a dance in a dream.

Police were patrolling, and seemed on the lookout for someone. They needn't look at him. Overhead the names of destinations clicked and changed, as though on a game board. Light exploded silently in a photo booth. Above the squealing of metal on rails a great vague voice boomed, echoing within the long iron shed. Horridge could never see where its owner was hiding.

He hurried past the Gents'. It was too public: there were always men watching surreptitiously, or moving behind him — and always a stench like perfumed urine, which must cling to one's clothes. He'd use the toilet in the cinema. He bought a newspaper: SHOCK REVELATION IN LIVERPOOL MURDER HUNT, its headline said.

The pavements looked slippery and unstable, glittering and wriggling with rain. Light lay glistening outside a pub, like slops. He hurried up the street beside the Odeon. Side streets made him nervous. Submarine glows drifted before him to be engulfed by the multicolored glare of London Road.

The Odeon's four cinemas were offering a Peter Sellers comedy, a Disney full-length cartoon, *Murder by Death*, and *The Rocky Horror Picture Show*. That was the one he wanted to see. Horror films took you out of yourself — they weren't too close to the truth.

Children raced about the foyer, knocking squat ashtray pedestals awry; others stood screaming, lost or frustrated. Children clamored for sweets and hot dogs and Pepsi-Cola. A salesgirl watched two boys furtively handling bars of chocolate. Horridge gave his ticket to a harassed usher, who tore it and gestured him vaguely onward, frowning at the children.

No time to use the toilet. He wanted to reach Screen 3 before the show began; he didn't like groping about in the dark. Once he'd touched a face, and a tongue had stirred like a worm within the cheek. After the blaze of the foyer the passage was dim. The large Screen 2 was in the middle; 3 must be on the left.

The small cinema was bright and empty: not even an usherette to be seen. Good — there would be nobody shouting and laughing at the monsters as a proof of masculinity. His seat creaked in the silence. Were they waiting for the cinema to fill? Wasn't he enough of an audience?

Beneath the red lights, the blue-green pelt of the floor and the seats threatened to turn violent. Floor and seats were tilted slightly to the right, though the screen was horizontal. He felt seasick. He shook open the newspaper, loudly and furiously.

> The man whose mutilated body was found in a Liverpool flat was a male prostitute, police revealed today.

That made him more sick. He didn't want to read on. But he must know all.

> The body of Norman Roylance (21) was found in a cupboard in his flat in Toxteth, Liverpool, on December 24. He had been bound and gagged. Police say that there were more than 30 razor wounds on the body.
>
> In a series of shock revelations, police gave us details of Roylance's life as a homosexual prostitute since the age of 15. (Full story on page 2.)
>
> Last month, also in the Toxteth area, the body of a young homosexual was found in a flat. He had also been bound and mutilated, and his body had been locked in a cupboard.
>
> Police are anxious to interview a man in his forties. He is described as being of medium height and stocky build. From descriptions, police have been able to issue this identikit portrait. HAVE YOU SEEN THIS MAN?

He stared at the sketched face. The flat eyes were neutral as a corpse's, but that was only slyness: they were hiding what lurked within them, as well they might. The face looked too small for the head. By holding itself stiff it hoped to conceal its real nature. In the flesh it wouldn't look exactly like that. That was its trick, to avoid being recognized! The empty eyes stared up at him, daring him to imagine their thoughts.

Shuddering, he turned the page. Its rustling was loud as an insomniac's blankets. Where the devil was the film? ONE YOUNG MAN'S LIFE ON THE STREETS was spread across page 2, but he felt queasy enough without reading that—if it was the truth. Who said the young man had been a prostitute? A victim, more likely. Young people weren't homosexual until they were corrupted—nobody was born that way. Horridge had his own idea about the murders: the man interfered with his helpless victims before he killed them. If he was a homosexual he was perverted enough for anything. Killing on Christmas Eve showed how unnatural he was. HAVE YOU SEEN THIS MAN?

He started. His neck felt spied upon. As he jerked round, a head dodged back from the projectionist's window. He'd paid to watch, not to be watched. He flourished the newspaper and read at random. An old man had been mugged by a gang of girls. That was what came of this Women's Liberation.

He heard the doors open. Someone was coming to double the audience! But it was an usherette. "Can I see your ticket, please?"

He always kept hold of his ticket; nobody was going to accuse him of not having paid. Did she mean to tell him he was in the wrong seat and herd him into another?

"Which film did you want to see?"

Good God, didn't they even know what they were showing? "The horror film," he said with brittle civility.

"You're in the wrong cinema. This is Screen 4."

If he argued they would start the film without him. He hurried down the passage, feeling hot and prickly. Illuminated numbered arrows pointed the way to each cinema. Well, he couldn't be expected to notice everything.

They were still showing the adverts. A lit bust, the head and shoulders of an ice cream girl, hovered above her tray. He muttered his way along a row, touching hair that twitched away, cloth that squirmed; a pool of tobacco smoke drifted sluggishly about his face. A soft-drink carton crunched beneath his heel. At last he reached the unoccupied seat.

He felt hemmed in by shoulders. What was drooping over the seat in front? As the screen flickered, it shifted. It was the empty head of a duffle coat. He settled himself, pressing his knees together so as not to touch anyone. At once the film began — and he found that it wasn't a horror film at all.

Was it supposed to be a musical? He'd been lured in under false pretenses. It began with a wedding, everyone breaking into song and dance. Then an engaged couple's car broke down: thunder, lightning, lashing rain, glimpses of an old dark house. Perhaps, after all — They were ushered to meet the mad scientist. Horridge gasped, appalled. The scientist's limp hands waved like snakes, his face moved blatantly. He was a homosexual.

This was a horror film, all right — far too horrible, and in the wrong way. Horridge tutted loudly, but the voice continued shrilling, the hands unfurled like unnatural flowers of flesh. The homosexual had surrounded himself with friends. Horridge could hardly tell them apart, nor did he want to: they were all the same species of filth.

The scientist created a muscle-man. Wouldn't it tear him apart if he touched it? The film refused to let that happen. Horridge complained, and was told to be quiet. How could anyone be interested in this — unless they were homosexuals themselves?

They must have known what the film was. Shoulders pressed against him, soft but muscular. He grew clammily warm all at once; the cinema was stuffed with flesh, the air was clogged with smoke, not all of which smelled like tobacco. Someone was thickly perfumed. Perhaps if he kept quiet they wouldn't bother him. His wet hands gripped his trembling knees.

What would they dare to show next? The homosexual was seducing the girl. How could she let such uncleanliness near her? Horridge closed his eyes, sickened — but at once he opened them, sure that he'd felt hot flesh edging closer in the dark. The homosexual was in the boy's room now. His silhouette moved on the curtain of the bed. Good God, they couldn't be about to —

He sprang to his feet before he knew he meant to. A sound filled his mouth like vomit. Nothing could make him sit through more of this. He forced his way out, struggling past legs, ignoring protests. He was trapped in a cage of flesh. Just let one of them touch him — they wouldn't touch anything else for a while. When he reached the doors his hands were shaking. He stumbled into the passage, among burly dark red pillars.

His nervousness hurried him to the Gents'. Someone was emerging. As he stood aside fretfully, he glimpsed the figure's long hair. He retreated, but he hadn't mistaken the sign: GENTLEMEN. He glared at the other, whose hair cascaded down his back and was spangled with rain.

He limped to the urinal stalls, a row of hollow oval heads, their lower lips protruding. As he stood at one, feeling at the mercy of his bladder, someone padded softly in. Did he hesitate behind Horridge before moving on?

Horridge ought to have used one of the cubicles. He didn't like the threat of being watched. He tried to hurry himself, but there seemed no end to the nervous flow. Unease gripped him by the back of the neck and forced his head to turn.

Had the man just turned away from watching? Horridge stared at the back of the head. In the clinical light the clipped tufts of black hair looked too vivid, unreal. The large square head was perched on the folds of the hood of the gray duffle coat.

He remembered the coat that had lain over the seat, head gaping. Had the man followed him because he'd protested at the film? He forced himself to finish, and struggled with the zip, which felt as though it meant to gnash its teeth.

He shoved upon the inner door. It cost him a few moments to realize that the door to the passage opened inward, and to grab the handle. Behind him the inner door halted half-open. It was being held.

He wrenched at the handle. Between the doors, the vestibule was claustrophobic as an airlock. His nervousness hindered the door. As he dragged it open, a large hand reached over his shoulder and laid itself flat on the wood.

He saw its hairs, black as an ape's. He saw the penumbra of moisture which outlined it on the door. It was inches from his face. He limped into the dim passage, clenching his eyes to see, and heard the man padding after him. He wouldn't be intimidated; the man had none of his friends with him now. He turned and stared straight into the man's eyes.

The face looked absurd on the large head: a small patch crowded with all the features, surrounded by luxuriant flesh. It gazed at Horridge for a moment, then it frowned. But it knew well enough why he was staring. It was the face he'd seen outside the house on Aigburth Drive, and spying from the window.

Was it the dim light that made it look indefinably different — or makeup? There was something about it, something he couldn't quite determine: something that reached deep into his guts and touched off a slow explosion of fear. As he fled, the threat of a nervous itch swarmed over the whole of his skin. His limp dragged at him.

He'd grasped the chill handle before he realized that his panic had driven him back to Screen 3. The unnatural voice squealed. He let go of the door as though it were the lid of a box of maggots.

Behind him, feet padded stealthily over the carpet. Horridge dodged toward the adjacent pair of doors. But was the man pursuing him? Perhaps he was returning to the cinema in search of victims —

At once Horridge knew. Revulsion surged through him, sweat burst out of his skin, gluing his clothes to him. The dim face that was bearing down on him was the face of the sketch in all the papers.

An expression was emerging onto the face. It seemed slow as corruption. Though he was fascinated, Horridge shuddered himself free. Before the expression could reveal itself, he hurled open the double doors.

Beyond them was another airlock. It was full of people, almost immobile beneath a stagnant spread of tobacco smoke. He struggled toward the far pair of doors. The hot thick cloth that blocked his way hardly yielded; people turned slowly to stare at him. He was panting, and deafened by his heartbeats. When he glanced back, he saw that the man was still following.

Horridge bumped into a stout woman. She raised a hand that could have engulfed his face in fat, and barred his way like a traffic policeman. "You just watch where you're going. There's a crippled lady here."

He had an urge to giggle wildly. He was being pursued by a murderer, as though he'd become trapped in one of the films — and nobody seemed to notice. But the absurdity wasn't reassuring, for his plight wasn't at all like a film: his clothes were sticking to him, his coat felt huge and cumbersome; the smell of his sweat suffocated him, he felt desperate for a bath. Even when delirious, he had never been so conscious of his body.

He squeezed past the woman, though she shouted, "Look at him, what's he think he's doing?" He dragged open one of the pair of doors. He hadn't reached an exit: he was in another cinema.

The long slope of rows of seats was full of an audience, staring at no film. Beneath red and green lights, the red and green pattern of the carpets jangled. Up the slope illuminated masks came drifting above ice cream trays. At the far end of the rows, he saw a luminous EXIT sign. An usherette touched his arm. "Can I see your ticket, please?"

The lights were dimming. She wouldn't have the chance to look too closely. He brandished the blurred sodden fragment of paper hastily at her. At once she said, "You're in the wrong cinema. You want— "

He pushed past her and stumbled toward what looked to be an empty row. Darkness flooded the cinema. The usherette was calling "Wait a minute, please, wait a minute!" The curtains parted, and a picture sprang onto the screen: Peter Sellers' face towered there, pretending to be a French policeman's. In the jerky light Horridge saw the man with the cramped face say something to the usherette, and come after him.

Horridge blundered along the row. It wasn't empty, after all. The children were reluctant to let him through. Fear ached in his stomach like gas, and filled his skull; his head seemed weightless, hardly part of him. The man couldn't harm him here, surely—but he could follow him home and find out where he lived.

He fell into the aisle. The wall slapped his palm, bruising it. The audience roared with laughter. He ran to the double doors. Another airlock. He fled through the dim purple box, and out. Beyond the double doors were double doors. He wrested them open. But the street was not beyond them: only laughter.

It was the cinema in which he'd first sat. The tilted screen was full of Peter Sellers' face, Orientally disguised. Was everything in league with the killer, to confuse him? An usherette advanced on him from the dark. The buzz of the indirect lighting seemed to crawl over his skin.

A bright arrow caught his eye: EXIT. He ran, dodging aside from a pillar, and grabbed the door to which he thought the arrow was pointing. Only the stare of the woman who emerged told him how mistaken he was.

As he fell back he heard the rain. Though his skin felt like moist unstable jelly, he forced himself to listen. Yes, it was rain, splashing faintly beyond a pair of doors beside him; it must be rain, it must. He banged the doors wide, glancing fearfully to see that there was nobody in sight behind him. He stumbled down a short stone passage, to a pair of doors locked with metal bars. He wrenched at the bars. He wrenched again, and the doors crashed open, freeing him.

Rain washed his face and stung his blinded eyes. His panic clung to him; he couldn't tell where he'd emerged. At last he saw how the side street led to the main road. He fled toward the lights. At the corner he blundered against a newspaper-stall — a carton that bore a pile of newspapers scattered with coins. The papers spilled, overlapping: HAVE YOU SEEN THIS MAN? MAN? MAN? Everything seemed to be addressing him.

He limped toward Lime Street, past the front of the cinema. There was no sign of the man in the bright foyer. Wind and rain swept across St. George's Plateau, past the stone lions and the diggings for the underground railway. He hurried downhill to the previous bus stop, and stood in shadow to be less conspicuous. The ache in his leg began to count the steps he'd taken today.

His panic was subsiding, or transforming. The nervousness that crept over his skin was more purposeful; it nagged him to act. He wished furiously that he hadn't fled. He should have called the manager, the police.

He didn't believe in coincidences. The more unlikely they seemed, the more that convinced him they were meant to happen. Shadows dripped around him; his sweat turned chill. His fingers worked in his pockets, frustrated. He had seen the killer three times now, in as many days. That was no coincidence. But what was he meant to do?

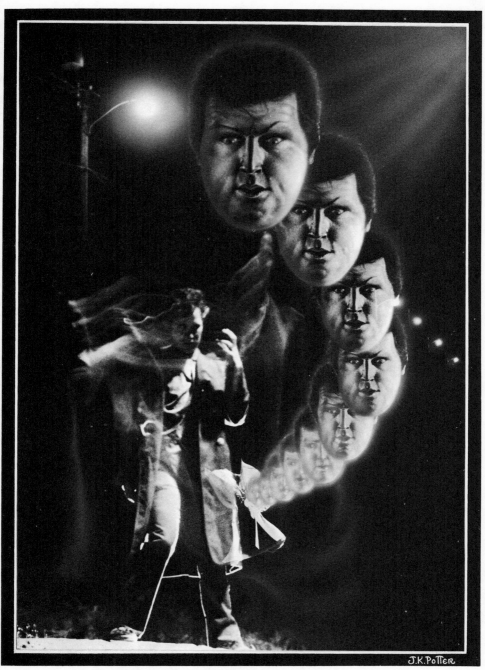

Everything seemed to be addressing him.

CHAPTER IV

"Edge Hill Public Library," Cathy said.

The telephone held its breath. For years she'd longed for the chance to say, "If this is an obscene phone call I'll just go and get a chair." But no doubt it was one of the boys they'd chased out for playing football with a book. "Edge Hill Library," she announced again.

"Is Mrs. Cathy Gardner there, please?"

Was her mother mocking her telephone voice, or had she genuinely failed to recognize her? "It's me," Cathy said.

"Oh, hello. Happy New Year." Perhaps her mother had been holding off the conversation while she thought of what to say. "Did you survive Christmas?"

"Yes, thanks. Just about," Cathy joked. "Happy New Year."

"Did he come?"

"Yes, on Boxing Day."

"What did he say about me this time?"

"Oh, he just wanted to know how you were." In fact Cathy's father had asked whether she'd returned to Lewis, who had left her for good shortly after the separation. He'd known the answer, but had wanted the reassurance, the secret delight.

"Did he. That was good of him." Her breathing became curt. Then she dismissed the subject, and said, "Have you thought any more about buying a house?"

"Yes, a bit." But she didn't think Peter had.

Did her mother sense that turn of her thoughts? "How are Peter's studies?"

"All right. He'll have more time when he's left the libraries."

Her mother's brief dissatisfied sound seemed unhappy — because Cathy wasn't being open? "I've got to go now. There are people waiting at the counter," Cathy said.

"Have you? Well, if you must go, you must." All of a sudden, as though she had been hoping they could talk longer, she said plaintively, "I hope you'll both come to see me soon."

"We will, mummy. Don't worry." The wire hissed emptily. She was about to repeat her promise when a click left her alone with the long anonymous whirr of the dial tone.

As she hurried to serve the queue, she felt dispirited. Was she due for a fit of depression? She felt heavy as a Christmas pudding. Feeling fat was often the first sign. Although she knew that it must end eventually, depression robbed her of all sense of time.

"Got any love books?" women were pleading. She showed them where the romances were kept separate. "Where's the football?" a boy demanded. He wasn't asking for his ball back; she pointed to the shelves where football books were filed, at 796.334 — you learned that classification quickly in Liverpool libraries. An old lady carrying a poodle like a tartan bag returned an overdue book; since nobody was looking, Cathy didn't charge her a fine. The man who always said, "Voters' list, please" as if instructing a servant tried to look as though he was first in the queue, and Cathy ignored him as long as she could.

She cleared returned books from beneath the counter, and fled as the hordes converged on the book-trolley. In a moment she'd join her colleagues, filing dishevelled books on the shelves. A woman laden with screaming infants screamed at them as she hunted through the newspapers for addresses of vacant flats. Cathy wouldn't have screamed — at least, she hoped not. She didn't want to have children in a flat.

Two little girls came to pester her. "Show us some Father Christmas books."

"Please."

"Please," they said, so soberly that she couldn't tell if they were making fun of her.

"I expect all the Father Christmases are out." But she went to the shelves. One little girl took her hand stickily and said, "You know your husband?"

"Yes, I believe we've been introduced."

Ignoring that, the little girl said, "He works here too, doesn't he?"

"He used to. But he's leaving the libraries soon."

She might as well have announced that Father Christmas had resigned. "Where will he work then?" the other child said incredulously.

"I don't know. Somewhere, I expect." She hoped so. She pointed at the shelves: "Nothing, I'm sorry. No Father Christmases at all."

"Show us some" — the little girl screwed up her face, to squeeze out a problem that would detain her — "some Rudolph the Red-Nosed Reindeers."

"No, you must find your own books now. Someone's waiting to be served."

It was the man who came into Sefton Park library: a nondescript man, except for his limp. He stared, as though she had no right to be here — as if she arranged where she was sent on relief! "Can I help you?" she said.

He seemed to be debating whether to retreat, like an embarrassed man faced with a girl assistant at a chemist's. If he wanted the librarian, let him ask: she was upstairs at her tea break. He controlled himself visibly, and said, "May I see a list of names and addresses for this area, please?"

He sounded too polite, as though concealing a dislike of her. "You want the voters' list," she said, glancing at the table where the rude man sat. "Are you looking for a particular street?"

Never before had she seen such intense distrust peering from anyone's eyes. She felt almost guilty. When he spoke, she could tell that he still didn't trust her. "Aigburth Drive," he said.

"Why, I live there," she would have said to many people — but she didn't feel like saying so to him. She felt wickedly delighted that he'd come to the wrong library. "You want the voters' list at Sefton Park," she said.

His eyes pinched narrow. Surely he didn't suspect her of lying. Maybe she was being paranoid, imagining suppressed violence in his voice as he said, "You must have it here as well."

"I'm afraid not." His continuing disbelief angered her. "If you'll just come over here," she said, "I'll ask that gentleman to let you see our list."

The rude man raised his head, hostile as a feeding animal. "No, no thank you," the limping man said hastily. "It's all right. Thank you for your help. You've been very helpful."

He limped out. The doors swung back and forth, back and forth, closing their gap. What a weird character! Her anger faded quickly — but not, she was pleased to find, before it had burned away the threat of depression. She joined her colleagues, who were muttering at stray books. In an odd way, the incident of the limping man had cheered her up. She always enjoyed mysteries.

CHAPTER V

As he fled onto Lodge Lane, Horridge gasped with relief. The crowd within the bus shelter stared at him through apertures framed by claws of glass. The girl had seemed to know more than she should. What reason could there be for her to know?

He trudged unevenly, cursing his display of panic. The man at the table had looked like an official, but there had been no reason for him to notice Horridge. By fleeing, Horridge had drawn attention to himself — and he must be inconspicuous now.

He trudged. His leg throbbed, and felt swollen. His thigh felt as though burdened with a clinging child. The memory of his flight through the cinemas was aching there. He had to plod and sway like a drunkard. He couldn't move faster than his doubts.

What had the girl been doing in that library? She wasn't supposed to be there. She might almost have been planted there to send him on this trudge, to give his doubts more time to trouble him. She had seemed all too ready to tell him that she couldn't help, without bothering to look in any index. How could she have known that he'd gone to that library so as to finish as quickly as possible what he had to do?

At last he managed to escape the faded street, the patrolling shoppers, the plague of shops that displayed dusty emptiness. At the roundabout he found he dared not pass the decayed house. He had to use the path just within the park, which followed the road but whose border of trees screened him from the house. He limped hastily by, distracting himself with a glimpse of a bench that had been turned to face away from the park, no doubt by vandals.

The lake was surrounded by fishermen, immobile as posts. If they'd nothing better to do they should go and clean up Cantril Farm, to make it fit for decent folk to live in. Why weren't they at work? No wonder the Social Security were suspicious, with all these people who didn't know right from wrong. But that was no reason to treat him as if he didn't know how to behave. Babble, babble. Was his mind trying to distract him from his purpose too?

It seemed so, for his thoughts tried to fasten on Lark Lane, to slow him. How like a village it was: a butcher's open-fronted shop with slabs, an old police station, an antique shop glowing brassily. It felt familiar, as though he had been here as a child — but he was sure he never had. Couldn't he linger? A fish and chip shop said it was "Chinese and English," which was a lie: it couldn't be both. Enough chuntering. Get on with the job that must be done.

Behind the library counter stood a bearded youth with far too much hair. No, he wasn't the goatish creature from the corrupt house. He tugged his beard as though ringing himself awake and said, "Can I help you?"

Exactly the girl's words. They were like automatons, not a pinch of character among them. "I want to consult the voters' list, please." Now that his request could be more specific he felt a little less uneasy.

"What street do you want?"

He wouldn't be caught like that twice. "I'll find that out for myself, thank you."

The youth groped out the list from beneath the counter. Through the dustily translucent plastic cover Horridge read AIGBURTH DRIVE, blurred as though drowned. He'd soon dredge it up. He sat as far as possible from the counter, in the junior wing. Surely the children wouldn't spy on him: Britain wasn't one of those countries yet, however many people wanted it to be. But he pretended to scrutinize several pages, in case anyone was watching. Only when his nervousness began to creep behind him, urging him to flee while he was still safe, did he turn to Aigburth Drive. He wasn't safe — he hadn't been since he had looked into the killer's eyes. He must make himself safe.

An instinct surer than his thoughts directed him to the exact spot on the page. His gaze fastened on the number of the house: it appeared eight times, alongside eight names. Lurking among them, pretending to be like the rest, was the name.

>   Harty, Brendan Sean (Flat 1)
>   Lunt, Aneurin Cornelius (Flat 2)
>   Craig, Roy (Flat 3)
>   Adamson, Frances Sybil (Flat 4)
>   Day, Patricia Anne (Flat 5)
>   Shone, Susan Gloria (Flat 5)
>   Gardner, Peter David (Flat 6)
>   Gardner, Catherine Angela (Flat 6)

Alongside the listings, consecutive numbers counted the names. Somewhere on such a list, Horridge must be numbered. No time to brood on that now. The killer lived on the middle floor, and his flat must be one of the two middle numbers — which singled his name out at once.

>   Roy Craig

It lay there challenging him to see through its disguise. It sounded too masculine, too strong: that betrayed it — that, and the fact that "Roy" was a little like "gay." That was what homosexuals called themselves, though Horridge was damned if he knew what they had to be gay about: it was an insult to the word.

Something else was struggling to emerge into his mind: a memory, a similarity — When he grasped it, he sniggered mirthlessly. Two children stared at him and hid, giggling. The name of the latest victim had been Roylance. That was no coincidence. Perhaps the killer's guilty conscience had made him leave that clue for those who weren't too blind to see.

He fumbled in his pockets. His pencil was shorter than his thumb, and as blunt. Still, it would write — but on what? He didn't want to draw attention to himself by asking for paper. Disentangling his birth certificate from the rest of his documents, he printed Roy Craig's name on the back. Then, from an obscure inkling that it might prove useful, he listed the names of the other tenants.

He stared at Craig's name, hidden in the official list. Why didn't it writhe maggotlike with shame? Let it stay as still as it liked — it couldn't hide from him now. "Thank you very much," he said at the counter, delighted with the way his politeness concealed his plan.

When he emerged, the cold seized him. His resolution began to shiver. He was provided with a telephone box too soon: a pair of them stood back to back not twenty paces from the library. He hadn't thought out what to say. He mustn't falter when he picked up the phone. Besides, the boxes stood between a Ladies' and a bus queue. Suppose he were overheard?

There was another box beyond the dual carriageway. The roadway was lethal with cars, and railings barred pedestrians from crossing — unless you leapt over, of course, assuming you were lucky enough not to have an injured leg. A subway trained pedestrians from one pavement to the other. Too much regimentation for his liking: it reminded him of Cantril Farm. There would be a phone box in Lark Lane.

But now he had faltered, his purpose turned liquid within him. Though he struggled with the feeling, he was heartened not to see a phone box in Lark Lane immediately. No need to feel guilty — he could use the delay to prepare his words. Interruptions distracted him: a butcher's cleaver chopped something brightly raw, a man trotting delicately ahead of Horridge with two tartaned poodles kept stopping to let his pets drip. All he could hold still in his mind was Roy Craig's name.

It was too good for the creature. How could names be so unfair? Decent people were made to sound like buffoons — such as John Horridge. "Horridge the Porridge" they'd used to chant at school, until he'd kicked and punched them: and then he was always blamed for fighting. "Horridge, you horror!" a teacher had roared, grabbing him by the collar, frowning at the smothered titters of the onlookers like a comedian pretending to be angry with his audience. For years Horridge had looked forward to leaving school. He'd expected life outside to be fairer.

Babble, babble. A glimpse hushed his memories: a side street, a tall red shape on the pavement, a cage with windows — a phone box. Apprehension plunged deep into his stomach. He advanced two lopsided steps, and saw that the box was occupied. He was reprieved. Angrily he forced himself to approach. He'd wait, and compose his speech while waiting. He was nearly at the box when a woman emerged from a car amid a fall of parcels and stood beside the box. She would have time for a good look at him. He retreated toward Aigburth Drive.

The road was empty of traffic. The tips of the bare trees swayed nervously; a few dogs played in the park. He was afraid to phone, was he? Scared to behave like a man? What was he, a lump of cringing slimy scum that slunk round corners and went limp whenever there was a problem to be faced? Wasn't he a man?

Ahead of him on the deserted pavement a telephone box stood soldierly. It seemed to march toward him as he walked. There could be no excuses now, nothing to tempt him to falter, nothing to intervene between him and the box. If he passed it he was a coward, less than a woman. Only yards beyond it lurked the house that concealed Roy Craig. If he passed that house without having phoned he would be guilty too, soiled, an accomplice. He strode forward unevenly and dragged open the door of the box.

There was no directory on the shelf. He couldn't use that as an excuse: he'd often heard the number on the radio, he had memorized it in case he ever needed it. Perhaps the phone wouldn't work. Furious with himself, he groped for a coin and dialed.

The silence gave him time to feel how near Craig's house was. It didn't matter. Craig couldn't spy on him: that window of the box was covered with a poster for domestic telephones, saying ISN'T IT WARMER AT HOME? The phone was ringing now: a pair of pulses, another. The sound was so close within his ear that it might have been his blood, throbbing unnaturally. If they didn't answer after six rings—

He heard no click, but where the next pulse should have been, a girl's voice said, "Merseyside Police, can I help you?"

The pay tone cut her off, a rapid peeping like the cry of a frantic bird. He thrust at the coin, which refused to slip in. It was bent, or the coin-box was faulty! He struggled with it while the tone babbled urgently and sweat covered him like a shower of hot ash. All at once the coin broke through into the slot. A silence followed which he dared not disturb.

"Merseyside Police, can I help you?"

She was still there. If he had lost her, he wouldn't have been able to call again. But she had given him no time to think of what to say. Jesus Mary and Joseph, whom should he ask for? When he spoke, it was only to fight off the suffocating frustration. "I want to speak to someone about the murder of Roylance."

He sounded absurd to himself: he might have been calling a shop to complain about damaged goods. But after a short pause she said, "Just hold on, I'll put you through to someone."

Waiting, he started nervously. Had the receiver turned live and dangerous? Eventually he realized that the irregular thumping which shook the plastic in his hand was the jerking of a nerve in his palm. The plastic was slippery with sweat. What was taking them so long? Were they tracing his call?

If they didn't answer by the time he'd counted ten, they'd had their chance. No, his mind couldn't sneak that excuse past him. The phone sucked at his ear and kept touching his lips like a plastic kiss, whenever he forgot to hold it and other people's germs away. Was somebody whispering amid the loud hiss? Were they sending a car to trap him?

It didn't matter. He must see this through. He knew he was right. He must act like a man. Instantly he saw how he could make sure he wasn't recognized. He shared a grin with himself in the disfigured mirror.

The man's voice leapt out as if to scare him. "Yes, sir, can I help you?"

All these people pretending to be so helpful! This time they needed help from him. "You want to know who murdered Roylance," Horridge said, making his voice as high and effeminate as he could.

"Yes, sir. We have that under investigation."

Horridge heard an almost imperceptible change in his tone. He was fooled, he thought Horridge was a pansy! "Well, I can tell you," Horridge said.

"Can I have your name and address, please?"

"No, you most certainly can not." He grinned back at himself between the tangled graffiti, delighted with his control of the situation. He was unaware now of his sweat, the stuffy box, the slippery burden in his hand.

"Take this down," he said, pulling out his birth certificate. "I won't repeat it. I'm going to tell you the name of the killer."

When he heard paper rustling, he read out Craig's name and address. "Have you got that?" he said tartly, and stood grinning at his grubby entangled reflection. What in heaven's name was he waiting for — to be trapped by the police?

The phone was halfway to the receiver when the policeman's voice arrested him. "May I ask where you got this information, sir?"

Horridge couldn't resist fooling him once more. Effeminately wistful, he said, "Roylance was my friend."

Stuffing his birth certificate into his pocket, he elbowed his way out of the box. He felt inflated by laughter. He must suppress it, in case it drew attention to him. Next time he mustn't hesitate so long, not when having acted felt like this. No longer was he conscious of his limp. He felt weightless with self-confidence.

He absorbed the view of the leafless trees against the pale bare sky. Nothing else had looked so clean to him since the quarry. Deliberately he walked toward Craig's house. He had nothing to fear now. It was Craig's turn to be afraid, just as his bound and helpless victims must have been. A breeze chilled Horridge's grin.

The sight of the bench that faced away from the park halted him. Did he dare? But there was nothing to be dared — only to be enjoyed. Craig couldn't touch him now. He crossed the road and sat on the bench. When the police arrived, he could pretend to be asleep. Eager as a child at his first pantomime, he waited for the show to begin.

He waited. The dark house squatted before him, sullen as a bully; it seemed to challenge him. He smiled tightly: he wasn't to be tricked into anything rash, he had the upper hand now. Whenever he gazed at the house for a while, it appeared to stir nervously.

Bedraggled leaves crawled along the pavement. The shadow of the house crept toward him like a stain. A glass dagger gleamed before him on the roadway, amid fragments of a bottle. How long had he been waiting? Since he'd sat down the shadow had crossed the road.

Perhaps the policeman hadn't believed him. Or perhaps he had, yet intended to do nothing. Horridge didn't even know his name; he had been just an anonymous official voice. What secret might the owner of that voice have had? Horridge's thoughts dragged his head down to stare at his shabby toe caps. He should have known better than to trust the police, after what they'd done to him.

He had still been at school; his father hadn't long been allowing him to help on the ladder at weekends and on summer evenings. The knocking at the front door had shaken the house. He'd heard his mother's sick enfeebled voice crying out upstairs, from where she was trapped in her bed: "What's wrong? What is it? What's the matter?"

Two policemen had wanted to know everything he knew about the cat burglaries. His father had tried to argue with them while his mother had cried out in the emptiness, unanswered. At last his father had given up, exhausted. "Go with them, John. Let them take your fingerprints. They'll soon see their mistake." But as he hurried upstairs to calm his wife, hadn't he glanced uncertainly at his son?

They'd questioned Horridge at the police station for two hours. They had seemed unable to believe that he hadn't heard about the burglaries, all of which had been of first-floor bedrooms. Because he minded his own business, they'd suspected him of lying. Eventually they had taken his fingerprints; then grudgingly they'd let him go. One of them had pointed at their copy of his prints. "Just remember — behave yourself." He had never found out who had given his name to the police; he had suspected everyone.

He jerked free of the trance of his memory. A car was slowing outside Craig's house. It halted there. It wasn't marked like a police car — but when the two men strode toward the house, purposeful but unhurried, Horridge knew at once what they were. He had been right to phone. Some people could be trusted, after all.

He narrowed his eyes unobtrusively, so as to appear to be sleeping, and watched them ring the bell. Suppose Craig were not at home? Suppose one of the other tenants saw the police and warned Craig to stay away? Then Horridge would have helped him to escape justice! He squeezed his eyes viciously shut, to punish himself.

He heard the clatter of a window, and opened them in time to see Craig leaning out like a gargoyle. The swollen face seemed to venture into the daylight reluctantly as a maggot's. "Who is it?" Craig called. His voice was deep enough to pass for a man's, but Horridge heard something wrong with his intonation.

The policemen had to step out from beneath the porch before he could see them. "Mr. Roy Craig?" one said, and displayed something in a small folder.

Craig hestitated, peering. "Just a moment," he said, and closed the window.

As the policemen waited, Horridge saw them exchange a meaningful nod. He hugged himself, not to keep out the cold but to make sure that none of his glee drained away. Mightn't there be a back way out of the house? At this moment Craig might be making his escape! For the love of heaven, why didn't one of them go round the back? He squirmed on the bench, restraining his urge to do their job for them.

The door in the porch faltered open. When he saw Craig being escorted into the darkness within, Horridge closed his eyes gently and grew calm. Only once before had he felt so secure — in his grandparents' cottage in Wales.

Some time later he heard the front door open. He let his eyes widen. No need to pretend to be asleep. He was greedy for the sight of Craig's arrest.

The policemen were emerging from the porch, but Craig stood in the inner doorway. Was he resisting arrest? Then why was he smiling? Was he so brazen that he could still smile? Not until Horridge realized that the policemen were apologizing did the truth seize him like paralysis.

It was as though the arrest had been turned on him — for one policeman was striding straight toward him. Horridge's legs shook; if he stood up, they would give way. If he fled, his limp would deliver him to them. He closed his eyes, pretending sleep, but his eyelids twitched violently. The policeman halted just beyond the pavement and gazed at him. Horridge couldn't catch his breath; the gaze was interminable, agonizing. Then the policeman kicked the fragments of the broken bottle into the gutter and returned to the car.

When the car had moved away, Horridge sat trembling on the bench, like an alcoholic tramp bereft of his drug. His mind felt empty and aching as a bully purged by sickness. Suddenly he realized that Craig could see him. The creature must be supremely confident now. Suppose he pursued Horridge home? Horridge jerked himself to his feet and fled toward Lodge Lane.

A bus was halted at the stop. While he limped toward the doors, the driver gazed at him as though he were a second-rate comedian. Horridge wouldn't have put it past him to drive off at the last moment — but he only made the engine roar impatiently.

Horridge clambered aboard panting and thrust the fare at the driver. The man only stared, waiting until at last he saw the notice:

EXACT FARES

PAY HERE

This driver does not accept money

That was a joke: never accepted what was offered, more like, with all their strikes and union meetings. As Horridge fumbled for the right change the driver watched indifferently, smug and stolid behind his official notice. He'd have liked to wipe the smugness off the man's face. At last he found the change and dropped it in the slot. Finally satisfied, the bus leapt away — but before he reached his seat Horridge had to stumble back, having forgotten to claim his ticket from the machine. He could never remember how to behave with this new system. They couldn't leave anything alone.

Around him passengers babbled. Nobody took any notice of him. Couldn't they see what he had been through? He felt as though he was in a madhouse. Was the whole world mad? Nobody seemed to care that a killer, perhaps a madman, was loose.

But of course the killer was a homosexual, which made everything all right. You mustn't do anything to upset homosexuals. Homosexuality was the most natural thing in the world: at least, that was what the government and the media — and now, apparently, the police — would like everyone to think. Horridge wouldn't have believed that the police, the so-called guardians of the law, could be so corrupted if he hadn't seen it for himself. They'd been quick enough to take him away on suspicion of burglary, but they mustn't touch Craig, oh no — not when he was a homosexual. After all, he'd only killed two people. Perhaps they were homosexuals themselves. What sort of identification might have been hidden in the folder which one of them had shown Craig?

When the bus reached West Derby Road he jabbed the bell-push viciously: pity it wasn't an eye. As the door faltered open, he glared at the driver. The man thought himself so secure, perched in his official box. He needed to be put in his place. But suppose Craig were trying to catch up with Horridge, to find out where he lived? He stepped hastily down.

He waited beneath what remained of a bus shelter. People hemmed him in with incessant vapid chatter. How could they prate such nonsense — unless they had something to hide? It must be meant to disguise their thoughts. Everyone was conspiring, or deluded by conspiracy. Only the other day he'd heard the latest filth that they were trying to make people swallow: that everyone was homosexual, whether consciously or not. He wasn't to be brainwashed into thinking that of himself. On the other hand, he was sure there were more homosexuals than would admit to it. Today's little spectacle proved that Craig had friends in high places.

A grubby bus to Cantril Farm arrived. Its grimy windows looked painted with fog. Downstairs people were smoking, despite the notices. You could get away with anything these days.

He sat, cramped into himself by the oppressive babbling. Friends in high places! They called that filth friendship! And their arguments were so pitiful. They tried to make out that because animals did it, it was natural: they wanted to behave like animals. They were a cancer on the human race. Perhaps their behavior was the source of cancer. So much money was spent on cancer research, yet nobody thought to look at the obvious. Couldn't they see that filth must breed worse filth? What men and women did together was bad enough.

The bus groaned through Tuebrook, past ragged gaps where streets had been ripped out as though they were infected teeth. Homosexuals must be close as Jews, protecting one another from normal people. Something had to be done about them before they took over completely. They ought to be put on an island where they couldn't contaminate anyone else — except that that was too good for them: no doubt they'd enjoy romping about naked all day.

Here was West Derby Village, blurred by the coated windows. Among the gleaming semi-detached houses, creamy white stone lions flourished flags on the gateposts of a park. The first time he had ridden this route, having accepted rehousing in Cantril Farm, that glimpse had delighted him. Cantril Farm had sounded like countryside: he'd thought that was where he was going.

Melwood Drive was lined with trees that soon fell behind, making way for council flats followed by an army barracks. At least there couldn't be any homosexuals in there: soldiers were men. Nevertheless the sight depressed him. The long low buildings with their regimented windows reminded him too much of Cantril Farm.

And here it was: home. He sniggered bitterly to himself. Within seconds Cantril Farm had closed around him, nothing to see in any direction but pebble-dashed walls, anonymous boxes for keeping people in, nothing to distinguish them but graffiti thick as vines. Over the lower roofs, tower blocks stood like guards. The estate looked like its purpose: to make everyone the same. Its name had tricked him into living here. It would be a good place to imprison all the homosexuals. That would soon teach them how to behave.

Over Christmas there had been no buses. He had been trapped in Cantril Farm. Yet compared with his situation now, that had been easy to bear. Never before except in nightmares had he felt so helpless. Frustration oozed through him like poison; its sourness filled his mouth. He gripped the bar of the seat in front of him until his whitened fingers trembled. What could he do in order to fight the unfairness of things? He was being carried back to prison, where Craig ought to be.

CHAPTER VI

As Horridge pulled out the stack of newspapers, something rattled deep in the chest of drawers.

He started; the newspapers jerked in his hands. The chest was suddenly as ominous as it had seemed when it had stood in his parents' bedroom, made dimmer by the huge shadows of the tassels on the lampshade. Those shadows had never been quite still. They'd hovered round the bed like a restless audience.

He had often wondered uneasily what his parents had kept in the looming chest next to the bed. After their deaths, when he'd dragged the chest away from the wall it had revealed its own shape on the aging wallpaper, like a patch of grass beneath a stone.

He laid the newspapers on the floor, then he inched out the bottom drawer. Perhaps the sound had been caused by something fallen from a drawer — but what could it be? Might it be a rodent, lurking in the darkness? The idea made his room seem unclean.

He knelt, and peered into the space left by the drawer. A long thin object lay in its depths: a bone? It didn't look alive, whatever it was, yet his fingers hesitated as they reached in: its texture might be unpleasant. But it proved to be cold metal, or a substance equally hard. He fished it out and gazed at it, bewildered. It was his father's cut-throat razor.

It must have been transferred inside the chest of drawers from his old home. After his father's death he had meant to throw away the razor but had been unable to find it. He remembered the loud scrape of the blade on his father's throat, the foam oozing down his face like spawn alive with hairs, the specks of blood.

He pushed the razor hastily away, but kept gazing. The timing of his find—now, when he felt so vulnerable, so desperately in need of self-defense—could not be ignored. He carried the razor to the bathroom, which was even more spacious than a telephone box, and washed it fastidiously.

The tap muttered and groaned. The plumbing had never sounded right. He could do nothing, and he certainly didn't intend to call the plumber whose van was often parked nearby: he wasn't about to put his inadequacies on show. He wiped the razor and laid it on top of the chest of drawers.

He read the newspapers. Here was the story of Craig's murderous career. Horridge had bought the most detailed reports, and kept them. He felt bound to know the worst, to learn how low the world could sink. You couldn't stay safe by keeping your eyes shut. The young men had been bound and helpless, soiled, mutilated. In the photographs they looked hardly more than children.

He read, moaning with horror. He writhed inwardly, frustrated by his helplessness. It was thought that the killer had enticed the young men from a public toilet used by homosexuals for picking up their victims. They called such places cottages. How could they be allowed to besmear words in that way?

He knew what a cottage ought to be: a place where one's parents retired, somewhere one could retreat from the grime and the clamor. He'd never known what had happened to the cottage after his grandparents had died. He remembered his grandfather, an old tree of a man, strong and quiet and gnarled.

Someone thumped on the window; the glass boomed. Nothing separated the window from the public walk except an unfenced patch of grass. His heart leapt unsteadily before he did. When he dragged the curtains apart, a gang of boys was running away. None of the boys round here was up to any good—nor the girls either. He glanced at the top of the chest of drawers. Just let them take care. He wasn't defenseless now.

He'd lost the thread of his memories. He would have liked to recall the cottage. He wished he had some photographs of Wales. Still, perhaps it was just as well that he couldn't see the cottage—no doubt it was overcrowded with young layabouts now, taking drugs and living off the country, as they called it. They lived off the country, right enough, but not in the way they meant the phrase.

He returned the papers to their drawer. Reading further would depress him too profoundly now. He stared through the window. He might as well have stared at the pane itself: out there were small marshes of muddy grass, separated by paths and hemmed in by anonymous walls, but none of that was visible — most of the lamps had been smashed. In the upstairs flat, a record throbbed as though savages were invading.

By the time he had washed himself, scrubbing his face until it blushed, the drums had stopped. The silence didn't enlarge his rooms, which seemed scarcely larger than interview cubicles, and as featureless. He'd left the walls plain white, thinking they would look clean. Often they made him feel trapped in nothingness.

When the water ceased jerking out of the tap, he heard mumbling somewhere in his flat. Had he left the radio on? No, the receiver was silent — and besides, surely the voice was too monotonous for the radio. It was beyond the bathroom wall. Was it speaking to him — trying to hypnotize him?

Eventually he realized that it was the sound of water in the pipes. It still didn't sound any less like a voice. Even when he closed his bedroom door he could hear the mumbling, as though an idiot were talking in his sleep.

Over the years he'd learned the source of every sound in his old home. The sounds had been familiar and comforting. He still didn't know where half the sounds here came from. It would take a damn sight more than that to scare him. As soon as he'd slipped the razor beneath his pillow he felt less vulnerable.

He lay in the dark, which robbed him of all sense of the size of his bedroom. He wished he could afford a new clock; the dark allowed the ticking to grow louder, louder. The sound was a four-beat rocking, too quick and harsh to be a lullaby. Roy Craig, kill-er. Roy Craig, kill-er. Couldn't it stop, just for a moment? Couldn't it at least slow down? Wouldn't it give him even a second of silence during which he might fall asleep?

He had no idea when it stopped: perhaps hours later. He was in the alley, among the stuffed dustbins. The girls surrounded him. As he backed against the wall, the rough stone plucked at his clothes. The bricks were hard and harsh; they felt like his fever dream, when his brain had seemed composed of chunks of rubble that ground together.

"Make it stand up," the girls were saying. The icy wall pressed against him. He was shivering; they must think he was afraid — and he was, for once his father had beaten him for handling himself. His body shook and throbbed, at the mercy of his panic. He stood helpless as he was seized by a painful orgasm.

He woke terrified, and pressed himself against the wall through the blankets, recoiling from the stain in the bed. For the love of God, why had that happened? It hadn't happened in the alley; he had been far too scared to achieve an erection. "Don't you be going with those girls," his father had used to say ominously, and Horridge hadn't wanted to; they had tricked and trapped him. Beyond the alley walls, frost had grown like lichen on the roofs of the outside toilets. "He can't make it stand up. He must be queer," the girls had said, and he'd listened appalled while they explained what that meant.

He felt as though he had been possessed in his sleep. He couldn't be blamed for that — but his bed felt invaded. Only once in his life had he masturbated, alone in his old home after his parents had died, his willpower enfeebled by dozing. The experience had been wholly unpleasant, pumping away as though to make a reluctant toilet work, to achieve the sudden uncontrollable flushing. How could people waste their time wallowing in sex? It wasn't as though it took much self-control to refrain. After all, one seldom had erections, and then only while asleep.

He was growing calmer, the side of the bed on which he'd taken refuge was beginning to feel safe, sleep was slowing down his thoughts — when, amid the ticking of the clock, he heard another sound.

Though his head was loud with blood, he raised it gently from the pillow. His hand slid directly and silently to grasp the handle of the razor. He managed to hold his body still as he listened.

There was no sound. Nor could he recall exactly what he had heard before. Perhaps it hadn't been a sound that he had sensed — but something had warned him that an intruder was creeping about nearby. Perhaps that had made him dream that he was helpless.

But he was not, even if Craig had come to silence him. He inched himself free of the blankets. Though his heel touched the stain, chill and slimy in the dark, he succeeded in setting his feet down noiselessly on the carpet. As he stood up, he felt for the blade. It emerged from the handle with a slight click.

He paced stealthily to the door. His fingerprints roamed its cold surface, and found the colder handle, which he turned minutely. It would be just like this place to betray him with an unexpected creak—but the door edged wide silently. He reached into the darkness, holding the blade in his other hand before his face, and twitched the light on.

The light surprised only the empty room. There was nowhere an intruder could hide; his furniture was sparse. He switched off the light at once. He wasn't satisfied. Somebody was up to no good nearby. He groped his way among the furniture, and peered between the curtains.

Outside, on the walk which passed his apology for a yard, was a light where no light should be. It was feeling its way along the fence on the opposite side of the walk. The figure that carried the torch was patting an object on the fence: a notice, where none had been when Horridge had come home.

What the devil was the fellow doing? What did the notice say? Surely it couldn't be Craig, not unless he had some mad plan to scare Horridge. But Horridge meant to find out what the man was up to. He felt his way back to the bedroom, and groped into his overcoat and shoes.

He eased open the outer door. His L-shaped flat walled off two sides of his meager yard: hardly even a yard, more a stray patch of concrete onto which the door opened. Over his door, stone steps led from the yard to the upstairs flat. He couldn't be brought any lower in the world than living below stairs.

Now, for once, he welcomed the stairs. They concealed him while he peered out. In his pocket he held the razor ajar and ready. He was nervously eager for action.

At first he could see nothing. All around him, concrete made the night massive and claustrophobic. Then he glimpsed a flickering. A passage led the walk past his outer wall and beneath the bridging upper floor. The torchlight was in that passage.

He limped rapidly yet stealthily to the end of his wall. The man was sticking a notice to the wall of the passage. Horridge gripped the handle in his pocket. "What are you doing?" he said loudly.

The man whirled; his hand dragged the notice awry. The torch-beam poked at Horridge's face, dazzling him. Then the man relaxed, or decided not to be intimidated. "You aren't blind, are you?" he demanded, and gestured at the notice with the light.

Above a caricature of a Negro family, the notice said SAY NO TO A BLACK BRITAIN! As Horridge squinted at him, the man's face emerged from the dazzle: eyes swollen out of proportion by thick spectacles, a withdrawn chin. He'd seen this man sometimes, reading the newspapers in Cantril Farm Library.

The man must have observed his approval of the notice, for he said, "Don't you think we should get rid of all these foreigners?"

Horridge nodded curtly. It wasn't the man's place to interrogate him. But the man continued, "Don't you think we ought to do something about all these layabouts sponging on the welfare state?"

Horridge didn't quite trust him. It was like brainwashing, this rapid stream of questions that demanded only agreement. They didn't sound like the man's own questions; Horridge suspected he'd learned them by rote. He couldn't think for himself.

A cold breeze made the cuffs of Horridge's pajama trousers shiver. All this was getting him nowhere. Why couldn't the fellow stand up and say what he knew was right, instead of skulking about under cover of darkness? Before the man could interrogate him further, Horridge demanded, "And what about homosexuals?"

The man's enormous eyes fluttered in their glass bowls, like startled fish. "I don't like them," he said.

Horridge pointed at the notice. "How is that sort of thing going to get rid of them?"

"Have you got a better way?"

Horridge had trapped himself. Though the man's triumphant stare enraged him, he couldn't reply. The man said, "Shall I take your name and address for some of our literature?"

"No, thank you. I'm quite capable of thinking for myself."

He stared until the man moved away. The torch-beam wavered on mud spiky with grass; it grew vague, and vanished. No, Horridge didn't want their pamphlets drawing attention to him — not while he had to decide what to do about Craig.

He locked himself into his flat. He knew of the movement which printed the notices. He might have joined that movement, if he had believed in belonging to groups — although he didn't care for the way they marched through areas where immigrants lived, to insult them: that was behaving like militant students. Militant! That meant to be like a soldier, but soldiers were on the side of law and order — not at all like students. Still, you couldn't blame the movement for marching: they wouldn't need to if people stayed in their own countries and behaved themselves instead of indulging in filthy practices in public lavoratories. There wouldn't have been a Hitler if there had been fewer Jews in Germany. The movement ought to get itself into the government, as he had.

He lay in bed, imagining the man with his light and his notices groping through the concrete maze. What could he hope to achieve by such furtiveness? Yet Horridge felt a little guilty. At least the man was trying to do something positive.

CHAPTER VII

When he woke, Horridge knew what he ought to do.

As he washed, he stared at himself in the mirror. He simply didn't look capable of carrying out such a plan. Sometimes when he looked in the mirror, he felt as though he couldn't recognize himself. Except for his slightly protruding ears, he would pass himself by unrecognized in a crowd. He flapped deodorant away from his face, afraid of inhaling the chemical.

He must buy milk. The bottle in the bucket of cold water beneath the sink was empty. He walked toward the shops near the bus terminus. Everywhere were fences, head-height, ankle-height, as though nobody knew how to behave unless they were made to. Maybe the fences had been put up for vandals to scribble on, with paint; the world was mad enough. Amid one tangle of graffiti he read KILLER.

Like his flat, the shopping street was L-shaped. Hardly a path in Cantril Farm ran visibly straight for more than a few yards; the walks sank into concrete valleys, or plunged straight through the hearts of tenements. The whole place reminded him of the mazes with which scientists tormented rats.

Above the shops three tiers of flats were stacked, a layer cake of concrete. Over the heavy metal mesh that protected the windows of the Trustee Savings Bank, iron bars were set — not so trusting, he thought wryly. A child was parked in the doorway of a betting shop, beside a sign LEADERS IN LEISURE. Puddles gathered litter in depressions in the concrete walk.

The walk was loud with shoppers. Let them babble if it did them any good. They'd rather chatter like monkeys than do anything constructive. But could he do more?

Yes, by God. He wouldn't be dragged down by Cantril Farm. He'd proved that he could act so long as he didn't hesitate. He felt dwindled by the tenements, but that wouldn't sap him.

Dull music trickled through the supermarket. Let it mumble — it wouldn't lull him. He bought a tin of corned beef to replace the one he'd used up for his Christmas dinner. You couldn't trust many foods now, not with all this experimenting with chemicals, all these amino acids he'd heard they put in foods. God only knew what foreign foods contained.

He hurried toward his flat. KILLER. There it was again, in a different place. No doubt they thought it clever to write such things. Television had a lot to answer for. But at the same time the word seemed addressed to him, urging him to act.

He drowned the bottle of milk in the bucket, and went out. For once he didn't fear losing his way; most of the walks led eventually to bus stops. Cantril Farm was constructed to herd people in the directions the planners wanted them to follow.

He waited opposite a post-box inscribed savagely as a totem pole. Above the tower blocks, the sky was featureless as whitewash. Nearby was a phone box — but he mustn't use one so close to home; they might trace him. Craig and the police didn't yet know where he lived; otherwise, why had they done nothing since trying to scare him outside Craig's house?

The bus was stuffed with a Saturday crowd. Among shopping bags on their parents' laps, children struggled like reluctant purchases. He had to stand; he refused to go upstairs into the stale smoke. Whenever the bus turned a corner, it threw his weight on his bad leg. Whenever the bus lurched, the low ceiling thumped his skull.

Please let the bus move faster, before he lost his nerve. But the driver was herding on more passengers, shouting, "Move further down the bus." The advancing crowd forced Horridge back. He had to sway when they did; he felt suffocated by bodies and the wails of children. Let the bus dawdle as long as it liked. By God, they wouldn't weaken him.

The bus turned out of Lime Street and rushed down the curve to the shoppers' stop. Those who had been seated joined the crowd in the aisle, hindering him. He was the tail end of the shuffling queue — just one of the crowd.

No, he was not, by God. He pushed his way out of the throng, ignoring the mutters of a knot of gossips. Beyond the boxed-in walkways that lowered over Williamson Square, two telephone boxes guarded each other's backs. In the square, people bought fruit from a barrow, set balloons adrift to draw attention to the plight of someone or other, sang folk songs beside a hat scattered with coins. He headed for the unoccupied box.

But a woman was bearing down on it, driving a poodle before her like a tartan shopping basket. He mustn't be made to wait, to falter! He ran lopsidedly, and grabbed the door. He met her glare, though his heart labored irregularly, until she stalked off in search of another phone.

Suppose there were no directory? Mightn't that mean that his purpose was mistaken? But the directory was on its shelf. He flicked the pages. No, their fluttering couldn't infect him. Craig. Craig, R. There were several—but only one at the address in Aigburth Drive.

He drew himself up straight, and dialed. Police cameras were posted all over the city center, spying. They had no reason to watch him, they wouldn't even notice him among the crowds. They certainly wouldn't be able to see what he was dialing. Could their vision be so sharp? He wished people wouldn't keep passing so near him.

As soon as he'd finished dialing, Craig's phone rang. Then—far too quickly, as if to take him off guard—the pay tone began.

Instinct convulsed his hand, which thrust in the coin. The shrill chattering was interrupted momentarily, then went on. Perhaps he'd been too hasty, and had wasted the coin. The tone stopped; the earpiece filled with silence. Was anyone there? Was somebody listening to him, stealthy as a hunter?

In a moment he heard the breathing. It was slow and heavy, but he knew it was only pretending to doze: no trapped beast could be more alert. Deep in it was a faint asthmatic wheeze. It seemed too wary to speak. Only after what felt like minutes, during which the breathing pressed close to Horridge's ear, did the voice say, "Yes?"

When speaking to the policemen, it had been deeper. Horridge bit his lip gleefully: Craig must be growing nervous. He oughtn't to speak. Craig knew that somebody was listening to him; silence would be more disturbing.

He was rationalizing his hesitation. He had found he couldn't speak;

disgust had gagged him. Craig's breathing must have pressed as close to the young men as he had— Horridge stared out of the box, at people feeding pigeons from the benches in the square, at a little girl chasing an apple that had rolled from the barrow. He was desperate for reassurance.

The plastic clung to him; Craig breathed in his ear. "Craig speaking," the voice said, a little higher, a little less sure of itself.

Horridge's lips twitched. His tongue forced them apart. He was preparing to say, "Had any good boys lately?" when Craig put down the phone.

He grimaced at the dead receiver, then he hurried out into the crowd. The side streets leading from the square were crowded as conveyor belts. He wandered, gazing at lifeless clothes in windows, enjoying the memory of Craig's unsureness. But he was growing frustrated. He hadn't done enough.

He must phone again, and speak. He couldn't do so here; Craig might have called his friends in the police, they might be searching for him. He sensed the presence of the cameras, perched somewhere overhead like hidden vultures. He needed to call from a place where he couldn't be watched, and with which he had no connection.

He climbed to the walkway and strolled toward the outward bus stop. Beneath him the swarming crowd looked as small as their minds, their purposes. Buses roared and squealed under the walkway. On the side of one a long notice said 70 INTO ONE WILL GO, and showed a long queue boarding a bus. There were only a few people in the queue, duplicated over and over again. They wouldn't make him into a duplicate.

At first the bus home wasn't crowded, except with shopping that sat next to passengers. Horridge watched the driver in the mirror. The man's lips moved as though he was talking to himself. He bared his teeth, licking them. Good God, was he mad? Perhaps he was simply trying to dislodge fragments of toffee.

As the bus bullied its way out of town, it grew full. Each time it slowed, it vibrated; the driver's face quivered as though the mirror were a pool. Wasn't that dangerous? People tramped upstairs, cigarettes panting in their mouths. The driver let a friend ride without paying. No wonder the company kept putting up fares!

The bus labored up Brunswick Road, beside which a few lonely street corners defended their territory amid a waste of mud and billboards. The woman who had just boarded the bus stood in the aisle,

scowling at the bag that dangled from her elbow and thumped her
hipbone.

Horridge stood up. "Excuse me, would you like to sit down?"

She stared, as though he were mad. That was Women's Lib for you.
How many of these women knew that to lib meant to castrate? She
sat down readily enough, for all that she appeared to resent his courtesy.

At once the driver said, "No standing. Seats upstairs."

Whom was he addressing? Horridge glanced at the woman, but
she avoided his look. At last he stared at the driver's reflected stare.
"Of course there's standing," he said, and pointed at the sign.

"No standing." The man sounded indifferent as a machine. As
soon as he'd driven past the traffic lights on top of the hill, he halted
the bus. "I've told you, no standing. This bus doesn't move until you
go upstairs."

Horridge felt everyone staring at him. He had been made a scapegoat, blamed for the delay. His skin felt as though they were sticking
pins into him. As he clambered upstairs, his limp had never been heavier.

The triumphant jerk of the bus made him almost lose his footing.
His foot dangled in mid-air. He remembered the ladder, the violent
lurch, his father dragging him down, his leg thumping the ground like
a hammer composed of flesh and fragile bone. That moment had made
sure he would never reach the top.

And now he was trudging upstairs at the whim of this petty employee
who thought his uniform made him all-powerful. He wouldn't do it.
He descended the stairs loudly and declared, "I'm not sitting in all
that smoke."

Some of the passengers groaned, as though he were a villain making
a stage entrance. "Then you can get off my bus," the driver said.

A bus stop which Horridge recognized was approaching. Rage
stiffened his face; he felt like a ventriloquist forced to imitate his dummy.
He managed to open his twitching lips, and to say, "That will be a
pleasure. Just let me off here and be quick about it."

As the bus stopped, the driver's face shivered. Horridge should
have challenged him with that—he wasn't fit to drive, he didn't even
check his mirror—but he wanted to be free of the suffocating disapproval
of the crowd. He wrenched at the folding doors. Was the driver retarding
them deliberately, to make a fool of him?

He gripped the pole of the bus stop. He wished he could have torn it out of the pavement, for a weapon. Nearby on a hoarding, a tobacco pipe larger than a man glowed and exhaled real smoke. Beside the hoarding stood a telephone box. His fury, and a sense of imminent release, rushed him to the phone. He dialed, and shoved the coin against the barrier, impatient for the pay tone.

"Yes?" the voice said warily before it was interrupted by the peeping.

Horridge bent over the receiver so that passers-by wouldn't be able to spy on him, and masked the mouthpiece with his birth certificate. "Roy Craig," he said. Though his voice was thick with disgust, he was savoring a sense of power.

"Yes, this is he."

Uncertainty made the voice rise, which excited Horridge: he would have it squealing before he'd finished. "You think you're quite safe tucked away in your flat, don't you?" he said. "We'll soon have you out in the open where everyone can see you."

Silence: not even the sound of breathing. Craig must have frozen like a trapped beast, hoping the hunter would think he wasn't there. A faint wheeze betrayed him. "The police may prefer to ignore what you're up to," Horridge said at once. "But I know."

The pitch of Craig's voice wavered; it sounded like a dizzy man on the edge of a fall. "What are you talking about?"

"Are you out of your depth? Am I confusing you? Oh dear." Relinquishing sarcasm, he said harshly, "Just remember that someone knows what you do to young boys—all of what you do to them."

"I've no idea what you're talking about."

"Haven't you? Shall I tell you?" Enraged, Horridge said, "You tie them up, and then—" He couldn't go on. "You filth. You obscene animal. You're not fit to live among human beings," he said.

He was losing control. His hand clenched on the receiver until the plastic creaked. He slammed the receiver into its cradle and shouldered his way out of the box, which had turned suffocating. A breeze cooled his burning face.

He'd achieved something. Craig was becoming more nervous. They were supposed to be so sensitive, these homosexuals. Horridge meant to nag at that sensitivity until it betrayed Craig—until Craig said too much to someone. Perhaps he would betray himself to one of the people in the house on Aigburth Drive. Surely they couldn't all be corrupt.

He stood at the bus stop. In the old days he would alight here from the homeward bus from town. He gazed across the dual carriageway, toward Boaler Street, beyond which he'd lived. Smouldering houses were heaped on mud, blocking his view.

The place was ruined. That troubled him less deeply than it might have; his sense of triumph was a cocoon. What did his street look like these days? Impulsively he crossed to the opposite pavement, resting his bad leg for a few moments on the central reservation. He wouldn't use the pedestrian subway. He'd had enough of subways in Cantril Farm.

Where the subway emerged, the Palladium cinema had stood. He remembered the Saturday matinees, the darkness swarming with other children, hair-pulling and fights in the flickering dimness, children sneaking to the exits to let in their friends who couldn't or didn't want to pay, the great unison cheer as the film appeared. Once, not long after he'd started school, he had sat dismayed and blushing while everyone else shrieked with laughter at Stan Laurel in a kilt, at the tailor trying to put his hand between his legs.

He made his way to Boaler Street, along a road between untidy pyramids which had been houses. Something drifted toward his face: a spider's strand? He gestured it away — but it was a telephone wire, hanging from its pole.

The far side of Boaler Street was intact, but the houseless pavement that faced it made the blocks of shops and houses look unguarded. Already some of the shop windows displayed debris. Half of the side of a house was covered by a poster that said TOLKEIN: DISCOVER HIS WORLD. The small butcher's was still standing: BOALER MEAT MARKET — GIANTS OF THE MEAT TRADE. That made him smile, as it always had.

He walked along his street. A few slates clung to roofs. Curtains swayed behind broken glass, but nobody was peering down at him. Once he had begun to climb the ladders he'd been able to see into all those bedrooms. Mr. and Mrs. Craven had kept a whip and a tawse behind the bed, Mr. Wallace had had Nazi medals in the back bedroom. He'd scrubbed their windows, he'd painted their bricks, and as he'd gazed down from the ladder the street and the people had seemed like his toys.

Here was his house. In the thin rectangle of earth that separated the house from the pavement, the hedge had grown long and spidery. All the doors were missing; he could see straight through the four empty frames to the jumbled back yard. The front room was bright with a mosaic of paper, tin cans, and peel.

What had they done to the end of the street? Beyond the crossroads there had been a similar terrace; he'd used to imagine he was gazing into a mirror. Now there was nothing but mud. He limped to the crossroads. Where four streets had stood, there was an enormous square of desolation, surrounded by derelict houses that looked shrunken by the waste. A sky the color of watered milk glared through the latticework of their stripped roofs. Smoke wandered over the mud, where puddles shone in ruts left by bulldozers.

He'd once played in these vanished streets. The view made him feel hollow — as hollow as he'd felt after his father's drunkenness had dragged him down. When his mother had become ill, his father had taken to drink. If Horridge had been given to self-indulgence, his father's behavior would have cured him.

His father had grown weak; he'd refused to face up to his duties. "Don't go out now. Go up and see your mother," he would say, in order to free himself for the pub. Horridge had sat by the gloomy bed, gazing at the pale collapsed face which he hardly recognized, hoping that she wouldn't wake, dreading the feeble plaintive plea: "Where's your father?" He had been his father's donkey, something on which to pile all the burdens.

After her death, the man had drunk more heavily — out of grief, or because now there was nothing to stop him? He'd begun to talk loosely as an imbecile. One day, searching for him in the pub, Horridge had overheard him. "It was worrying about the boy that killed her. Sometimes I wonder if he's my son. Maybe they gave us someone else's baby by mistake. Never in my life before have the police been to my house."

Horridge had fled unnoticed, but the sense of injustice had clung to him. All the street corner gossips had fallen silent as he'd approached. Everyone blamed him. But gradually, as he walked, he'd come to the conclusion that his father must have killed her. That was why he was so anxious to shift the blame. Perhaps, in his drunkenness, he'd fed her too much medicine.

He had never told his father that he'd heard. He'd behaved as though nothing had happened — polite but aloof. It had strained his nerves; he'd dreaded hearing his father enter the house, the cue for him to begin pretending. He wasn't qualified for any other job, and he knew nobody besides his father who would take him on.

Did his father sense this change, or had he grown maudlin since his wife's death? He'd begun to fawn on Horridge, to hug him drunkenly, calling him "son" for the first time in his life. But when the new batch of business cards was printed they'd advertised HORRIDGE, not HORRIDGE AND SON. His son wasn't a man, he was only a tool to be used without acknowledgment.

Had his son's aloofness made him drink more heavily? He had begun drinking on the job, and that had caused the fall. Horridge had heard his sudden incoherent shout below him, that might have been a warning or a threat; he'd felt the support of the ladder wrenched from beneath him, the terrifying impact of the ground. Even before the pain grew, he'd known that his leg was irreparably damaged.

When they released him from the hospital, he'd found his father intolerable. The man had kept apologizing, clinging hotly to him, breathing stale beer into his face. From disliking physical contact, Horridge had grown to loathe and fear it. Never before had the house seemed so cramped. It was full of his father's sounds, threatening to close in on him. He had felt physically menaced.

Often he would spend the evening immobile in his chair, listening for the threat of the key in the lock, his father's drunken blundering into the house. "I'm sorry," his father would always begin, like the first ritual words of a confession. "I'll make it up to you." He'd taken Horridge on jobs, to carry the paint and to do such work as didn't need a ladder. Most of all Horridge had detested his charity.

Drink had killed him. There had hardly been space in the front room for the crowd around the coffin. All the women who lived in the street had wept around Horridge. "Don't you get lonely. Come in and see us whenever you want. We'll look after you." How many of them had talked about him behind his back? They were as bad as his father, lying there looking peaceful and gentle, the hypocrite. Gazing at his father's sunken face, Horridge had been unable to remember anything good about him. He'd become merely an object, incapable of menacing.

Once the crowd and the coffin had left, the house had seemed the right size at last. Horridge had strode through it, occupying all the rooms. He had finally become a man, with his own house. He'd felt triumphant and free.

He hadn't long felt so — not when he'd realized that there was no money to come from his father, who had squandered it on drink. He'd applied for jobs, but even when he concealed his limp they had noticed it. At last he'd had to rely on the government's grudging charity. His father had dragged him down to that.

No need to depress himself. He'd achieved something today. The derelict houses looked like a low fence, pitifully incapable of containing the desolation that had already reached them. Smoke roved the mud as though in search of the destroyed streets. He turned his back on the waste.

The hedge swayed over the pavement outside his house. He made for the roadway to avoid it. Could he really pass his house without going in one last time? He glanced up at the front bedroom, into which he'd moved his bed when the house was his. Through the broken window peered a burst football.

He'd kick that ball out, if he did nothing else. He picked his way into the front room, over the doorstep scaly with broken slate. Water grew upon a stain on the ceiling, drew itself together, dangled, dripped. The wallpaper had been clawed down — by animals, or by people?

Between the communicating doorways of the front and back rooms the stairs climbed, hemmed in by walls. Fallen plaster crunched underfoot. The sensation reminded him of fever, of the impression that his skin was encrusted and crawling. He could hardly recognize the house; never before had it felt so grubby — as though it had been buried and disinterred.

A mattress drooped over the top of the stairs, bristling with rusty springs. He had never seen it before. Since he had been lured out by the housing planners, someone must have been sleeping here. And there was movement in the back bedroom, the skirt of someone who was trying to hide. It was wallpaper, flapping in a breeze.

He paced carefully into the front bedroom. Water had burst the paper overhead, which trailed sodden streamers. The scraps of paper which clung to the walls looked entirely unfamiliar. Had the absence of doors and house numbers tricked him into the wrong house? Or had that pattern lurked beneath the wallpaper all the time he had slept in this room?

Some of the floorboards were missing; pieces of timber lay on the gap-toothed floor. He picked up a piece of wood to test his footing. As he straightened up, he saw the three bent nails still protruding from beneath the windowsill, like the legs of a rusty spider. So this was his room. What was that in the middle of the floor, where his bed had stood? He peered incredulously. His mouth filled with disgust. It was a heap of filth.

His father had beaten him several times for wetting his bed. Horridge had felt that that part of his body was out to get the better of him, to soil him. Now someone had fouled his room. Nothing could have robbed him of his house and all its memories more viciously.

As he stumbled forward inadvertently, he saw the cat. It was crouched in the corner nearest the door, waiting for him to vacate the doorway so that it could flee. It looked dirty and shapeless as the stuffing of the torn mattress. He knew that it was the culprit that had soiled his house.

He advanced delicately, raising the piece of wood. It seemed vitally important to kill the creature. He had almost reached it when it leapt. He whirled, and brought the club crashing down. It tore a hole in the wall; plaster rained on the boards. He heard the cat scuttling downstairs and out.

He stood in the derelict room, gnawing a splinter out of his hand. His teeth ripped at the skin, as though to drain his fury. "Filth. Filth. Filth," he snarled.

He hurried to the dual carriageway. His limp swayed him violently, but his rage urged him on: he must be rid of it. He made himself wait for the pay tone before thrusting in the coin. "Just you remember I'm never far away," he said without giving Craig a chance to speak, and felt powerful at once. "You'd be surprised how close I am to you."

CHAPTER VIII

For the next few days he listened to the radio. Whenever it tried to sidle beyond audibility he reeled it back. Old Beatles songs. Music and memories of the 'thirties. Couldn't they face up to the present? He listened to every news report—but there was no word of Craig.

He read the papers in Cantril Farm Library, but they had no more to offer. On an impulse he asked to see the voters' list. There was his name, lined up with the rest, pinned down by its number. Each day he was first for the papers, until he found the man with the fishbowl eyes waiting at the table. Horridge left at once. He was taking no risks.

Of course Craig betrayed himself by his silence. Had he not been guilty, he would have reported the calls to the police. But mightn't he have reported them? Might the police have forbidden the press to mention the calls, while they hunted the caller? Let them hunt. If they'd known where to find Horridge they would have arrested him by now. The listing of his name made him feel indefinably vulnerable.

Craig's refusal to betray himself to witnesses frustrated him. He couldn't call again, in case the police had tapped Craig's phone. He must find another way to speed things up. Suppose they traced him somehow before Craig broke!

With the razor he cut out all the photographs of the victims from the newspapers. The photographs were too flimsy; they might be overlooked. On the kitchen windowsill he found an old tube of glue, curled up like a grub. He mounted the photographs on pieces of cardboard. That night he dreamed that he was playing in the quarry.

Next day the sky was flat as ice, and drained of color. Everything looked frail, and made him nervous. At least the buses seemed to be on his side: one came at once to take him out of Cantril Farm; his connection arrived at the Shiel Road bus stop just as he limped up. They gave him no time to doubt. He would be fine so long as he didn't start brooding. The police wouldn't be watching the house — they had no reason.

Nevertheless he couldn't walk straight past the house. He had to detour through the park to reach the telephone box. Now that he didn't intend to speak, the threat of hearing Craig's voice unnerved him. But there was no answer. As he'd hoped, Craig was not at home.

He'd taken only a few steps toward the house when he averted his face and crossed the road to dodge behind a tree. Suppose his calls had disturbed Craig so much that he was refusing to answer the phone? Peering round the tree, he saw that the front door was ajar within the porch. Couldn't he put the photographs in an open envelope and drop it in the hall? Perhaps he could write Craig's name on the envelope.

That was idiotic. The photographs must be placed outside Craig's door, and one ought to be protruding from beneath the door, as though Craig had dropped them. If a neighbor found them, that would give him something to explain. If Craig himself found them, he might well blame someone in the building; that would prey on his mind.

Horridge stared across the road. Craig's curtains were parted; they looked luxuriously thick. Wasn't there a glint beyond them, as of eyes watching? Wasn't there a dark bulk that contained the glint, like a large head? Perhaps Craig was sitting in the dim room, afraid to show his face.

Horridge stared until his eyes felt parched, willing Craig to emerge. Beneath his gaze the house seemed to twitch, unnerving him. The glary sky made the trees look thin and brittle. He felt drained of purpose.

A postman poked letters through the front door. Why didn't the man go in and leave them in the hall? Later a woman slipped a handful of pamphlets through the door. Neither arrival moved the dark shape with the glinting eyes, if they were eyes. By now Horridge was watching aimlessly, emptily. He'd wasted hours. What if those visitors had been detectives, disguised in order to guard the house? He turned dully and went to look at the reflections by the bandstand.

A crisp-bag swollen by bubbles floated in the water. Nothing was clean: perhaps nothing had been since the quarry. He had stepped down through the roughly carved gap and had halted, gazing at the massive cliff, shining gray in the sunlight. He'd felt alone with the bright surfaces of rock, and free. Even the rubble underfoot had been spotless. The strength of the quarry had seemed to fill him. Each day he'd played for hours, a bandit in his lair, a soldier maneuvering, until his grandfather called him to dinner. Why had that week ever had to end?

Because he'd grown up, that was why. He had more important things to do than stand moping by the water. And by God, he knew how he could succeed. He could stand in the porch and ring Craig's doorbell. If Craig were at home he would hear the window opening, but Craig wouldn't be able to see him. He hurried down the avenue toward the obelisk, disregarding the twinges in his leg.

A figure was idling along Aigburth Drive. Horridge slowed, to let him trudge out of sight. He turned, hair trailing over his shoulders, and stared at Horridge. It was the student with the shifty eyes, whom he'd seen talking to Craig.

His eyes were blank, preoccupied; he seemed hardly able to see across the road. No doubt he was plodding home to his drugs. Horridge heard the door slam, though it didn't look as though the youth had closed it properly. Had he noticed Horridge? Probably not — but he'd certainly prevented him from carrying out his plan. Weighed down by rage, he limped away.

When he reached his flat, the morose boy who lived overhead was kicking a football against the twilit fence. Often he did nothing else all day: thud, thud, thud. "Haven't you anything better to do?" Horridge snarled. The boy gaped after him. With his gangling limbs and small head the boy looked insect-like, performing some instinctive ritual with the ball.

Horridge was struggling with his attacker in a cramped dark place. When he woke, his arms were tied. The indifferent ticking of the clock made him feel more alone and helpless as he writhed convulsively in the dark. Before he was free he realized he was only tangled in the blankets, but that lessened his fear not at all.

Sleep had deserted him. He lay trying to conquer his fears. He was going to do Craig's work for him, was he? Was he going to terrify himself into waiting to be trapped by the police? Not bloody likely. He wasn't an invalid, to lie awaiting the worst. For once he had the chance to achieve something. He'd see it through, whatever the consequences.

Wind hissed through the maze of concrete wastes of Cantril Farm. Again the sky resembled ice; it looked thin, treacherous. The bus took its time in arriving. Alighting at the corner of Shiel Road and West Derby Road, he called Craig's number. There was no reply.

The second bus left him on Lodge Lane. Mightn't Craig have come home by now? At last he found an undamaged phone. Still no reply. But by the time he reached the house — Suppose he went in and Craig returned while — He forced himself toward the park. His doubts dragged at him.

He was dawdling in the hope that something would hinder him. Nothing would, except himself — and he wouldn't allow that. He walked past the house without detouring. That would show he meant business. He called a last time. No reply.

He walked between the stone gateposts, slowly in order to conceal his limp. There was no gate; grass sprouted above the hinge on the post, like unkempt hair behind a rusty ear. The short drive curved up to the front door, then down to another pair of empty posts. Within that semicircle, the lumpy ground was ragged with grass. The uneven hedge drooped over it, and leaned over the wall toward the pavement. The place seemed as neglected as Horridge's old home.

He eased open the door to the porch, which was almost as roomy as his bathroom. Hiding within was a large empty cracked vase. The porch seemed dusty, desolate, which made him feel all the more an intruder. He wasn't to be cowed. He crept in, and stood with a clang on the shoe-scraper. Wind slammed the porch door at once.

His heart's jerk seized him. Never mind. No more distractions. He stared at the list beside the doorbells: Harty, a blank, Adamson, Craig — He thrust at the bell-push hastily, though his finger was shaking so much he feared he would miss. He heard the faint ringing. Good: if Craig were home, he would be able to hear the window without opening the porch door.

There was silence, except for the shuddering of the glass of the porch in the wind. Should he ring again, to make sure? Suppose that brought Craig out of hiding — to the door instead of to the window?

He was trying to distract himself. He must go straight in, up to the landing. Craig's door would be on the right. To drop the photographs and push one partly beneath the door would take him only seconds. No more dawdling and cowardice! He thrust at the front door. He thrust harder, then he stared at it. It took him moments to see, and longer to accept, that the door was locked. Only the shadow of the porch made it seem ajar.

He managed not to pound on the door. "God. Oh dear God, please, no," he moaned. He clamped his hands over his ears, digging his fingers into his scalp, trapping himself with the thumps of his blood — so that he failed to hear the porch door opening behind him.

"If you want Roy Craig," a voice said, "he's out."

It wasn't Craig. It was a woman's voice, though husky. She had trapped him in the porch, in the dim grubby box. His skin felt as though swarming with dust. All at once he glimpsed his dream vividly. He had been struggling in a wardrobe with an unseen enemy who was too strong for him. He found the razor in his pocket, and clutched it.

He couldn't turn, for he would be unable to speak. His face was beyond his control. It had grown stiff as a mask, and he had no idea how it looked. His lips felt like thick bars, imprisoning his tongue. His hand trembled in his pocket. It at least could move.

"Are you a friend of Roy Craig's?" the voice said.

CHAPTER IX

It was the first week of Fanny's exhibition. She'd managed to bear the first days. Apart from interviews with the media, from which she'd emerged edited and contradicting herself, she had felt ignored. She'd stood like a wallflower, overhearing comments on her work. "Isn't that sweet?" "Very Lowryish, aren't they?" "Don't you feel these naives are a bit limited?" "Aren't primitives a little out of date?"

Two days had been enough. She'd felt pent up, unemployed. She ought to work instead of mooching in the hope of overhearing compliments. A new painting grew in her mind: visitors to an art gallery. She would rather paint them than watch them. How many had visited the exhibition because they felt that they ought to be seen doing so?

It distressed her to dislike people. All the more reason to stay home and paint: she could feel more affection and sympathy for her subjects that way—these subjects, anyway. The third day she began sketching; by the fourth, her ideas were too urgent to wait for more sketches. Figures gazed at paintings and tried to imitate their poses. Some of the gallery visitors had white sticks, and were being escorted. One long-haired man scratched his head and poked his fingers in his eyes.

Just as she was painting most intensely, Roy Craig came to unburden himself to her. What he had to say disturbed her—but she couldn't stay depressed for long while she was painting. When he left, she painted on. Some of the faces gazing at the pictures were rapt, wistful or absolutely calm, with great wide eyes.

Then, buttocksbumanarse, she ran out of some of the colors— just because she was painting so well! She sketched for the rest of the evening, to make sure her ideas didn't vanish and to prevent herself from brooding over Roy's tale.

Next day she went downtown early, to the artists' suppliers in Bold Street. Shops displayed hats like pale blue wicker baskets. A delicatessen boasted caviar. A woman gazed at an overfed leather suite and said to her husband, "Looks terribly cheap, don't you think?"

Fanny was glad not to be trying to appeal to them. They must be locked into their opinions, their conviction of what was Art and Good and Tasteful. Perhaps they might even spare time for Art which had Something to Say. She giggled at herself: she sounded like Winnie-the-Pooh with a headache.

The bus home dropped her by the tower block. She glanced along Lodge Lane, toward the terraced houses huddled together, their only front step the pavement. There was the audience she wanted to reach — the poorer people. They would criticize her work honestly. She could seldom distinguish the genuine opinions of the gallery visitors, if they had any.

She'd displayed her work in some of the community centers, in a fish and chip shop, in the Upper Parly Arts Center. But nobody had ever asked the price, though she'd hoped people would be pleasantly surprised: she had wanted them to be able to buy. Were they content with their garish luster pottery, their 3-D religious plaques that performed a little dance when you moved, their portrait of a woman with a blue-green face that sold at Boots the Chemists in its thousands? Wasn't there any way she could reach them?

There was only one way to try, and that was to keep painting. Figures came alive in her mind. They grew closer, more economically depicted. She knew exactly what she would paint as soon as she reached home. She strode eagerly into the drive.

A man was poking at Roy's bell. He stood, head cocked — like what sort of bird? Now he was vainly shoving the front door. Of course Roy was at work; the civil service's Christmas holiday was over.

Why was the man so impatient? She remembered what Roy had said about the police visit. Did this man have something to do with the persecution? "If you want Roy Craig," she said, "he's out."

He didn't turn, though his shoulder blades drew together beneath the gray dilapidated coat, making her think again of a bird. She must have startled him. Had she mistaken the bell he was ringing? "Are you a friend of Roy Craig's?" she said.

Was he deaf? Had it been the intrusive breeze rather than her voice that had made his shoulders move? He seemed unaware of her. He stood motionless, his right hand bulging his coat pocket. Ought she to touch his shoulder? Somehow she must make her presence known.

Then he began to turn. He looked stiff as a dummy on a turntable. She was fascinated, and at the same time rather unnerved. Here came his face on his pivoting body: fortyish, bland and scrubbed, with protruding ears. Here came his eyes to stare fixedly at her. They were an astonishing baby blue.

His stare abashed her. It and his face were secret as a baby's. Why didn't she advance to the front door, or stand aside to let him out of the porch? The grip of his stare was forcing her to speak, yet she didn't know what to say. She had never in her life felt so uncomfortable.

"I'm sorry," she managed to stammer. "I didn't mean to pry. I'm sure you've a good reason to be here."

A faint smile crept over his face, but left his eyes untouched; if anything, their scrutiny grew sharper. An insight seized her. She blurted, "You're a policeman, aren't you?"

His face stiffened. His hand moved in his pocket like a Hollywood detective's. He looked to be struggling to control his face. What could be trying to emerge? All at once a grin tugged his mouth wide. His eyes twinkled as though she were a favorite child. "Not quite," he said.

She remembered what she'd meant to suggest to Roy, that he ought to hire— "You're a private detective," she said.

"That's it. You've got me." His voice was light; the constant nimble changes of its tone made her think of a ballerina's footwork. She heard how she had delighted him. "What a perceptive woman you are," he said.

"I have to be. I'm an artist." For a moment, without any definable reason, she was uncomfortably suspicious of him. She'd told him what he was, instead of making him tell her. "Roy has told me all about the reason he's hired you," she said carefully. "We often talk. He lives just across the landing."

"Of course, the artist. Miss Frances Adamson, I believe."

She was enormously relieved: she could trust him. "Most of my friends call me Fanny," she said, "but Roy thinks it's rude."

He raised his eyebrows and smiled to himself. She noticed that his visible hand was trembling. And his shoulders had tried to shrug off the draft. "Sorry," she said, closing them both into the porch, "It must be a cold job sometimes."

"I suppose so." He was staring at the door as though she might have locked him in. "But the suffering's worthwhile."

"I'm just going to make a cup of tea. Would you like one?"

Roy believed that it had been someone in the house who had called the police, because they didn't like his living there. She found herself growing suspicious of people she'd taken for granted, and that distressed her. Perhaps the detective could prove their suspicions wrong, and rid her of her paranoia.

He was staring at the door. His hand stirred in his pocket. Remembering bad films, she had to suppress a giggle. Suddenly he smiled at her, eyes wide. "Thank you," he said. "That would be very useful."

In the hall she noticed he was limping slightly. His glance seemed to challenge her. "Is that real?" she blurted.

"What do you think?"

When he walked upstairs ahead of her, slowly as a mannequin, the limp had vanished. "No," she said admiringly. It was a subtle way for him to look less like a detective.

She unlocked her flat. God, this was what you called an exhibition. Still, no doubt van Gogh hadn't been the tidiest person in the world, dropping ears everywhere. The floor was scattered with magazines and newspapers from which she'd clipped images. Lumps of modelling clay with which she'd been experimenting occupied a sheet of plastic on the table. She threw her keys beside them.

The postcard on the mantelpiece nagged at her. "See you on Jan 15." Perhaps they would; she hadn't yet decided. Her exhibition wouldn't be over by then — but people came to look at her paintings, not at her. Why should she deny herself a week in Wales just to oblige people who didn't really like her work?

No time for reflection now. She had a visitor. "Take your coat off," she suggested.

"No, thank you." He was glancing everywhere in the room — his was a full-time job, like hers. "What's that?" he asked, pointing.

"Oh, nothing. Just clay for shaping. Sometimes I feel I'd like to work in clay, but I'm not very good."

"Aren't you?" His tone sounded satirical.

"Well, I don't mean as an artist," she said. Was she defending herself unnecessarily? "I have an exhibition running at the moment. Though I'm not sure what that proves." Her intermittent self-deprecation and his wide-eyed gaze were making her chatter. "I want to appeal to the underprivileged, you see. But all I seem to get is the usual gallery crowd.

"And what kind of people are they?"

She'd said too much; she didn't want to sound completely ungrateful for her audience. "Oh, just the sort of people who visit galleries."

He grinned faintly. Of course, as a detective he must be amused by her apparent inability to describe people. Did he really think that as an artist she wouldn't have an eye for people? She couldn't be bothered to start an argument. "I'll put the kettle on," she said.

When she returned, he was handling a lump of clay. No wonder he was a detective—he had to use his curiosity somehow! "Did you do that?" he said over his shoulder as soon as she came in.

He jerked his head toward the metal bird. He sounded almost accusing. "No," she said wistfully. "A friend." Tony had sculpted it especially for her, and she treasured it—but at the same time it helped remind her that two artists couldn't live comfortably together, not in her experience.

The detective's voice brought her out of her memories. "Damnation," he muttered without turning. "I've got your clay under my nails. May I wash my hands?"

"Of course you can. There's soap in the kitchen."

He went slowly, as though still parading the absence of his limp. "Can you find it?" she called. "Just by the knives in the sink."

Receiving no reply, she was making to show him when he said beyond the door, "Have I dropped my notebook out there?"

She searched the floor. Anything could hide amid the collage of her flat. "I don't think so," she called at last. "What does it look like?"

He emerged, and went to the table. "Here it is," he said. Her view was blocked, but she saw him slip an object into his pocket.

She brought him tea, milked and sugared. Four spoonfuls! What a sweet tooth! It was like one of the inevitable idiosyncrasies novelists gave their detectives. She headed at once for the subject she wanted to discuss. "Isn't it dreadful, playing a trick like that on Roy," she said. "You wouldn't think there'd be such bigotry these days."

"You'd be surprised how some people still feel."

"Of course the police didn't think he had anything to do with these murders, but having them check was upsetting enough."

His bright quick eyes fixed her. "Is that all he told you?"

"Just about the police. Why, is there something else?"

His lips grew thin, reproving her. "I'm sorry," she said. "Of course you mustn't tell me. It's just that this whole affair has been worrying me too. Roy thinks someone in the house was responsible. You don't think that, do you?"

He gazed at her. After a while he said, "Yes, I'm afraid someone in this building is definitely implicated."

She stared depressed into her tea. Its whirling, a roulette of bubbles, slowed. She felt that ill luck and viciousness had invaded the house. She couldn't control her suspicions: the culprit must be the almost invisible man on the ground floor, The Bell With No Name. The names she and Cathy had given him didn't seem so funny now.

The detective finished his tea and handed her the cup. "I'll tell Roy you were here, shall I?" she said.

At once his hand burrowed into his pocket. He must be making sure he hadn't forgotten his notebook again. "Look," he said abruptly, "I'd like to ask a favor of you. I shouldn't really have told you as much as I have. Would you mind not mentioning you saw me?"

It might lose him his assignment, at that. No doubt his faded overcoat was only a kind of disguise, but at that moment it made him look rather pitiful, vulnerable. "It was my fault," she said. "I wouldn't let you out of the porch. All right, I promise I won't tell him."

She watched him down the stairs. Now the slowness of his walk looked triumphant, a march. Before closing the front door he glanced up at her. "Thank you for everything," he called.

CHAPTER X

Horridge closed the dictionary and gazed at it as though it were a treasure chest. Around him people searched the library shelves for adventure, horror, romance, crime. None of them was aware of his triumph. He sat gazing out at Cantril Farm, smiling to himself.

The dictionary gave only one definition of "fanny": buttocks. That in itself showed how corrupt the painter was, to change her name to that — corrupted by Craig, perhaps. But the next entry in the dictionary was even more suggestive. Fanny Adams had been a girl murdered and cut up in 1812. Could any other coincidence have linked the painter to Craig so closely? Why, if you looked at it correctly, it even confirmed that Craig was the killer.

Not that confirmation was needed. Once again the creature had betrayed himself by silence: he hadn't told the woman about Horridge's phone calls. So she wasn't wholly in his confidence — but that didn't make her any less contemptible. No pang of sympathy for her would distract Horridge from what he planned to do.

He'd seen at once what kind of woman she was, with her face made up to look younger than forty, her oversized earrings that looked rusted by her red hair, her blouse flamboyant as a scrawled wall: a woman with no taste or breeding. Everything had confirmed his first impression: the audience she boasted of wanting to reach, the shirking class; her outrage that poor defenseless Craig was being made to see what people thought of him; her painting itself, all that modern rubbish — it was entirely typical that she couldn't even describe people when asked. Of course that was something he could be thankful for.

Most inexcusable of all had been her suggestion that he was a friend of Craig's—though he was grudgingly grateful to her for telling him that he was a detective. She'd seemed almost eager to help him triumph. He'd enjoyed few things so much as deluding her. Everything had been on his side, for a change. After his ruse in her flat, he felt sure of victory.

Now he must visit old Mr. Fearon. Suppose Mr. Fearon was dead? It had been years since Horridge had seen him. Still, he felt too justified to believe he would be thwarted now. He returned the dictionary to its shelf, patting its spine gratefully, and left.

He'd learned Mr. Fearon's address by heart the day he had met the old man in the L-shaped street of shops and recognized him from years ago in Boaler Street. He knew nobody else in Cantril Farm. He'd clung to that knowledge in case he ever needed it.

Passing buses marked the main road. When he headed for it, buildings constantly blocked his way. Beside the path, grassed patches were sown with broken glass. He read the names on the blocks of flats and houses: Cremorne Hey, Boode Croft, Custley Hey. What kind of language was that? Were they trying to get rid of English?

Now he could see his destination, on the far side of the main road. He couldn't go straight to it, though a path led across grass to a gap in the railings. He'd been tricked by these paths before: they led you onto the main road and abandoned you there, on the wrong side of the railings, without a pavement. Sometimes he thought that the planners had faked those paths, to teach people to obey without questioning.

He had to follow the walkway, a dried-up valley of concrete which plunged beneath the road. The tunnel was treacherous with mud and litter; the walls were untidy webs of graffiti. All the overhead lights had been ripped out. He stumbled through, holding his breath; the place smelled like an open sewer.

On the far side he clambered up concrete steps. Fragments of glass squeaked and cracked underfoot. Nearly there now. But did the name on the wall before him refer to the entire block? And where was 81?

He hurried beside the pebble-dashed wall, past displayed rooms. He peered through passages that opened between flats. There it was, at the far side of an inner square of concrete: an L-shaped flat, exposed at both ends by passages. Once before he'd found himself on this side of the main road, and had determined to see where Mr. Fearon lived. The location reminded him of his own.

He made for the flat. Somewhere there was a faint metallic screeching. He was beneath the concrete stairway to the upper flat, and ready to knock on the door, before he saw that this wasn't 81 at all. He recoiled, disoriented. Then he saw that the corners of the square were identical. He'd simply mistaken the corner—but none of the flats was 81.

He could feel his nerves tightening like a net. Had he come too far, beyond the territory whose name he'd read on the wall? There must be dozens of places in the concrete maze that looked just like 81. A dread which he'd tried to suppress was creeping into his thoughts— that sometime, perhaps in fog, he would come home and be unable to distinguish his own flat.

Anonymity surrounded him. The muffled screeching persisted, scraping at his nerves. That was the only sign of life here: the voice of a machine. What kind of machine? A bacon-slicer—no, not quite. Suddenly he remembered that he'd heard such a sound on Boaler Street, in Mr. Fearon's shop.

He limped toward the sound. Beyond one passage was a square which seemed indistinguishable from the square he was leaving. From a corner flat came the screeching. He had to approach close before he could read the number, on an oval plaque smaller than an egg: 81. He hadn't strayed from the right path for long.

He knocked, knocked louder. The screeching faltered, and failed. After a while the blue flowers on the plastic curtains stirred, and an old face peered between them. The flowers sagged back into place; the face reappeared, blurred and surrounded by separated blobs of its flesh, in the frosted glass of the door. At last the door opened.

The old man gripped the doorframe, both barring the way and supporting himself, and glared a challenge. Did he think Horridge was a complaining neighbor? He was silent for so long that Horridge wasn't sure he recognized him. Could this face really have been Mr. Fearon's before it had shrunken inward so? Then the old man said, "You're Frank Horridge's son."

It didn't sound like an invitation to enter—more like the solution to an annoying problem. A frown joined his stare, urging his visitor to come to the point. Horridge had hoped to ask him a favor in memory of Boaler Street, but hadn't expected him to be so crabby. He could only say like any other customer, "Could you cut me some keys?"

The old man looked suspicious. Had he forgotten how Horridge knew he cut keys? At last he grumbled, "I'm not supposed to do that at home, you know." But he relinquished the doorframe and turned his back on Horridge, who ventured to follow him.

In the main room the overhead light blazed. Dusty tassels dangled from the lampshade. Bluish daylight seeped through the curtains. Mr. Fearon pulled back a shabby screen to reveal his cutter's tools, as though he had been hiding them from the portrait of Christ on the wall, gazing out of the glittery rays of his halo. The business seemed furtive—but Horridge refused to be made to feel like a criminal. What he was doing was right and necessary.

He took out the molds. He had a moment of panic: suppose they had been squashed out of shape in his pocket? At first he'd protected them with the cards that bore the photographs, and now they were wrapped in newspaper. He unwrapped them and handed them over.

The old man hardly glanced at them. "These are for your flat, are they?"

"Yes, of course. I made these impressions a long time ago, in case I ever lost my keys."

"It's the first place I've seen round here with two Yale locks in it."

Horridge felt as though a steel trap had sprung in his belly. "I like to keep my bedroom locked." His polite, determinedly unoffended tone sounded guilty to him.

"You don't want to go locking interior doors. If you have burglars they'll only break the locks and cause more damage."

That was none of his business. Though his body felt tightly entangled in nerves, Horridge refused to answer. After a while the old man stared hard at the molds. "What kind of clay is this?"

"Just some that I used to play with."

He hadn't anticipated that question; his lie was jerky, nervous. But his reference to the past seemed to mellow Mr. Fearon. "Aye, those were the days," the old man said. "It was a good street. You knew everyone then. Not like this bloody transit camp." The sense of shared memories made him more friendly. "All right, I'll make your keys for you. I'll whiz round to you with them tomorrow. Whereabouts do you live?"

Nobody must know where he lived, not now. The skin of Horridge's face felt as though it were shrinking. "If it's all the same to you," he managed to say between stiffening lips, "I'll wait for them."

"Well, it's not the same to me at all. It's a damned long job, son. Did you know that?"

"No, I didn't. I'm sorry." Before the old man could win the conversation, he added hastily, "It's urgent, you see. I can't get into the house without it."

"You'll just want the front door key, then. Which one is that?"

Oh God. God, no. Could the old man see the sweat exploding all over Horridge's body? "I won't be able to get into my bedroom either," he complained.

"You're in a bad way, aren't you?"

Unsure what the comment referred to, Horridge didn't dare answer. "All right, I'll do it now," the old man sighed at last, shaking his head. "Just you wait there and don't start getting restless. This is going to take longer than you think."

He plodded behind the screen, and drew it closed behind him. Eventually he emerged, bearing some object which he concealed from Horridge, and trudged into the kitchen. Horridge heard the flare of gas, and its monotonous breath, sometimes interrupted. After a considerable time Mr. Fearon pottered back. The screen creaked shut.

His comings and goings seemed to dawdle on for hours. Each time he appeared he made some remark, as though he'd spent the interval thinking of it. "I suppose you still miss your father. Always good for a laugh, old Frank." "There aren't many like him these days." "Brought you up single-handed, and looked after you when you had the accident, with never a word of complaint."

Horridge could only agree inarticulately; he felt at the mercy of the old man's goodwill. Once Mr. Fearon said, "Getting much work?" Perhaps he was growing senile. And once, to Horridge's dismay, he said, "Just keep your ears open for the door. I've got someone coming for keys."

The cramped room, the old man's small sounds which Horridge could neither ignore nor interpret, his infuriating slowness, his secrecy which preyed on Horridge's imagination — everything reminded him of life with his father. His hands moved restlessly, neither quite opening nor becoming fists: he felt he was a puppet of his nerves. When the metallic shrieking began, it seemed to drill deep into his teeth. At least it meant that the ordeal was almost over, for the old man soon emerged with two keys.

Horridge clasped them gratefully. "How much do I owe you?"

"How much is it worth to you?"

What was that supposed to mean? What did his stare imply? Perhaps that he wouldn't ask a direct question so long as his customer wasn't too blatant. Angry to be made to feel guilt, but helpless, Horridge had no idea what to reply.

At last the old man said wearily, "Oh, give us two quid. That won't break you, will it?"

Perhaps he'd hoped to be offered more — but he could be no poorer than Horridge. He crumpled the notes in his hand as if they were litter, and plodded to let Horridge out. But Horridge said, "I'd like my impressions back, please."

"Right enough, you wouldn't want to be leaving them. They're no use to anyone now, son. I had to crack them."

"I'd still like the clay."

Not until he was crossing the third square of concrete patched with uncombed grass did he realize why Mr. Fearon had stared sideways at him. The old man felt suspected now: he thought Horridge hadn't trusted him to dispose of the clay. Horridge grinned to himself as he limped to the shops. Mr. Fearon wouldn't dare betray him.

Now he must act fast, just in case the painter mentioned him to Craig despite her promise. After all, why had so many pieces been cut out of the newspapers in her flat? Could she have been making sure that none of her visitors saw Craig's face? He bought a plastic wallet full of marker pens, and hurried to his flat.

He lifted his newspapers from their lair. Eventually he found the photograph: the wardrobe in which the first victim had been discovered, with one word hacked out of the wood of the door: BITCH.

He stared at his blank piece of cardboard, then he grinned. Of course! He took it to the window, and gazed at the graffiti that crawled over the fence. He'd never thought he would be grateful for that eyesore. But now, as he wrote BITCH with the pens, he copied the discords of color, adding flourishes and elaborations as his memory prompted. At last he pinned the notice to his bedroom door, and admired his handiwork. It reminded him of the paintings that cluttered the walls in the painter's flat. He grinned, wiping his hands. He was convinced, and he was sure his victim would be: the writing looked exactly like Fanny Adamson's signature.

CHAPTER XI

Craig had one foot in the bath when the telephone rang.

The water was warm around his ankle. Should he answer the call, and perhaps be made to feel worse? By the time he had dried his foot and inserted it into his slipper, the ringing had ceased. He sank into the water, grateful for its soothing embrace. He'd had a bad enough day already.

There had been another letter from the intolerable pensioner. Craig's colleagues read out their hostile correspondence, or passed it around the long Inland Revenue office, but the letters depressed him too much for that. "Maybe if you have time between your cups of tea you'll deign to work out how much tax you owe me on these dividends." That was bearable; years ago, bitterly gleeful, Craig had written DIFFICULT TAXPAYER in red ink on the man's control card. But there was always the postscript: "Haven't you anyone in your department who can write legibly?" "When are you going to buy me new glasses?" Craig knew his poor handwriting was growing worse — hardly surprising, under all the circumstances.

Still, he might have read the letter out if he had been sure of his colleagues, except that he no longer knew himself. One police visit and three phone calls had done that. Not since his marriage had he felt so uncertain how to behave.

He tried to relax, to feel like the water. At least the third-floor discotheque wasn't thumping overhead; they must all be out, thank heaven. Though he admired Cathy: a capable woman. She needed to be, with that husband of hers.

Had that been true of Daphne? Perhaps she hadn't been quite

capable enough. Memories floated up. Of late they had been uncomfortably vivid, sharp with guilt. Perhaps the lulling of the water might soften them. He knew he couldn't elude them.

Had he really wanted to marry? He'd thought so then, but had that come of a need to prove he could have a girl friend? Still, he'd grown fond of Daphne; they'd talked and hummed Mozart together, to the amusement of their colleagues; in restaurants, they were happy to be quiet together as well as to chat. Best of all, she'd seemed content with affection rather than outright sex.

Marriage had released her sexuality. Sometimes he had satisfied her, more often they'd lain side by side, dummies in a bedroom display. He'd known she was brooding on why she didn't appeal to him — but he had been trying not to believe what was wrong. Surely one teenage relationship couldn't have exerted such a hold over him.

Had it been desperation which had made him at last go drinking with Nelson, a colleague who he'd known was homosexual? Had he simply wanted to discuss his troubles, or to be taken to the club?

The club had shown him what he was. Despite the shock of unfamiliarity, despite his shrinking from the shrieks of the flamboyant, before the evening was over he had felt at home. He'd been able at last to be open — but how was this helping his marriage? That doubt had stiffened his movements, tripped up his speech.

He'd begun to wonder if an affair might help. Would he feel less unfaithful to Daphne with a man than with another woman? Would it help him to be less inhibited with her? The plan had seemed furtive, almost squalid — like the toilets which the desperate used, where you could hear intruders approaching before it was too late.

One night the solution had seized him. He and Daphne had been sitting by the gas fire, the only warmth they seemed able to share. He had been thinking drowsily about the club. All at once he'd grown randy. As he grabbed Daphne's hand she had gazed incredulously at him. They'd made love violently and urgently. Hidden within his closed eyelids there had been a young man.

His ruse had worked for months. Sometimes, as they lay embraced, he'd wanted to tell her about himself. Might she have understood a confession? His lips had locked in his words. He was feeling too peaceful. Maybe next time.

Then, without warning, the young man had vanished like a magician's exposed trick. Craig had been alone with the void within his eyelids. "Sorry. I'm sorry," he'd muttered to Daphne, invisible beneath him.

He hadn't wanted to return to the club; it would have been like an addiction. Instead he had bought magazines. He'd gazed at the nude young men until they were fixed in his memory. Had he been tiring of the strain of marriage? Couldn't he have found a more secret place for the magazines?

When he'd come home, Daphne was standing at his desk, which had been their wedding present from her aunt. Her shoulders grew stiff as a judge, and he'd seen that the bottom drawer was fully open. Yet at first she'd sounded incongruously apologetic. "I was looking for drawing-pins," she'd said.

He'd never kept them in that drawer. He had been unable to speak, and her anguished inward expression had prevented him from going to her. "This can't be you," she'd said low, as if praying tonelessly. "You're keeping these books for someone else, aren't you? You can't be that. I won't believe it."

She hadn't wept. Perhaps her unshed tears had become the ice that froze her into herself. When he'd offered to help make dinner she had said, "Please just stay away." Serving dinner, she'd avoided his touch. He had never been so intensely aware of her.

That night, and every night until she'd returned to her parents, he had lain cramped and sleepless on the couch. She'd achieved a quick move to another Inland Revenue district. Almost her last words to him had been, "I think I could have borne it if it had been another woman."

The water was cooling. He rose wallowing from the murk, and hoped those memories were gurgling down the drain, which sounded like an injured throat. Had Daphne married again? He wouldn't like to have spoiled her life.

He swaddled himself in his towelling robe. He shaved, and stung his cheeks with Brut after shave. Oh you brute, he mocked his reflection. Who could care for that old bag of a face? It looked pouchy as a hamster's. Going to the club tonight would be not only a regression but a waste of time.

Still, he began dressing. Usually the main room seemed comfortably spacious; the heavy curtains helped it seem so, as well as protecting his sleep from any hint of light. Now the room looked emptily large. His only companions were the photographs.

One was of Daphne. Just before she had found the magazines she'd had her hair cropped very short. Had she been prompted by her subconscious? At the time, she had never looked so attractive to him. Now, gazing with a faint calm smile out of the frame, she looked like Joan of Arc in the films.

Her expression would never change, nor would it reach him. He slipped a record from its sleeve: Beethoven's last quartet, Opus 135. The stylus settled delicately on the rim. Even the first bars, which sounded more complex every time he heard them, failed to distract him from the photograph of Paul.

Left alone, Craig had known neither what he wanted to be nor how he appeared to others. Sometimes he'd behaved exaggeratedly male, sometimes a camp gesture had caught him unawares. When he'd set out to act camp, to put an end to speculations, his gestures had grown stiff, parodic. His colleagues had been bewildered by him.

He'd returned to the club, though he no longer felt at home. Then one night, just as the dim coagulated light and the camp squeals that slashed the roar of conversation were becoming unbearable, he'd seen Paul.

The young man had been leaning on the bar, looking like a model who'd been forgotten by an art class. His expression was bored: posing wasn't his style, he'd agreed to model only because he'd been asked — but was that expression defensive? A sweet ache, wholly unfamiliar, had grown between Craig's stomach and his genitals: panic and yearning. He'd had to force himself to shoulder his way along the bar.

When at last he'd glanced at Craig the young man's boredom had been visibly deliberate. "You look as though you feel out of place," Craig had said.

The young man stared: was Craig about to jeer? At last he'd said, "Maybe I do."

"So do I," Craig had said, smiling with profound relief.

The peace which they'd experienced together then had been the seed of their relationship. Not long afterward, Paul had moved into Craig's flat. For months Craig had felt stable, calm, invulnerable — at least, as much so as he ever had.

Paul had been a plasterer. Once, when he'd worked on Craig's bathroom wall, Craig had watched him: his complete involvement in his skill, his graceful deftness, the economy of his craftsmanship. Craig had thought he'd never seen greater artistry.

But Paul's work had separated them. He had never wanted his workmates to come to the flat. When he went drinking with them, which was often, he had never invited Craig. It hadn't mattered to Craig—but it had troubled Paul, who had stayed out drinking more frequently, sometimes not returning to Craig the same night.

One midnight he'd tramped in, punching the wall to steady himself. "I can't stand this." His voice had been drunkenly menacing. "I'm going back home." He'd dragged his suitcases about, shoving Craig away, and had thumped downstairs with the suitcases full, to yell for a taxi.

Craig had moved to Aigburth Drive, to forget. He didn't need sex, it involved too much pain and loss, it made him too vulnerable. He was content to stay within himself. He had a few close friends who shared his tastes in music. He liked his colleagues well enough, though their only notion of art seemed to be films, which he thought vulgar and sensational: he hadn't been to a cinema for ten years. His work was demanding and sometimes unpleasant, but bearable. He was able to sleep at night.

Then the police had visited his flat.

At first, despite the initial shock, their visit hadn't disturbed him. He could tell that they knew he was gay, but they seemed to accept that without censuring him. When they had satisfied themselves that he wasn't the man they were hunting, they'd told him of the anonymous call.

No, he'd told them when he could speak: he had no enemies that he knew of. His mind was calling him a liar. It must be someone in the house: who else could have a motive?

He hadn't needed the menacing calls to confirm his fears. Those calls had depressed him so much he hadn't reported them to the police. It didn't matter who had been calling: weighed down by distress, he couldn't yearn for revenge. Even his thick curtains couldn't help him sleep. It wouldn't take many more calls to make him leave this flat.

The phone rang.

He started. One buttonhole of his jacket gaped while his fingers wrenched convulsively at the button. His heart scurried, his breath began to wheeze. The second movement of the Beethoven ended with an abrupt *forte* chord, isolating the shrill bell. Was it his tormentor calling? He lifted the pickup arm gently from between movements, slowly enough that before he could reach the phone, it fell silent.

But this was dreadful. He was afraid to answer his own phone. He couldn't feel safe even in his flat. At work stray remarks made him feel insecure. "The queers are better off now they can be treated medically." "They'd be all right if they left children alone" (as if all heteros did!). Even his colleagues who liked to think themselves tolerant made a joke of gay ads in the newspapers, as though nobody listening could possibly be gay. They were like Peter Gardner upstairs — his generation was supposed to be tolerant, yet he always stood away from Craig as though he might catch something. Fanny across the landing was one of the few with whom Craig could be open without fearing they would think he was making a pass.

Not that he cared for all homosexuals. He disliked the flamboyant gays; they lacked taste and discretion. He disliked the empty cleverness of others, their nervous brittle wit and ostentatious culture. Men who wept in public, even over the deaths of friends, embarrassed him. It was all so simple: he belonged nowhere.

He played the slow movement of the Beethoven as he finished dressing. No other music moved him so profoundly: its calm, its plaintive sweetness that achieved resignation. Often he felt that it contained all that Beethoven had wanted to say when he had known he was dying.

The music calmed him, to an extent. Perhaps after all he might meet someone tonight. He didn't insist on a "real man," whatever that was, as some did; he simply wanted someone who would make him feel peaceful.

He glimpsed himself in the mirror. Who would bother with that wheezing middle-aged bag, who didn't know himself what he wanted to be? No doubt he'd spend the evening vying with the others in hollow wit. He had nowhere else to go; there were no concerts tonight. He sleeved the Beethoven, and checked automatically that the records were in order in their cabinet.

The landing was chill. He was glad of his thick overcoat; it promised to be a cold night. He poked the time-switch, then ducked back into his flat to confirm that the lights were out before he closed the door. His breath rasped as he hurried resoundingly downstairs.

The light clicked off just as he reached the hall, which allowed him to see someone's silhouette on the glass of the front door. He heard a key scrabbling; it sounded clumsy as a dog's claws. He strode to open the door for whoever it was.

Even when he opened it, the man in the porch remained little more than a silhouette. Craig stepped back a pace to let him enter, but the man stood, neither advancing nor moving aside. Though he was within arm's reach, Craig could make out nothing of his face. All he could distinguish was that the man's right hand had plunged into his coat pocket.

Craig paced forward. The cold that seeped into the porch seized him. Surely this man didn't live here. Why should he have a key? The calls had made Craig nervous. "What do you want?" he demanded, more sharply than he'd intended.

He heard a faint click, and the man's right hand made a violent lunge toward his face.

For a moment the gesture seemed to have offered more violence than it had achieved. Something had flashed beneath Craig's eyes, but hadn't touched him. His throat was very cold. As he recoiled, his hand moved instinctively to draw his collar shut.

Then he realized that he couldn't swallow. His neck felt unfamiliar, no longer merely cold. Good God, the man had attacked him—he'd whipped him across the windpipe with a piece of metal; that must be the source of this rapidly growing ache.

Only when his fingers touched his neck did he realize that the man had cut his throat.

He twitched open the blade. . . .

CHAPTER XII

Horridge felt so confident that he made the first call from Cantril
Farm. Craig was either not at home or lurking. Horridge made his way
to the bus stop. Even the unlit walks, overlooked by blinded neon lamps,
hardly bothered him now that he could defend himself.

The bus was crowded with young couples, dressed with what passed
for smartness these days: they looked cheap to him. No doubt they
were all off to get drunk. Let them waste their time if that was all they
cared about. Some people had more important things to do.

The notice made him uncomfortable. He'd slipped it down the front
of his trousers, having nowhere else to hide it. But the discomfort was
worthwhile. This time he would get through to Craig. He had some
bits of clay to attach to the notice; that would convince Craig it was
the painter's work. Either he would betray himself by accusing her,
or this new distrust would be unbearable.

If only Horridge were able to confront him directly! He found these
underhand methods slightly disturbing. Anything was justified under
the circumstances. He hurried along Lodge Lane, past gateposts that
led to mud which sprouted litter, toward Aigburth Drive.

He called again from the box near the house, waiting only a few
seconds before he replaced the phone. After all, Craig's window was
dark. Even Craig would hardly be hiding in the dark. Or might he?
Horridge had to remind himself that he was dealing with a madman.
Never before had he noticed how meager and how widely spaced the
lamps were along Aigburth Drive.

No need to worry. Craig was out, he must be. Horridge needn't be
bothered about anyone else. If he encountered the painter, he had only

to tell her that he was visiting Craig. Nobody else would recognize him.

He popped a sweet into his mouth, to encourage himself. Then he made his way slowly up the drive. In the pale light the house looked like a bony ghost of itself. Within the curve of the drive, the ground was ragged with shadows of grass and hedge. He shivered; the night was very cold.

There was a light in the house.

The glass of the front door was bright. He faltered, clutching the razor in his pocket. The glass turned black. What did that mean? Was someone waiting for him in the dark? Perhaps he ought to come back later — but he knew perfectly well that once he retreated he wouldn't be able to return. No need to be afraid. Nobody could harm him. He was armed.

His shadow rushed at the porch door. He managed to disentangle the keys from the razor. He closed the porch door behind him; he wasn't about to be startled by its slam. He groped at the lock with the key. It felt wrong. Was the key upside-down? It must be the wrong key. Yes, because the other slipped easily into the slot. Before he could turn the key, the door tugged it from his hand. Darkness gaped before him, and Craig stood there.

The man's dark bulk loomed over him. The dim white light from the street made Craig's face look plastic, even more unhealthy. Horridge's lips dragged his mouth open in a silent scream. His hand fumbled in his pocket.

Craig fell back a pace. Why, he was afraid! And he had every right to be. Could Horridge force a showdown? But the small gray face on the swollen head was peering at him, bearing down on him. "What do you want?" the voice said, high and menacing.

The porch felt shrunken, suffocating. He was trapped. He knew exactly how Craig's victims must have felt. As the large head advanced toward him, it occurred to him that it must be bloated by disease; that explained the disproportion of the face. From the huge black overcoat that was about to engulf him seeped a faint sly scent.

He twitched open the razor, and slashed. At the last moment he had to close his eyes. At first the cut felt surprisingly easy, then he encountered an obstruction like an unexpected bone in a piece of meat, which made him shudder. But the blade soon cut free.

He opened his eyes. Craig stood clutching his throat. His eyes and mouth looked slack, no doubt with astonishment. He was at Horridge's mercy now. But he was by no means dead, and he must be: Horridge mustn't leave him like this. As he backed into the hall Horridge followed him and cut at his fingers, in an attempt to expose his throat.

Craig was growling faintly, like the animal he was. Then Horridge realized he wasn't quite growling; it was more like a muffled gargling. There was no need to worry about it — it was clearly the loudest noise he could make.

Suddenly Craig surged forward, shouldering him aside. His strength terrified Horridge: had he to drain all that? Craig stumbled into the porch. Only just in time did Horridge realize that he intended to ring the bells to summon help. Horridge limped after him and grabbed the coat sleeve of his uninjured hand. He had to cut deep into the fingers before they recoiled from their groping for the bells.

He went for Craig's throat again, forcing him into the hall. Each time Craig tried to grapple with him, he retreated; he wouldn't have been able to bear the touch of the glistening hands. Still, he was able to watch without squeamishness. What he was doing was necessary. They must do worse in slaughterhouses.

He'd reached Craig's throat several times now. The man turned unsteadily and made for the stairs. He was moving as though his legs were crippled. By God, was he mocking Horridge? Perhaps his movements showed that he was weakening at last. Horridge cut at the side of his neck. When Craig turned, moving as though he were blind drunk, Horridge easily avoided his hands and pushed him by the shoulder back against the wall.

The man lolled there at the foot of the stairs. Horridge felt a kind of detached pity: he ought to be put out of his misery, like any diseased animal. At the same time, the creature's growing weakness disgusted him. He cut unobstructed at Craig's throat. Fewer than six cuts, and Craig slid almost silently down the wall to squat on the floor. His head slumped forward. Surely he wouldn't have been able to bear any weight on that throat if he had been alive.

Glancing at his own hands, Horridge couldn't suppress a shudder. It was only blood, even if diseased; and there wasn't much of it, luckily. About Craig he felt nothing but relief. Alive, the man had been beneath contempt; dead, he was less than an object. Horridge perched the razor on Craig's shoulder while he wiped his hands. Then he wrapped the razor in the stained handkerchief and slipped it into his coat pocket.

God, the front door was still open. Anyone might have come in and discovered him. He was sure he was alone in the building; otherwise, surely someone would have wanted to know what was making all the noise. Luck had been on his side, because of the rightness of his purpose, but he mustn't tempt fate now.

When he reached the porch, he saw that his coat was spattered with blood.

There were surprisingly few stains, under the circumstances; and none was very large. But oh God, how could he conceal them? He couldn't throw his coat away. All his documents were in the pockets, and he mustn't risk carrying them openly. Around him the porch grew oppressive.

The solution made him grin widely. As he took off his coat the sleeves pulled themselves inside out, to help him. He buttoned the coat again, tartan side outward. Looking down at himself, he couldn't help gasping. Such blood as had seeped through had been absorbed by the tartan; the pattern concealed it. Could anything else have proved so conclusively that he had been meant to kill Craig?

Before he emerged into the porch, he pulled out his notice. Snatching his keys, he closed the front door quietly. As he strolled along Aigburth Drive, feeling invulnerable in his tartan disguise, he tore the notice into tiny pieces and sowed them in the gutter. It amused him to be leaving a trail that nobody could follow. A breeze carried the scraps into the park.

On the first bus he felt the beginnings of panic — the stains weren't quite the same color as the tartan — but nobody looked at him twice. He relaxed, smiling secretly. It just showed how blind everyone was. A good job there was someone left who could still see.

Something tapped against his teeth. It was the sweet, almost untouched. He sucked it as though it were a prize. It helped him ignore his faint nausea at the thought of Craig's blood within his coat.

His throat felt strange. A sensation was mounting there. For an uneasy moment he couldn't tell what it was. Then he sucked the sweet harder, to keep down his wry mirth. He could feel how spasmodic and uncontrollable it would be. But really, he couldn't blame himself. Even if he had planned for years he could never have devised a more appropriate death for Craig. Life was fair, after all.

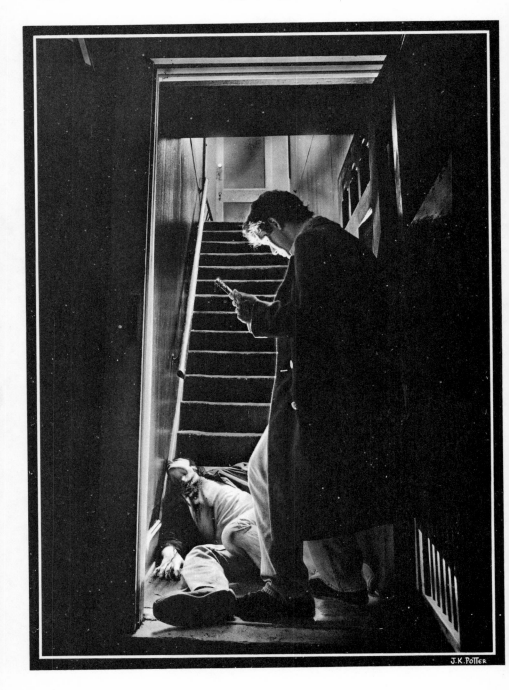

He lolled there at the foot of the stairs.

CHAPTER XIII

Just as Cathy reached the landing, the door opened. Light leapt out at her. Her hand jerked; a potato jumped out of her shopping bag and rolled downstairs, loud as a severed head in an absurd horror film. It seemed no louder than her heart, for she'd thought for a moment that it was Mr. Craig's door that had opened.

"I didn't mean to startle you," Fanny said. "I'm sorry."

"That's all right, Fanny. I'm just being stupid."

"No, you aren't. I feel the same way about the house now."

Then for God's sake let her keep it to herself. Cathy groped about the dim half-landing for the potato, averting her gaze from the wall at the foot of the stairs. That was stupid too — there was nothing to see. She would be all right so long as she didn't think about it.

Fanny stood as though awaiting the password for the stairs. Cathy made to hurry by; she didn't want to talk just now — not about that, anyway. But Fanny said, "Do you want a coffee?"

"I'd better not, thanks. Peter will be home soon." She couldn't think of a better excuse.

"Come in for just a little while. There's something I've got to talk about."

Cathy sidled toward the top staircase, to make her next refusal easier. Then she saw that Fanny's wardrobe was open. It looked empty, apart from the flowered overalls Fanny often wore when painting. Clothes gathered in a suitcase on the floor. "You aren't moving, are you?" Cathy demanded, dismayed.

Fanny stepped back into her room, so that Cathy had to follow her for a reply. "No, but I've got to get away for a while. Some friends have invited me."

"When are you going?" Cathy was taken aback by her own wistfulness.

"The day after tomorrow."

"But your exhibition won't be over then, will it?"

"It'll have to look after itself. I've got to go, Cathy." She seemed almost to be apologizing for leaving her in the house. "I haven't been able to paint since. I'll be all right once I've been away." As though to emphasize her own restraint she said, "Mr. Harty's moving, you know."

On Friday night he had been waiting in the hall when Cathy and Peter had come home. He'd seemed almost to blame them and the other tenants for having left him alone in the house to deal with the situation. He had been in his toilet when he'd heard scuffling in the hall and had thought a drunk had got in. When he'd looked out at last he hadn't recognized the man propped against the dim wall. He'd called the police to tell them that a drunk had passed out. Only when they'd lifted the slumped head—

"Are you sure you wouldn't like a cup of coffee?" Fanny said.

"No, really. What did you want?" Cathy wished she didn't sound so irritable.

Fanny glanced at her unfinished painting of people in a gallery. She tidied a dress which lolled from her suitcase, neck gaping. Then she seemed to run out of distractions. "You know that Roy—" She faltered, perhaps at having to speak his name. "Did you know that someone was trying to drive him out of the house?"

Of course Cathy didn't—she had hardly known him. "Why should anyone want to do that?" she demanded.

"You know he was gay."

"We assumed so. You don't mean they wanted him out because of that?"

"They must have. They called the police and tried to make out he was a criminal."

"God, how disgusting. How can people be like that?" She was growing uneasy: who might the culprit be? "But the police didn't arrest him," she said, and wished that were reassuring.

"No, but he was upset, you can imagine. I'm not supposed to tell anyone this, but—he hired a detective."

"Oh." Cathy wasn't anxious to help the conversation, which seemed more and more threatening.

"I met him once. He didn't look like a detective. Of course that helped him do his job."

Fanny seemed glad to avoid the point too. "What did he look like?" Cathy said, to delay further.

"Like that," Fanny said, pointing.

From the foreground of the picture of the gallery—insofar as you could speak of a foreground amid the painting's jokes about perspective—a man's face gazed. It looked glowingly scrubbed, like a little boy's before a party. His vividly blue eyes fastened on his audience, scrutinizing them. His thoughts were unreadable.

"Why, I know him," Cathy said. "He comes into the library."

"Well, there's no reason why he shouldn't," Fanny said. She sounded nervous.

"No, of course not. He has a limp, doesn't he?"

"He puts it on sometimes as a disguise." They were drifting away from Fanny's point. She said abruptly, "He was sure it was someone living here who wanted Roy out."

"That's terrible." She sounded less outraged than numbed.

"I know. But do you think that's the worst of it?"

"What do you mean?" Vague panic roughened her voice.

"Oh, I don't know, Cathy." Plainly she did, but had been hoping not to have to be specific. "Suppose whoever wanted to get rid of Roy didn't stop at calling the police? Suppose they—"

"Oh, no. I don't think so, Fanny." She interrupted quickly: she didn't want to hear. "Nobody here could have, not that. It isn't the same sort of thing, is it? Someone who makes anonymous phone calls isn't going to—to act. It must have been two different people."

Fanny's look of doubt forced her to continue. "Don't you think it must have been someone Mr. Craig was involved with who—killed him?" Each phrase struggled not to leave her mouth. "It sounded like a crime of passion, don't you think so? They do things like that sometimes. I suppose having to be secretive puts a strain on them. Sometimes their emotions must be too much for them. It's a different world."

"I hoped you'd say something like that." Fanny looked ready to smile. "So you don't think I should tell the police about the detective?"

She'd reached her point at last, though for a moment it seemed

that she'd lurched away. "I don't see why you should," Cathy said
eventually. "Presumably if he knows anything that might help them,
he'll go to them himself."

"Of course he will." Fanny was smiling, and seemed eager to be
active. "Well, I mustn't keep you. Thanks a lot, Cathy. You've made
me feel a great deal better."

Cathy couldn't return the compliment. She climbed the stairs hastily,
before the time-switch overtook her. Her steps sounded isolated; the
emptiness of Mr. Craig's room seemed to have affected the house.
Which room hid his persecutor? Whose face was a mask?

Peter came home shortly after she did; she heard him go into
the main room. She turned down the moussaka on the stove, and
followed him. He was sprawled on the bed, reading *The Savage Sword
of Conan.* "Oh, hello," he said, as though faintly surprised to see her
but hardly caring.

"Don't read for a minute. I want to talk to you."

"Oh, Christ. Can't it wait? I won't have a chance to read this
tomorrow if we're going to see my parents."

"Well, they are your parents." She sat on the bed, and captured
his irritable hands. "Just listen," she said, and told him Fanny's tale.

As soon as she'd finished, he pulled his hands away. Had he been
impatient to do so? He didn't like her to touch him so often now. Had
marriage separated Ben and Celia too? "So what do you want me to
do about it?" he said to her story.

"I'm not sure. What do you think we ought to do?"

"Nothing. Bugger all, that's what I think. She just wants you to
do something so she doesn't have to. What are you suggesting, we go
to the police?"

She hadn't considered the notion seriously — but perhaps it might
be safest, at that. "Well, no chance," he said. "There've been too many
fuzz around the house. You start inviting them up here, just watch them
sniff out my dope. They've got me paranoid enough."

"We ought to start looking for a house of our own."

"Sometime. No point until I've finished University. Listen," he said,
taking her hands, "don't get paranoid. We'll be all right here for another
year or so. Nothing else is going to happen. It's a good house."

So he did know how she felt, and was actually responding. He
stroked her hair as she rested her cheek on his chest. She didn't wan

to move, for their shared moments were becoming rarer — she wasn't sure why. Did that happen in all marriages? She'd have to move soon, to tend the moussaka.

"Hey, listen." He patted her cheek. "Christ, I've just had an idea."

She sat up eagerly. "You say old Harty's leaving," he said. "I'll bet he was the guy who set the fuzz on Craig."

She sagged a little; she'd hoped he meant to talk about moving. "Just think about it," he urged her. "He didn't seem too upset on Friday night, when you think what he must have seen. I'll bet he was glad someone got Craig."

Perhaps he was right, or perhaps the caller had been the other man on the ground floor: he was anonymous enough. Both ideas depressed her. "I've got to look after the dinner," she said, standing up.

"Smells good." Had that cost him an effort? He seemed disappointed that his theory hadn't cheered her up. "Things are going to be all right," he insisted. "Let's just stay away from the law, okay? We won't need them."

CHAPTER XIV

Today the sun was bright between the tower blocks. Even the blocks looked clean as bone. Glass gleamed like jagged dew among the grass blades. Passing cars exploded silently with light, and touched off explosions in the windows of flats. It was warm enough for Horridge to go out without his coat and buy a new one.

On Saturday morning, when he'd risen from his soundest sleep for years, he'd thought of continuing to wear the reversible, tartan outward. Craig's blood would be a secret badge of his achievement. But when he'd slipped his arms into the sleeves, the coat had felt clammy. He'd struggled out of it and had hung it in the wardrobe. To throw it away might have attracted attention.

He went downtown to the Army and Navy Stores, which seemed least expensive. Government Surplus raincoats—pale, almost white—were selling cheap. He tried one on, and found that it made him look like a detective in an old film. That amused him: now that he didn't need to play detective, it was a good disguise.

He bought the coat, then limped in search of newspapers, taking care not to buy more than one at any stall. He wandered amid the crowds for a while, enjoying his disguise, until a twinge of nervousness urged him home. Suppose someone broke into his flat while his documents were in the wardrobe? Besides, he had to find out what lies the newspapers were telling about him today.

He spread the new ones on the table, together with the earlier reports. Today the lies, where there were any reports at all, were lurking inside the papers. On Saturday there had been headlines so large and black they might have been shouting at illiterates, which no doubt they were. NEW RAZOR HORROR. ANOTHER HOMOSEXUAL SLASHING. NEW LIVERPOOL SLASHING HORROR. They sounded like slogans for trashy films.

His anger was mounting. He'd paid good money to read this rubbish about himself — to see his exploit served up as entertainment to the mob. But the reports were worse. Today's said only that enquiries were proceeding, but the earlier ones had had far too much to say. He scrabbled papers aside, and found the worst:

> Police today issued a statement about the murder of Roy Craig, of Aigburth Drive, Liverpool.
> It was revealed that Mr. Craig was well known in Liverpool's homosexual community. For this reason

What community? Where was it supposed to be? Lurking in some dark place, afraid to venture out into the light — its members knew that if decent people knew about it, they wouldn't let it exist for long. Community, indeed! Animals couldn't form communities!

> For this reason, police are considering the theory that his death was a "carbon copy" murder, inspired by the murders of two homosexuals in Liverpool last year.

What were they trying to insinuate? That Horridge couldn't think for himself? That he was a homosexual? They'd better be careful what they were saying! He hurled the newspaper to the floor, but it floated down lazily, mocking him. He grabbed the day's *Liverpool Daily Post*. What had they to say for themselves? Before he could find a report, the editorial caught his eye:

> Often, in its demands that crimes should be solved instantly or always prevented, the public seems to forget the difficulties under which our police labor. Undermanned, with a multitude of taxing and often thankless tasks

He restrained his fist before it had crumpled more than a corner of the page. How much had the paper been paid to say that? They were all in it together, insinuating filth about him. He knew what the so-called difficulties of the police were: that they were incompetent, or worse.

He'd read enough lying for today. He swept the papers together in a heap. Had some pages sneaked into the wrong papers? It didn't matter; they were all the same. He was snatching up pages that had escaped the heap, and piling them indiscriminately on top, when he saw the report that he had missed in the latest batch:

> Police are still investigating the murder of a Liverpool homosexual on Friday night.
>
> Later that night, on Princes Avenue in Liverpool, an unprovoked attack was made on a colored man by three youths. He was cut about the face with a razor, and later had to receive seven stitches. This incident occurred about a mile from the scene of the murder.

Horridge stared at the cramped box of print. He felt as though its frame had closed about him. What were they trying to do? "Unprovoked attack" indeed — what had a foreigner been doing out so late, unless he was up to no good? Yet that thought didn't prevent the report from distressing him. They'd made him sound like a young thug, terrorizing people. Was that how his achievement sounded?

His fist thumped the table; the newspapers trembled. No, by God. He was no thug. He was one of the few who still stood up for what was right — and he'd write to them to tell them so. No; letters could be traced. He'd phone them.

Then he grinned. His closed lips tightened over his teeth; his eyes stretched wide. He sat forward, trapping his legs beneath the table. No, he'd do no phoning. That was precisely what they wanted. All their lies and insinuations were meant to make him betray himself. Let them try. He wasn't Craig, to be distressed so easily.

He dumped the newspapers in the drawer. He didn't know why he bothered keeping them, except to remind him how sly people were. Well, they could stay shut up in there. They had nothing to tell him. He was turning away when he remembered the editorial.

Gradually his mouth widened into a smile. Of course, he hadn't been thinking straight. Their confusion had almost infected him. His mounting glee couldn't be contained by the small room. He must walk, it didn't matter where.

Mightn't people notice his new coat and wonder why he had bought it? It didn't matter. People bought new coats sometimes, even people as badly off as he. Nobody could suspect anything — not when even the police were so mistaken.

He walked, alert with gladness. His relief possessed him; everything looked interesting. His first idea had been right after all: the police were simply incompetent. Each of their theories led them further from him. They would never think to search for someone like him. He was safe.

He enjoyed all he saw. He grinned to himself at the sight of a minute general store housed in a shabby caravan in a parking space. Even the scenic area, which had used to infuriate him, only amused him now: the benches that commanded a view of caged saplings, children's deserted swings, a few low humps of grassy earth, all walled around by Cantril Farm barracks. There must be somewhere he could enjoy himself more fully. Where could he go?

He'd join the library. He hadn't borrowed a book for years. He ought to do more reading—there were few enough people left who could read. He climbed the ramp to the library. Women passed him, carrying baskets full of books. Perhaps that showed there was still hope for them, if only they wouldn't delude themselves with fiction.

The fish-eyed man was hogging the newspapers. Now the tables were turned: he'd achieved far less than Horridge. Horridge grinned openly at him, but the man looked quickly away. Hadn't he the courage to acknowledge his feelings? That was a weakness Horridge need no longer fear in himself.

He scanned the shelves. He would choose his books, then join. Fiction, fiction, fiction. Adventure and horror were mixed on the shelves, as though one might be a consequence of the other. Detective stories displayed fingerprints on their spines. He grunted low with mirth. That was the one way the police might have caught him, since they already had his fingerprints, but he'd left none on Craig. He'd touched only Craig's coat, and they couldn't take fingerprints from cloth. There must be hundreds of fingerprints on the outer doors; they'd never distinguish his. Apart from that—

All at once his face grew cold as plastic. Sweat coated his forehead. He was sure he must have turned pale. His fist clenched in his pocket, and he heard the razor click shut. He hadn't realized it was ajar; he might have cut his fingers. He could lop them all off without releasing himself from the trap into which he had fallen.

He'd left his fingerprints all over the painter's flat.

CHAPTER XV

As Peter and Cathy emerged from the van two women strolled by, humming tunelessly. Everyone around here in Childwall hummed defensively as they passed you, Cathy had noticed. They glanced at Peter, then at her. They resembled birds: brightly feathered heads, sharp intolerant faces. They seemed to be thinking: what did this young couple mean by cluttering this street of snugly paired houses with their tatty van, with Peter's cartoon on the side like a faded bloom of flower power left over from the 'sixties? What right had they to invade this tidy garden, with its family of gnomes, its viny trellises, its carriage-lamp beside the front door?

Peter rang the bell and leaned against the lamplit wall. He looked as though he were waiting on a stage set, bored with the part he was to play. Cathy was thinking that perhaps his parents hadn't heard about Craig's death. If they had, surely they would know not to seem too anxious; it would only harden Peter's stubbornness.

His father opened the door. She could see that he'd heard: he looked both determined and faintly embarrassed, like someone bearing his urine specimen through a hospital. He said only, "Some of your mother's friends are here."

He took Cathy's coat, but Peter kept on his old denim jacket. A delicately painted plaster saint watched over the hall table from a shelf. "Has the paper come?" Peter's mother called.

"No," his father said, adding to Cathy, "You used to be able to rely on people."

"Is that Peter?"

"Yes," Cathy called. It wasn't worth feeling annoyed.

In the living room, Peter's mother and an elderly couple sat neatly as a window display in their trim suits. His father took his place on the sofa beside his mother, symmetrically. Their conversation seemed light and fragile as the best china, from which they were sipping. They were discussing the Royal Family. "Didn't Princess Anne look lovely?" the elderly woman said to Cathy.

On television, or in a newspaper? "Oh yes," Cathy said agreeably. You shouldn't attack other people's beliefs without good reason. About her only thought on royalty was that, in being constantly surrounded by a false environment — royal toilets that were built for their coming and then, once they'd used them, torn down — they had something in common with schizophrenics.

The discussion petered out. To Cathy it sounded like chat about characters in a television series. The elderly woman set down her teacup delicately and said, "So this is Peter and his wife. Hasn't he grown, Gerald?"

"He has," said her husband.

"Tell Mr. and Mrs. Dutton what you're studying, Peter," his mother said.

"Conspiracy Theory and Applied Paranoia."

Cathy's toes curled up; her nails slid within her shoes. But Mrs. Dutton said, "Are you? You must need to be clever for that. Mustn't he, Gerald?"

"He must. Very nice."

Peter's father was silent. Clearly he wanted the elderly couple to leave so that he could come to the point. Peter was on edge with the careful politeness that limited the conversation. Both tensions worried her nerves.

God, no! She grabbed Peter's wrist, but Mrs. Dutton said, "That's a funny-looking cigarette. Is it a new brand?"

"I roll my own. Herbal tobacco. Not addictive like cancer sticks."

"Oh, why do you want to smoke?" his mother complained. "You never used to. Please don't smoke now, at any rate. Your father's getting a cold."

Reluctantly he put it away. Cathy dug her nails into his wrist. The four were too deep in a new discussion to notice. "Mrs. Wright said she thought a jumble sale was a good idea," Mrs. Dutton said. "But do you know what she said? She said she didn't want any old books.

I said some old books are very good books. We shouldn't sniff at books that are going to take a child to Lourdes, I said."

"I had to sit through that film once, with Jennifer Jones," Peter muttered. "I had to go with the school. It was supposed to be a treat."

"Jennifer Jones?" his father said, cupping his ear. "I saw it during the war. Lovely."

At last the Duttons left. Peter's parents marched back into the room. At once his father said, "What's this we hear about someone's being murdered in your road?"

Don't correct him! Cathy pleaded with Peter. But he seemed determined to liven up the conversation, for he said, "In our house, you mean."

"Oh no," his mother said. Her anguish sounded close to hysteria.

His father held up one hand, to hear all the evidence. "Exactly what happened?"

"He was queer. Someone caught him in the hall and cut him up. Zz-it! Skatch! Ss-kack!" he said like one of his comics, and brandished an invisible razor. "Well, you did say exactly."

His parents frowned at him, as though someone had made him up or perhaps as though they were imagining his excesses, which would fade away for lack of attention. "We weren't aware you were living among homosexuals," his father said.

"Oh, he was a very warm and wonderful human being."

"If they weren't making everything legal these days there'd be less trouble."

"You reckon if you make something illegal people don't do it?"

Peter was reaching in his pocket. Cathy made to grab his wrist. His mother said plaintively, "You're going to move, Peter, aren't you?"

His hand emerged empty, since the argument had changed. "What for? It's a good flat, and the rent's low. We wouldn't get another like that."

"Yes, and now we can see why the rent's low," his mother said. "You could live here until you found somewhere decent, if money's the problem. We'd look after you."

Was it an accident of words, or was she criticizing Cathy? Peter glanced at Cathy as he said, "We're all right where we are."

"You do what *you* think best," his father said. (Rather than consulting Cathy?) "But it can't be doing you any good to live there, among all these drug-takers that we read about."

Peter stood up. His grimace might have been a suppressed grin. "Where are you off?" his mother said mechanically.

His footsteps clumped upstairs. "You can see we're right, can't you," his mother told Cathy. Not that Cathy disagreed — but if she had, they would have blamed her for his obstinacy. She was beginning to glimpse their view of her.

His mother took framed photographs from the sideboard, where they interrupted ranks of plates. "That's Peter when he was little." Cathy hadn't seen these before; his mother must have a large stock, so as to be able to change the display. She was treating Cathy as she might have treated any visitor — in order to avoid hearing her thoughts about the argument?

Peter's childish face beamed smugly out of its frame. Did his parents cling to this image of him so as not to see what he'd become? Perhaps they still saw this image in him — perhaps they ignored the rest of him, as they'd ignored his living with Cathy before they were married. If they suspected anything about him, no doubt they blamed her for it.

Peter reappeared, and saw the photographs. "Oh Jesus, put that stuff away."

Cathy tugged his beard playfully. "We're just delving into your guilty past." His mother frowned as though that were an insult.

"Well, don't," he snapped, and turned to his father. "Anyway, what's wrong with people taking drugs? Just because they aren't legal yet — "

"Subject closed," his father said: refusing to be distracted, or determined not to have an argument disturb his home? "I think we've made our feelings plain about your living there," he said. "I hope you'll take them to heart. In time you'll see we're right. I only hope it won't be too late."

Silence filled the room, oppressive as humidity. It made Cathy nervous, and she rose. "Where are you off?" said Peter's mother.

She dawdled in the bathroom, surrounded by the scent of air freshener. A pink fluffy cover disguised the toilet as a large stumpy flower or a toy with a soft head. The room seemed almost intolerably polite.

She trudged downstairs, past miniatures like windows on a better world. Below her in the hall, something fell with a thud. Momentarily the stairs were steep and dizzying. Then she saw it was the newspaper, delivered at last. She hurried down and grabbed it; it might help break the awkward silence. "Here's the paper," she called.

RAZOR KILLER CAUGHT

At first she hardly dared read on. She hadn't been able to read any of the reports of Mr. Craig's death. But if the headline meant what it seemed to mean— Her gaze snatched nervously at the words. By the time she reached the living room she was smiling. "They've caught him," she said.

All three stared silently. "The man who did the killings," she stammered, excited. "The police have got him. They're sure he's the one."

"Well, fine. About time," Peter said.

His parents were less easily convinced. They read the report together, frowning. Eventually his father looked up. "That does seem satisfactory, I'll admit." His relief prompted him to say, "Shall we have a game of whist?"

Peter's mother shook her head at her son; her forehead stayed pinched. "It still isn't a nice area. I don't like to think of you living there."

"We aren't going to stay there forever. But Christ, nothing else is going to happen." He grimaced at her, annoyed by her concern. "Nobody else is going to be killed."

CHAPTER XVI

RAZOR KILLER CAUGHT

The man responsible for the slashing to death of three Liverpool men has been caught, police announced today.

They gave his name as Harold Nickelby (28) of Toxteth, Liverpool.

Confession

According to a police spokesman, Nickelby was seen by a young policeman loitering near a public lavatory known to be frequented by homosexuals.

When the policeman, who had noticed his resemblance to the identikit picture recently issued by police, asked Nickelby to accompany him, Nickelby is alleged to have said, "Don't bother checking. I am the man you want."

When cautioned, he is alleged to have said, "I'll be glad when it's over. I need to be put away."

Preying

Nickelby is being held by police in connection with the killings of Tommy Hale on 16 November, Norman Roylance on 24 December, and Roy Craig on 9 January.

Nickelby, who is unemployed, is said by police to have a history of unprovoked violence.

According to the police spokesman, Nickelby said he was "glad to be stopped" because the killing of Craig had been "preying on his mind." He is alleged to have said that he felt

compelled to return several times to the house on Aigburth Drive
where the murder was committed.

Horridge glared at the newspaper. Twilight was seeping into his
flat, insidious as mist; his surroundings grew dim. They thought they
could dim his mind so easily, did they? They must think he was mad,
to be tricked so simply.

Making out that Craig's death had been a copy had had no effect —
so now they were trying this ruse on him. Had they arrested an innocent
man as a scapegoat? They were capable of that, he knew only too well.
But no, he was sure that Nickelby didn't exist — you could tell the book
from which they'd borrowed his name.

Their methods were so obvious. If they tried to catch criminals
that way, God help the country. Most blatant of all was the purpose of
their last line. They wanted to sneak into his mind the idea of returning
to Aigburth Drive. Did they really think he'd go back so that they
could catch him?

But he had to go back, to wipe away his fingerprints.

Suppose the painter had already shown the police? Like them, she'd
tried to suggest he was a homosexual: might they be in league? But
then the police would have arrested him by now. No doubt her daubing
occupied her time. Besides, why should the police have let her into
their secret? She must think Craig's executioner had been arrested.

She had no cause to go to the police before she went away. But
was she going away? Might the words on the card he'd glimpsed have
meant that her friends were to visit her?

Babble, babble. He'd watch the house until he saw her leave. But
the police might be watching for him. Babble, babble. They couldn't
watch all the time, if they were as undermanned and overworked as
they liked people to believe. He'd spot them if they were about: he'd
keep an eye open for suspicious characters.

Tomorrow. Wasn't that when she was going? Surely that was right.
His memory wasn't trying to betray him. He struggled to project the
image of the card in his mind. There it was, on the mantelpiece, in
the rubbish dump of a flat. But he couldn't read the end of the line.
See you on, on See you on

Twilight brought the walls creeping toward him. They boxed in
his mind. Abruptly he stood up, and went walking. The paths were

hardly visible. Once he strayed onto a squelching verge. Low fences glimmered like decaying wood in a marsh; the tower blocks looked like tombs — few lights relieved their massiveness. See you on Jan See you on Jan

He wished he could flee to the country. Silhouettes with hollow footsteps tramped overhead on concrete walkways between buildings. Must he live the rest of his life in this prison camp? He thought he remembered where the cottage was, but he dreaded finding out who lived there now — if it hadn't been pulled down. Besides, he'd once tried walking in the country after his fall. Within an hour he had been near to crying out with the pain in his leg.

Children ran home from school along the dim paths, careless of whom they knocked down. When he lurched aside from one gang they laughed at him as though he were the simpleton whom everyone had mocked when Horridge was a child. Horridge had never been sure that the creature was so simple; he'd known enough to play with himself. Could anyone have made such inhuman sounds in public unless he'd been pretending to be simple? If he had really been so stupid, then he should have been put out of his misery.

They needn't think Horridge was a simpleton — not the children, nor the police. He could see more clearly than any of them, including the housewives who trudged home laden with baskets, trying to look burdened as women in the paddy fields: they didn't impress him.

A face poked forward from the dimness at him. She lived near his flat. He felt as though she'd punched him in the stomach. She must be wondering why he was strolling; he never did so in Cantril Farm. He mustn't do anything out of the ordinary. Anyone might be watching.

He hurried home. Not too fast! If he passed her, she would observe that too. He watched dimness engulf her. See you on Jan On Jan On Jan Her door clicked shut. Surely it was too dark for anyone else to see him. He ran like an injured child trying to win a game of hide and seek.

As he switched on the light, he saw it: Jan 15. All at once it was vivid, for he remembered how they hadn't written 15th — they didn't sound English. You couldn't expect her friends to be worth knowing; one of them had been Craig. See you on Jan 15.

He listened to the radio, to hear whether they were in league with the police. Yes, here came the lies: the fictitious Nickelby was the culprit, killing Craig had been too much for him. Let them play their game if it amused them. The news was followed by weather reports. "Heavy rain," the newsreader said. "Poor visibility."

Horridge stumbled to his feet and grabbed the radio as though it had begun ticking. He turned up the volume. Had he misheard? The suave voice read the reports; each one received the same careful false inflections. He switched off the set, almost wrenching the knob loose. The man hadn't been saying "visibility" at all. He had been saying "disability."

He managed to douse his fury. He'd more important things to think of than their cheap vicious tricks. He must remember everywhere he'd touched. Then he could go in quickly, wipe away his prints, and go straight out. He'd be too quick for the police.

The door and the doorknob. No doubt his prints were mixed with Craig's. He squirmed, disgusted. Craig and the painter must have had some doubly unnatural relationship. He was too tense to finish his dinner. He scraped half a piece of toast into the bin. Baked beans oozed down the plate, discomforting him.

He'd touched several of her pieces of clay before selecting two. Did clay hold fingerprints? He'd take the pieces away, just in case. She wouldn't have moved them — she was too untidy. Luck hadn't deserted him altogether, surely.

He finished the list in his mind. What could he do now until he grew tired? He ought to have borrowed a library book before fleeing. At last he switched on the radio. Perhaps they'd exhausted their tricks for tonight — or could they tell when he was listening?

There was nothing he cared to hear. Radio Merseyside was blaring jazz, Radio City was snarling pop music. Elsewhere was a murder play. Here were bland songs of yesteryear, soothing, reassuring, false. On the station that was meant for serious music was cacophony. Clang! Bong! Ping! It sounded like a herd of savages let loose in an ironmonger's.

He lay in bed and tried to sleep. He must be wide awake tomorrow. The clock was chanting: see you on Jan, see you on Jan. His mind listed places he must wipe, over and over. Had he forgotten one? The door. The doorknob. The table. The chair in which he'd sat. The cup — he must wipe all the cups, to make sure. The kitchen door and its handles. The tap. The knife with which he'd cut open the clay to receive the

keys. The spoons — he'd stirred his tea. Wasn't listing things supposed
to help you sleep? The door. The doorknob. The table.

He slipped the key into the door. It was the right key; as soon
as he'd entered the hall he had clenched his fist around the front door's.
The door of the flat refused to budge. He grasped the knob and shoved.
He must wipe that last of all.

The door jerked wide. He eased it shut behind him. Apart from
its jumble, the flat seemed deserted. A face stared at him from the
painting of the art gallery. He ignored it — no time for distractions.
He would start in the kitchen and work outwards.

When he opened the kitchen door, the painter was at the sink.

She turned and saw him. Her mouth fell ajar. His hand struggled
in his pocket; his documents cascaded out, onto the floor. His birth
certificate displayed his name. As she gazed at that, he fumbled open
the razor.

When she saw the blade, her mouth gaped. A scream rose in her
throat, like the shrill of a train rushing up a tunnel, but it wasn't quick
enough. He slashed her cheek. Her face tore like canvas, and a multicolored torrent spilled out, drenching him. He was covered with paint
sticky as glue.

He woke with a cry that clung to his ears. It frightened him, for
it didn't sound human. What was digging into his neck through the
pillow, like a hidden bone? He had to drag himself free of his nightmare
before he remembered that it was the razor. He lunged for the switch.
The light showed that it was scarcely midnight. The clock raised its
voice mockingly. He still had hours to suffer.

He was covered with paint sticky as glue.

CHAPTER XVII

Fanny was struggling to close her suitcase when she heard footsteps on the front drive.

It had to close. There was nothing she could leave out. She sat on the case, which felt like a hard lumpy bed, and dragged the zip shut while the case was overpowered. Its teeth bit an empty sleeve. Who was on the drive? Just let her deal with the case—if she gave it a respite it would never close. She poked the sleeve back, but a dress emerged from the far end of the case like a soggy Jack-in-the-box. "Get in, fustilungs," she snarled and heaving the case to her, flapped the dress into place and thumped herself down on the lid. She closed the case after a loud struggle and rested on it, panting.

She hurried to the window. Nobody was to be seen, even when she lifted the sash and leaned out. It must have been the postman. She went in search of the letters.

Except for shadows, the stairs were deserted. She ought to be less nervous now that Roy's killer had been caught, but there was a shadow at the foot of the stairs—a blurred version of the strut between the front-door panes, perhaps—which unnerved her. Besides, whoever had sent the police to Roy must still be lurking somewhere in the house.

She sorted the strewn letters on top of the cupboard in which the electricity meters chattered among themselves. She felt an odd pang of apprehension: perhaps there might be a letter for Roy. No—but there was one for her.

It was from a girl she knew at the gallery. She dawdled upstairs, slitting the envelope with her nails. Did they want to know why she'd been avoiding the gallery? The page was obscured by its own shadows.

Was she misreading it? Surely — But the brightness in her flat confirmed what she thought she'd read. More than half her paintings had been sold.

She sat beside her case, trying to absorb the news. It was incredible. She could bring down her prices spectacularly now, in order to appeal to the people she wanted to reach.

Didn't she want to reach those who had bought her work? Her heel tapped a floorboard, urging her to answer, ticking off the seconds she had left. Was there such a thing as a wrong audience for one's work, or a wrong reason to like it? Perhaps — but, she thought abruptly, it wasn't up to her to judge. According to the letter, the gallery visitors realized that her name on the paintings was an intentional joke. Few people had before.

She must hurry, or she'd miss her train. She opened the curtains wider, to make sure no burglars thought she was pretending to have gone away. Sunlight gleamed in the detective's eyes.

Might he have been wrong? He hadn't offered any evidence that Roy's persecutor lived in the house. Mightn't it have been the man whom the police had caught? Even detectives could be wrong. She draped the painting to protect it from the sun.

She propped the letter on the mantelpiece, behind the card. The card fluttered to the floor. No time to pick it up. She strode about quickly. Gas off. Toilet flushed. Windows shut. Which coat to wear? The heavy one — it might be cold in Wales. Efficiently she buttoned herself up: snap, snap, snap. God, her case was heavy. She slid it out of the flat, glanced back once, and slammed the door.

In the park, trees feathered the chalk-blue sky. As she walked, branches disentangled themselves gradually and silently to reveal how complex the patterns were. At the end of the avenue the obelisk stood, clean as shell. Everything made her feel restful.

She was singing the *William Tell Overture* as she turned out of Aigburth Drive. "Ya-ta-tum, ya-ta-tum, ya-ta-tyum-tyum-tyum." A man recoiled from her; his two Pekingese, their faces like furry Oriental demons, tried to snap at her ankles. So much for melody, she thought, giggling.

She plodded along Sefton Park Road. "God, you're a weight," she told her case. "I wish you were old enough to walk by yourself." It wasn't only the case that was slowing her down: she was suddenly full of ideas for her gallery picture. Wasn't the painting too bitchy? Some of her new ideas were more genial.

Ought she to go back? She rested her suitcase and gazed like a pavement artist at the flagstones. Shouldn't she spend just an hour with her painting? But then she'd have to send a telegram to say she would be late. Besides, she wouldn't be able to predict how long she would be busy. She hefted her case. She'd sketch her ideas on the train journey.

What time was the train? She dropped her case at the bus stop. Was her memory five minutes fast or slow? She rummaged in her pockets. Don't say the timetable was in her other coat. When she shouted her annoyance, people in the queue stared or ostentatiously ignored her. Because of all the distractions, she had left her train ticket in the flat.

She hurried home furiously. Her case thumped her leg, challenging her to carry it further. "All right," she growled, "you just wait." Where were all the taxis?

It was a good thing she'd had to return: although she thought she'd made sure they were open, she'd left the curtains drawn. So that was what selling did to her concentration! She fought the front door. Come on, damn it! The lock seemed not to recognize her key. At last she reached the stairs, which looked indistinct as a dusty attic. She climbed them anyway — it would have wasted time to go back to the time-switch.

Her suitcase accompanied her: bump, bump. Not until she reached her landing did she see how redundant its clambering was. She could have left the case in the hall. She didn't need company on the dim stairs.

"Just don't start playing me up," she told her lock. The key turned easily; the door opened, revealing dusk within. Everything was overlaid with the purple of the curtains. How could she remember the room as having been so much brighter?

There was her ticket, waiting amid the clutter on the table for her to choose which coat to wear. She stuffed it into her pocket. Faces hid beneath the cloth that draped her painting. But she'd covered the painting to keep it from the light — because the curtains had been wide.

Something else was wrong.

She stared about. Something was out of place. The lurking faces. The cuttings, and the newspapers with their rectangular holes. Clay on the table. The closed doors to the kitchen and the bathroom. The

card on the mantelpiece. But she'd left that card on the floor where
it had fallen.

The card held her gaze for minutes. She fought to distrust her
memory. Although the card might have fallen after being replaced,
the reverse was impossible. Someone had been in her room. When she
glimpsed the looming unfamiliar shape, she whirled. It was her suitcase,
squatting outside the door.

Now she couldn't turn away. The depths of her mind were crying
that worse was to be seen. Where? There was the door, which showed
no evidence of having been forced; beyond it was the landing, guarded
by her case. There was nothing else—

There was no sign of the metal bird which Tony had sculpted for
her.

After a time which seemed paralyzed as her thoughts, she dragged
her case into the flat and closed the door. She sat on the case, staring
emptily. The theft had violated her flat. She felt soiled, as though after
a rape.

She glanced dully at her watch. No chance now of catching the
train. In any case, she wouldn't have been able to go. She must call
the police, and send a telegram. The dismal tasks burdened her mind;
her head drooped.

The thief must have slipped in as soon as she'd left. Must it have
been one of the other tenants? Who else would have had the oppor-
tunity? If only Cathy weren't out at work—she couldn't trust anyone
else in the house. Was the thief Roy's persecutor? Surely he would have
taken more than the sculpture, unless he had meant only to distress
her. Did he want the whole house to himself?

Still, she didn't know that he had stolen nothing else. She must
check before calling the police. She rose wearily. Confronted by the
bathroom door, she was all at once uneasy: suppose he were hiding
in there like a ghost train's dummy, poised? Then by God, she'd scare
him more than he had unnerved her. She wrenched the door wide.

She heard a noise within, small but sharp. She glared about, but
could see nothing. Nobody could hide behind the bunched shower
curtains. The only movement was of water, gathering lazily at the mouth
of the tap, preparing to fall and pronounce another small sharp drip.

Stupid! She opened the kitchen door angrily. Nothing visible had
been touched. Her memory of how the room had looked fitted snugly

over it. One tap was straining to drip into the metal sink, but she wiped its mouth with a finger. Swiftly she checked cupboards and drawers.

So the thief had taken only the sculpture—unless he'd gone into the capacious wardrobe. There was nothing in there worth stealing; she had virtually stripped it when filling her case. Still, she'd better make sure. She was upset enough without looking foolish to the police.

The double doors were ajar, although she thought she'd closed them. She pulled them wide. Dimness, faintly purple, lay within. Her hanging overalls were huddled in the left-hand corner, as if for companionship. Their hangers squeaked, startled. At first the swaying of the flowered overalls obscured what else was in the wardrobe.

It was the metal bird, hovering waist-high in front of the overalls. It gleamed dully. So he hadn't stolen it, after all! Why had he hidden it there, in one of the pockets? What was that meant to achieve?

It wasn't in a pocket. Something else held it in mid-air. Nor were the overalls swaying only because she had disturbed them. Protruding from the foremost sleeve, holding the bird's slim body, she saw a hand.

"Come out," she cried, as she might have if a mischievous child had startled her.

The flowers flapped outward; a dim figure came at her. Before she could make out the face above the overall, the metal bird darted toward her. Its jagged beak pecked deep into her forehead.

CHAPTER XVIII

Horridge limped along the path on the edge of the park. On the pavement across the road, a postman hurried in the opposite direction. Trees interrupted Horridge's glimpses of the house, which looked deserted. The painter's window gleamed emptily. Did that mean she had left?

Abruptly her face appeared in the window. He flinched behind a tree; bark scraped his shoulders through his raincoat. He heard the rattle of the sash. She was leaning out to peer, but apparently not for him. Nevertheless he shrank behind the tree again, heart clenching.

At the sound of the sash he peered out. The window was empty. He limped hastily to the telephone box. A stench of tobacco smoke surrounded him like halitosis; the unwashed windows robbed him of light. His heart jerked, trying to get the better of him, to scare him. It wouldn't succeed, any more than the painter would. He gripped the razor in his pocket.

Had he been right to leave his documents in the reversible? Surely they'd be safe enough in the wardrobe—nobody would want to steal that coat. There was no point in taking risks, in carrying papers that would identify him.

The thought made him feel already trapped. The glass of the box looked coated with smoke: was that exuding the oppressive stench? The silence of the phone seemed threatening, as though its shrill were poised to leap at him. His eyes felt feverish, pimply with insomnia. He began to shuffle and stamp nervously, like an imprisoned beast.

Movement halted him. The porch door had opened. When it had displayed its gap for a while, a suitcase emerged. Carrying it—yes, it was the painter! His grin gleamed in one of the few patches of the mirror that were still clear of graffiti.

She might pass the box, and see him! He seized the phone. Dial, for the love of God. Anything. Of course—he knew one number that wouldn't answer. He dialed Craig's flat, and imagined the phone crying in the empty room. The trick amused him, yet made him feel inexplicably nervous. When he replaced the receiver, he had to bang it into place several times before the minute trilling stopped.

The painter was turning out of Aigburth Drive. No, she wasn't coming back. Never mind skulking in his hidey-hole. He had a job to do.

He advanced toward the house. Gravel squirmed underfoot. Six windows glinted at him. Wasn't it spiders that had six eyes? No need to make himself nervous—nobody was left in there who could recognize him.

The key was right first time. He tried to tiptoe upstairs. The stairs were a vindictive sounding-board: listen, he's limping, they shouted. He fought to regulate his steps. Was the door opposite the painter's threatening to open? Most unlikely, he thought, grinning.

The painter's room blazed out at him, like the springing of a trap. He closed the door quickly behind him. The room was too bright; it displayed him. He sidled to the window and drew the curtains. The room filled with purple twilight, which seemed unhealthy to him. Had Craig and the painter committed secret filth in that light? They would never do so again.

Where was the card? Though he'd seen her suitcase, he needed reassuring. At last he found it, lying on the floor beneath the bony ashen cage of the gas fire. He propped the card on the mantelpiece. See you on Jan 15. He was safe.

He limped into the kitchen. Knives first. Seizing a tea-towel, he pulled open the kitchen drawers. A chorus of rattling announced the knives. Each time he took one out, its neighbors chattered metallically. The noise unnerved him, and might deafen him to warnings. He pushed the kitchen door wide.

As he returned to the drawer, he heard footsteps on the gravel drive. He froze; the knife trembled in his hand. He flung the knife into the drawer and ran to the bay window, almost knocking over a draped painting. He clawed aside the edge of curtain, which felt cold and slippery. Through the gap he glimpsed the painter entering the porch.

Oh dear God, no! Instinctively he grasped the razor. Perhaps she'd returned for her letters, and would go straight out again. He heard the front door open. Then, accompanied by what sounded like a gang of echoes, she came trudging upstairs.

He couldn't use the razor; Craig had taken so long—he couldn't go through that again. He stared about, and saw the bird. It was metal, and sharp. Certainly it looked more like a weapon than a work of art. He grabbed it, and was heartened by its solidity.

The clambering sounded like a drunken giant's. God, where could he hide? He stumbled to the door beside the kitchen. There was no concealment in the bathroom, nor anywhere amid the stove and sink and cupboards. He jerked the door shut.

The footsteps reached the landing with a thud. Could he hide behind the door and strike her down? Suppose someone else was in the building, and heard? There was only one hiding place. He dragged the wardrobe doors open, and climbed within.

He left the doors ajar. He couldn't bear to be imprisoned in total darkness, with the dusty smell of wood. Besides, he must hear what she was up to. She was dragging an object toward the flat—her case? As he retreated into the depths a hanger tapped him on the shoulder, creaking, and dangled an overall.

He remembered Craig's stains on his coat. He couldn't afford a repetition of that. Snatching the overall from its wire shoulders, he buttoned himself up swiftly.

Her key slithered into the lock. Was she talking to herself? She mustn't be quite right in the head—but that was true of all these so-called creative people. How many of them were homosexuals? Tchaikowsky had been. Horridge could have done without his music— he would have preferred the world to be clean. His mind was chattering to leave no room for seeds of panic.

He heard her stride to the table. There was a sound of cloth— maybe she'd put something in her pocket. Leave now, go away, get out! Now she wasn't moving. Was she staring at the wardrobe? Had she seen the gap between the doors?

He was paralyzed. If he moved she would hear him. Sweat boiled out of him, pricking his skin; the overall clung to him. It was too small, and oppressed him with his own feverish heat. His hand clenched on the slim metal body.

She was leaving, thank God. He heard the dragging of the case and the slam of the door. The bird dropped from his unclenching hand. Why couldn't he hear her on the stairs? He was ready to risk movement, since he felt the threat of cramp, when he heard her steps — still in the flat.

Did she know he was there? His limbs twitched, tugged by pangs of cramp. Sweat glued his clothes and the overall to him. He felt unclean, as though she'd made him soil himself. Hatred grew in him.

Her slow tread paced around the room. He was becoming convinced that she knew he was there — that she was playing a game, just as Craig must have played with his helpless victims. He heard her opening doors. Sweat pierced him like shards of ice.

She was approaching the wardrobe. He was trapped. The doors opened. They admitted only meager light, which framed her silhouette. Despite the twinging of his limbs, he stood absolutely still. Perhaps she wouldn't see him.

His bad leg betrayed him. Cramp jerked it awry. He stumbled a little; hangers jangled. The silhouette came peering toward him out of the purple twilight, its halo of red hair darkly smoldering. "Come out," the painter's voice snapped like a domineering teacher's.

Cramp and self-disgust and panic convulsed his arm. The bird flew up and leapt at her. He heard and felt the beak go into her, but the silhouette showed nothing.

He watched the silhouette sink to its knees. He had to strike again at the top of its head before it would fall out of his way. At least its voice was silent; perhaps it had been too surprised to cry out.

He stepped hastily over her. In the purple twilight her face looked unreal. That made even the leaking of her head bearable; it was easy to imagine that dye from her hair was staining her face.

The dye might seep through to the floorboards. It would help if she weren't found for a while, to give him time to plan. Everyone would assume she was on holiday. He grabbed her beneath the arms to heave her into the wardrobe.

It was as though she were making herself heavy. He could scarcely move her; her grossness disgusted him. Her head lolled back, staining his overall. Once, when he tried to shift his grip, one of her breasts flopped into his hand. He recoiled shuddering, and with an effort fueled by panic flung her into the wardrobe.

Then he realized that he had felt a pulse in her breast.

He picked up the metal bird, and closed his eyes. It had to be done. In any case, she was corrupt: she believed that everyone, including him, was homosexual. God only knew what she and Craig had done together.

He opened his eyes minutely, to see exactly where her head was. Then he struck until his arm was tired. He could tell he'd done enough, by a change in the quality of the blows. That dismayed him, but it was easy not to think about it. He threw the metal bird into the wardrobe without looking.

Beneath the scattered stained newspapers the floor was clean. He bundled the papers together with the overall and hurled the bundle into the wardrobe. The snap of the doors sounded final, satisfying.

He patrolled carefully. The knives. The spoons. The taps. The kitchen door and handle. Couldn't he take his time now, to be thoroughly convinced that he'd missed nothing? But the wardrobe disturbed him indefinably. It looked exactly like an ordinary wardrobe. You couldn't trust appearances.

At least he'd left no prints in there; the metal bird must be too rough to take them. He wiped the other places that he'd listed, and shied the tea-towel into the kitchen. On the landing, he scrubbed the doorknob with his handkerchief.

Aigburth Drive was deserted. Nobody was spying from behind the trees. Horridge strolled down to the lake and enjoyed the still reflections. He'd intended them to calm him; but once he had left the wardrobe behind he had grown quickly peaceful, without external help. He felt relieved that he had done all he needed to do. He felt invulnerable.

When he emerged from the park, the house no longer looked unnaturally alive. Whatever had possessed it had been exorcised. It was quiet now, just another aging house. Still there was no sign of watchers. The police had missed their last chance to capture him. He strolled away delighted, hardly limping.

In the purple twilight her face looked unreal.

CHAPTER XIX

A van large as a room stood outside the house. Men were furnishing the van from Mr. Harty's flat. "Are you going tonight?" Cathy asked him. Her own plaintiveness dismayed her.

"Yes, I am."

Peter dropped the shopping bag about which he'd been complaining mutely all the way from Lodge Lane. "You've found somewhere better then, have you?"

"I'm afraid that anywhere else would be better now, so far as I'm concerned. But yes, I'm going to a pleasant flat. I should think about a move yourselves if I were you."

"Sometime," Peter muttered, stooping reluctantly to the bag.

The van was growling, eager for its run. "Goodbye, Mrs. Gardner, Mr. Gardner," Mr. Harty said.

Echoes seemed to be invading the stairs. It was as though a plague of desertion were spreading through the house. At least Fanny wasn't gone forever. Halfway up the stairs, intuition too vague to define halted Cathy. Had Fanny returned? There was nothing to hear, and she couldn't knock while Peter was watching: that would need too much explanation.

As she unpacked the shopping she said, "I want to see Frank and Angie."

"When?" He tried not to hear by making plastic crackle.

"Tonight."

"Oh come on. Jesus *Christ*, we only saw them on New Year's Eve."

"I thought you quite liked them."

"What? I can stand them sometimes, when I have to. They'd be all right if they were younger, maybe. I mean, we might just as well go to your mother's."

Her mother had rung her today, in case she needed reassurance. Cathy would have liked to visit her, but her concern would only annoy Peter. Besides, she didn't think much of him at the best of times; neither she nor Cathy's father nor Lewis had liked him—he resembled none of them. Was that why Cathy had married him?

"I'm not going to argue," she said. "I want to go. I want to talk."

Irritability roughened his voice; he must have a cannabis hangover. "So talk to me, for Christ's sake."

How? Their private language had died, and very little had replaced it. "I rang Angie this afternoon," she said. "They're expecting us."

He gobbled his dinner without comment. When she washed up he wiped a few plates and smoked a joint. Before he could roll another she said, "I want to go now."

She drove the van past Penny Lane. Boys stood eating out of newspapers. Beside her, Peter swayed like a bag of shopping. It was a good job that he couldn't drive. On Allerton Road couples were window shopping; a young man staggered out of a wine store, bearing a carton of bottles of spirits to his sports car. Shops or petitions barred pubs from the area.

Queens Drive was an avenue of trees and sodium lamp-standards. The Halliwells' Cortina occupied their driveway. Each semi-detached house was guarded by a large car.

The doorbell chimed a half-hour. Soon Angie appeared in a long dress entwined with cotton vines. The hall walls were crowded: a nostalgic pub mirror, Frank in an old school photograph, the *Desiderata*: "Go placidly amid the noise and haste, and remember what peace there may be in silence. . . ."

Angie finished massaging Frank's neck. "I didn't know you had massage parlors round here," Peter said. He stood frowning at Angie's Royal Family portrait album, at the very fat new leather suite. When he sat down, his chair was audibly rude to him.

Frank opened the flap of the bar counter: homemade, of glossy pine. "Cathy, what would you like to drink?"

"A huge gin and tonic."

"Peter?"

"What, a little drinkie?" His tone stopped just short of mocking. "Beer's all right," he said.

"I know what *you* want," Frank told his wife, pouring tequila. *"Et pour moi—le vin!"* he announced gravely.

Unbuttoning his waistcoat, he sank into his chair, which humphed. "I hear you're thinking of buying a house," he said to Peter.

"You hear wrong."

"That isn't what I said, Frank. He knows what computers are talking about but doesn't understand me," Angie complained.

"Sorry, sorry. Still, it's worth thinking about," Frank said. "Apart from all the other advantages, property is an investment."

"Don't give me that stuff, brother. I've had one capitalist at me today already."

Cathy shifted uneasily; her chair made sure that everyone noticed. "How about you?" Frank asked her. "How do you feel?"

"I'd like to move soon. I want a house before we have children."

"Mm." His eyes flickered: he didn't want Angie reminded of their barrenness. "That looked a promising house we passed the other night," he said to Angie. "In that road."

"Which road?"

"Er—oh, you know."

"I don't"

"Of course you do. You know."

"Which one?"

"You know." He was almost squeaking—he sounded like a man determined to overcome a language barrier by shouting, anything to steer them away from the subject of children.

"Husbands." Angie's grimace was gentle. Had she known what he was doing? She was glancing about at her collection of elaborately ethnic dolls, most of which he'd bought. One, which was shaped like a fat skittle, unscrewed to yield up a smaller which unscrewed too, until a whole family emerged.

Peter looked bored, excluded. "When are you finishing work?" Angie asked him.

"Tomorrow."

"Eighteen more months as a student, isn't it? Will you be glad when it's over?"

"I don't know. It isn't a bad life."

"Living off us poor overtaxed workers, you mean?"

She smiled to show that was a joke, but his voice was low as a dog's warning as he said, "I thought all the workers were on the factory floor. That's who I'd call workers."

"That doesn't say much for your library work then, does it?"

"Right."

Angie frowned, then shrugged. "You'll manage while he isn't working, will you?"

"I expect so. We've been all right so far. Touch wood," she added, touching Peter's head.

He recoiled; his dislike shocked through her, like electricity. She hadn't meant anything. "Come and see what I'm making for supper," Angie said.

In the kitchen she said, "What's wrong, Cathy?"

"Oh, Angie, I want a house. I don't like the flat anymore." She felt close to weeping. "I try to save for the deposit. But if we move to another flat I may not be able to save."

"Maybe you could look for just a small house. You've got to start somewhere. They might give you a mortgage even if Peter's not working. They can't all be male chauvinists." She gazed at Cathy. "What's really wrong?"

"I wish I knew. Peter and I seem to be getting on each other's nerves so much."

"You're bound to be nervous after what happened, even now they've caught him."

"That's what I try to tell myself. But it's so horrible." She was weeping. "I keep thinking of my parents. They got so they couldn't bear to be in the same room together."

Angie hugged her, trying to contain and calm her trembling. "These things happen. Listen, I'm going to tell you something. When we found we couldn't have children we couldn't stand each other for a while. Do you know what it was? We couldn't bear secretly blaming each other. Eventually we had to talk it out, and that brought us closer than we were before. But believe me, Cathy, for a while we felt like separating."

Perhaps she and Peter were just going through a phase. A child might mature Peter, make him aware of his responsibilities. Maybe she ought to find a small house and take him to see it. "Thanks, Angie," she said, and kissed her. "I needed cheering up."

Down the hall the television announced the news. "He'd have the box on all night if I didn't stop him," Angie said.

"I hope you switch off before the National Anthem. Otherwise you get bad luck."

"Watch it. You'll end up as bad as Trotsky in there. Let's go and interrupt them before there's a war."

They hurried in the pub mirror, ready for another drink. " — in a police raid on a London house," the announcer said.

"Bastards," Peter muttered.

Frank glanced quizzically at him. "I take it you aren't fond of the police?"

"What do you think? It shows up what you were saying, doesn't it? You tell me what use it is to own property when the fuzz can break in."

"But they won't, unless you break the law."

Peter's eyes grew thin. "You're in favor of drug raids as well, are you?"

"Will you get us another drink?" Angie said, to separate them.

"The law must be upheld. I'd rather have a visit from the police than have my house invaded by a mob of anarchists."

Peter stared as though Frank were possessed. "You know what you are? You're a fuckingfascist." It sounded like a single word.

"Well, if you feel that way — "

"Don't worry." Had he meant to achieve this from the start? "We're going," he said, rising quickly. "Or at least I am."

Let him walk home: serve him right — but Cathy remembered what Angie had told her. Perhaps she and Peter could talk out all that was wrong. "I'm sorry," she told Frank, who refused to look at anyone. "Maybe Angie will be able to explain. I'll phone you," she promised Angie.

Before she reached Penny Lane she had to halt the van; her hands were shaking. Slabs of light lay beneath shop windows. Empty shoes bunched in a window, like fruit. The deserted pavements looked bleak. Everyone was at home or out enjoying themselves.

"If he didn't want an argument why did he give me that shit? I bet he thought I'd have to be all middle-class and polite. No chance, brother."

Once her hands were controllable she ground her heel into the accelerator and drove home. As she opened the porch door, a man with a lopsided face whom she had never seen before emerged. The house would be overrun with strangers now. Nothing could have changed its atmosphere more jarringly. Oh, when could they move? Peter strode into the hall without switching on the light. As though to escape the threatened discussion, he climbed into the resounding dark.

CHAPTER XX

"Here's the man," a woman said. "You've had it now."

But Peter was only replacing a book on the shelves. He resented being made into an ogre. It was the woman's job to control her child, not his.

He dawdled to the counter. His colleagues were serving a queue; the counter resembled a conveyor belt piled with books. The staff fished book cards from metal trays, hoping the correct reader's ticket would be attached. "What is your name, please?" "Open your books while you're waiting, please." "And your name is?" "Your name? Your *name?*"

It was all a con. They made their job so important — perhaps they needed to convince themselves. Put people behind a counter or in a uniform and they'd enjoy their power. The more insignificant the job, the more rigidly they exerted their power. "Please don't turn down the corners of pages. We haven't much money to spend on books, you know." The old lady trudged away, looking bewildered, humiliated, resentful.

The temptation of petty power affected Peter too. One reader always cleared his throat before his name: "Huh — Barnes." It sounded hyphenated. "Pardon?" Peter would say, to make him omit the cough — but he never had. Nor could he meet your gaze while saying his name. Afterward Peter had detested his own trivial sadism.

A massive woman with a face like a boxer's advanced on him. "Can I have that book?" She jabbed a finger thick as his thumb at the trolley in the staff area.

"We'll be putting the books on the shelves in a minute." His position behind the counter allowed him to fear nobody.

It was all false. The job let him play a role, avoid himself. Wasn't that true of all jobs? The minute hand snipped away the time to five o'clock. Soon he would be free. Cathy had suggested he work in the libraries. The only good thing had been meeting Anne and Sue, and smoking with them in the staffroom.

An old lady struggled up to him, trying to manage a pile of books and a poodle like a woolly toy with eyes bright yet inexpressive as the stones in its collar. "Do you like my little doggie? You can stroke him. He won't bite."

God forbid. He grabbed the books as they spilled. *Nurse Nightingale's Last Doctor. Operation—In Search of Love. Two Against the World.* "That's a lovely book. I expect it wouldn't be your style, though."

Why did she bother saying so? Why must she be so oppressively *nice*? "Thank you so much," she said when at last he extracted her tickets. "Say goodbye to the nice man, Hercules," she said, waving its paw. Peter felt as though he'd been forced to swallow a mixture of sugar, saccharin, and molasses. He was full of loathing.

Jesus, where was five o'clock? The clock's hands appeared to shift minutely, but perhaps that was an echo of his acid trips. A queue passed sluggishly along the counter; they were all coming in now that it was nearly closing time. "Open your books, please. One on top of the other."

Quarter to five. All the windows were boarded up, and protected further by heavy wire mesh. You couldn't lock people and their problems out, any more than you could lock them away. He wished he'd had a joint—except that would have made him feel more oppressed, shut in with the artificial light in daylight. No wonder kids broke the windows when the city council spent so much on building a new library, yet expected them to live in shit and tower blocks.

The librarian patrolled, intoning, "Closing in five minutes." An old man woke grumbling; another shuffled newspaper pages together like huge unwieldy cards. Some children ran in to dare the notice: NO CHILDREN ALLOWED IN THE LIBRARY WITHOUT TICKETS OR NOT IN THE COMPANY OF AN ADULT. One of the staff chased them, calling, "Now then, now then," like a stage policeman. He was playing a game as much as they were, Peter thought.

"We're closed, I'm sorry," the librarian said, barring the way of a group of men. "Closed, I'm sorry. Closed." Peter had heard the men talking in the pub next door; they were communists, unemployed. One of these days they won't be able to lock you out, brothers.

"Goodbye, Peter," the librarian said. "I hope you do well with your studies."

"See you," Peter said generally, and "See you, brother," to long-haired Mike, who read the *New Statesman*.

He strolled along Great Homer Street. The line of shops, low boxes of orange brick, dwindled behind him; some of them were already locked in metal, impregnable as safes. Opposite them on a patch of waste stood two market stalls, scrawny frameworks of tubular steel, picked almost clean of merchandise. He wouldn't be seeing those sights again. He was free.

Girls stood beneath a tower block. "There's the library man," one said.

"Where?" another hooted. "That's a girl."

Ah, irresistible Liverpool humor, the famous Scouse wit, the instant quips. Their squeals of laughter set the back of his neck ablaze. He ought to have retorted, "If I'm a girl then what the fuck does that make you?" Often he replayed scenes in his head and gained the advantage — more often since taking acid.

The bus labored uphill, away from the Mersey. Back there, stars were drowning — lights on the river, blurred by mist. Ahead, floodlights blazed over Anfield football ground, a glare of lightning prolonged for hours. Football fans piled onto the bus.

Ranks of lit shops passed close on both sides. Scarved fans disembarked. A newcomer asked Peter, "What's the score?"

"Half an ounce of Moroccan hash." Pretending frustrated him, and nothing interested him less than football. Sometimes his refusal to pretend landed him in fights — at least, with the threat of them. This time he didn't need to worm his way out. The man sidled away, shaking his head, to question someone else.

Lights sank into fog. West Derby Road. Boaler Street. The gay porn bookshop on Holt Road. Lodge Lane. Trees stirred dimly in Sefton Park, like the onset of a trip. He hoped Cathy was out shopping; he liked coming home to an empty flat. When he'd lived with his parents he could always retreat into his room when he grew irritable.

The flat was as empty as the house sounded: good. He had still to grow used to this new experience, marriage. It had seemed to promise total security, an end to all problems — but it felt less real than living with Cathy had. It weighed him down with bourgeois ambitions and the fear of failure. He was wary of giving himself to the marriage, in case he did something wrong.

Was he being lazy? He released the vacuum cleaner from its cupboard and led it about, snatching at dust. "Darkies all work on the Mississippi," he sang. When he'd finished he felt virtuous. Time for a joint.

He crumbled the resin. Where had Cathy put his books now? Her idea of tidying was to clear things out of sight; it didn't matter if you couldn't find them. There they were, hiding in a corner. Most were library books, which he'd borrowed as a member of staff. One day he'd return them — maybe.

Most were set books for the University. He must do some reading. Nineteenth-Century Litteratchah. Dickens — Christ, what a turgid turd. "Discuss the effects on Dickens' style of the tension between melodrama and social comment." Should he write something now, while Cathy wasn't here to distract him? But the flat seemed distractingly large and silent. If he played a record, the music would carry his thoughts away. He'd get his head straight soon. He could work during the rest of the vacation.

He felt the cannabis take hold. Time slowed. The sound of a passing car became an event in itself, prolonged and fascinating. He reached for an unread *Silver Surfer*, and admired the sleek metallic curves of the inhuman superhero. "Leave comics alone," his parents had used to say. "They're beneath you." He hadn't looked at a comic for years, until one day when he was wandering stoned.

Now Cathy disapproved. Couldn't she see that in time the comics might buy them a house? Often he went to the Comics Marts, to share a few joints and to marvel at the comics dealers' prices. He wanted a house as much as she did: he'd like a room to himself. But they had no chance of a mortgage now. Christ, why would he want to trap her here? He had more reason to want to move than she had. He thought he might have seen the killer before he'd murdered Craig, and had done nothing.

The first time he'd seen the man watching Craig — when Craig had been complaining about the stereo — he'd known the two of them were involved. He hadn't needed to glimpse the man lurking among the trees to confirm it. One of Craig's ex-boyfriends, no doubt. Peter had wondered what he was up to, but hadn't been about to get mixed up with those people: Craig had always disturbed him, with his simultaneous heftiness and grace, the qualities of Oliver Hardy. Perhaps if Craig had been open about what he was, he would have been less alienating.

Whoever the man was, he had something to hide; he must have, to have conned Fanny into thinking he was a detective. Maybe he just hadn't wanted her to know he was gay. Stupid cow — she was as stupid as her name. She deserved the same as had happened to Craig.

He shuddered. He'd had a brief vivid image of the killing. Shit, he couldn't have prevented it. The joint was setting his thoughts adrift; they floated over one another, overlapping. Suddenly he saw Craig against the wall. His mouth and his flesh were gaping. Peter felt the razor part his own skin.

He jerked himself free of the trance with a start like awakening. His stomach felt hollow with abrupt vertigo. Christ, that had been like acid; he hadn't realized the dope was so strong. Maybe he needed a walk in the country, to calm his head.

That reminded him. He dialed, and at last Jim's stoned voice said slowly and warily, "Who is it?"

"It's Peter. Did you score that acid?"

Jim sounded lugubrious and muffled, as though talking in his sleep. "It's supposed to be coming tonight."

"Oh, great. Will you keep me a tab? I'll come around later."

When Cathy came in, sinking on the bed as her bag of potatoes sagged on the floor, he said, "Want to go out tonight?"

"Oh, yes." She sat up. "Where?"

"Jim's got some good stuff." No need for her to know that it was acid.

"Oh." She sank back. "I thought you might mean to look at houses."

"Houses? Houses?" he gurgled in a strangled Monty Python voice. The cannabis forced him to observe his behavior. It was a way of avoiding discussion, but he had to struggle to free himself of the voice; his throat seemed to contract around it. "Not tonight," he said irritably. "The stuff won't wait."

"Peter, for heaven's sake. You'll smoke all our money."

"Ah ha!" That was a cue for his Freak Brothers quote. "Dope will get you through times of no money," he said, and raised his voice as she trudged sighing to the kitchen, "better than money will get you through times of no dope." It occurred to him that he needn't feel mean for wanting his own room. Clearly she did too.

CHAPTER XXI

"Are you coming?" Peter said.

It wasn't worth making the automatic pun. Why should she bother to go with him? She moved about, rapidly tidying. He glared when she touched his comics. "You put them away so you know where they are," she suggested.

"I will later. Are you coming?"

Halfway downstairs she halted. Good Lord, surely she could bear staying alone in the flat. She had plenty to read. There was nothing duller than a roomful of people waiting to score. She might visit Frank and Angie. Peter wouldn't have far to walk. Suppose he were stopped by the police? She was faltering outside Fanny's door when the light ran out of time, and clicked off.

At once she was sure that Fanny's room was occupied.

It couldn't be Fanny. How could Fanny infect her with such fear? She felt as though she had been struck blind. She backed away, and found she had lost her bearings. She was afraid of falling down the precipitous stairs, but she was terrified of touching something in the dark. "Peter," she called, holding her voice rigid. "Put the light on."

The silence which surrounded her wasn't quite silence. There was a faint creaking whose source she tried not to guess. Was it coming from more than one direction? Were Fanny's and Mr. Craig's doors opening stealthily, trapping her between them? Who was creeping out to close in on her from both sides? "Peter, will you put the light on!" she cried.

The click was unexpectedly close to her. He had been tiptoeing upstairs, to pounce. Both doors were closed, and insisted that they hadn't opened. Seeing her expression, he said, "Hey, what trip were you on there?"

She tramped out and started the van. She barely waited for him to slide the door shut before she drove off. In the park trees were embedded in night, like fossils. She couldn't have stayed alone in the house. Depression was gaining on her, slowing her time.

From Sefton Park Road she turned onto Croxteth Road. Traffic lights counted off the time it took her: green, amber, red. Couples with bottles converged on a tall house; aloft, music thumped. She wished she were going to that party, or one like it. She turned left into Hartington Road.

As she drove, houses and gardens dwindled on both sides. Doorbells of flats showed names less often. A door leaned out of a broken window as if it were searching for visitors. Gray faces peered through net curtains like cobweb; they looked unsure of themselves as ghosts. "Don't park outside," Peter said.

Fern Grove was closed off by pebble-dashed bollards like petrified tree stumps. Eventually she found an open side road. She felt conspiratorial, but it was less exciting than dispiriting.

The house had no front garden. A swollen unkempt privet hedge concealed the front window. A path whose gravel held still underfoot led between a few patchy fist-sized stones to a large front door beside a stack of two bay windows. Red light smoldered through the curtains and through the panes of the door.

At last the bell brought someone into the crimson hall. His head looked boiling with wiry curls. Eventually his hand found the latch. "Peace, Jim," Peter said. "You know Cathy."

"Yeah." He sounded as though he wasn't sure or didn't care. Peter stepped in, glancing warily at the street, and urged her to be quick.

Red light filled the house, thick as jam. Her eyes felt coated with it; she had to prove to herself that she could breathe. Upstairs someone was singing — no, wailing: "Oh shit shit shit." Was it a bad trip? Another voice tried to interrupt, low and soothing.

Jim gestured them loosely into the front room. In the clotted light, people sat on threadbare furniture or floor cushions. Their tangled hair looked like spaghetti dangling in the sauce of the filth. "Hi" or "Yeah" they muttered, or raised lethargic hands. The dim walls were cluttered: mandala posters, science fiction book covers enlarged, posters for rock concerts, a large damp patch of wallpaper. Joss-sticks protruded fuming from small metal stands.

She sat with Peter on a cushion. Jim perched on a limping wooden chair. The bars of a feeble electric fire were indistinguishable from the light. Nobody said anything. Everyone watched a man whose hair swayed about his face as he rolled a joint. His movements were slow and careful as a celebrating priest's.

Ten minutes later he licked the paper shut. In five more minutes he'd inserted cardboard in the mouth of the joint. A further minute passed before he lit the twisted end. He inhaled, closing his eyes prayerfully.

Everyone watched in a kind of stoned respectful silence. Incomprehensible wails seeped through the ceiling. When was Peter going to get down to business? Delaying was part of the ritual; you had to pretend you weren't here to score, only to smoke. It might be hours before he asked Jim.

She refused the joint when it reached her at last; she was depressed enough. Someone split open a cigarette to roll another. Conversation began. Had it needed the cannabis to coax it out? The passing of the joint filled the long pauses.

"They seized eight kilos on the docks today."

"Bad news."

"There's supposed to be some very excellent Lebanese hash coming from London."

"Probably came through Liverpool first."

"That'll put the price up."

"Thirty pounds an ounce."

"Bad news."

"Inflation."

All that had consumed ten minutes. Words were slowing; heads nodded. One of Jim's commune returned from the kitchen with a dish of biscuits: hash cookies, or a vegetarian recipe? His long nails were underlined with dirt. Cathy gestured the dish onward without touching it. She thought of the health food café on Hardman Street, full of thin morosely virtuous young men.

Another joint was rolled. She felt cramped and utterly bored. Once she'd seen *Fantasia* at the Royal Court. The back stalls had been packed with muted families of theater-goers; Peter and his friends had occupied the front three rows, passing joints and cheering when the cartoon mushrooms danced. She'd felt little affinity with either group.

Was that a faint desperate screaming overhead? In the thick light, the damp patch on the wall glistened red. Blurred by the dimness, the bloody shadows looked unnervingly shapeless. She felt a twinge of the panic she had suffered on the landing.

Perhaps Peter sensed her unease. Sounding embarrassed, he said, "Hey, Jim, did you get that stuff?"

"Yeah," Jim said mournfully. "I've got some Congo bush too, if you want."

They wandered off to use the scales. If Peter hadn't been expecting grass, what had he meant to score? A joint was making its round. What the hell—Peter would be half an hour at least, no doubt. When the joint was handed to her to pass on, she inhaled heavily.

She felt the cannabis reach into her brain. That was enough: she was driving. Too late: the joint had released all the thoughts she wanted to suppress. They seized her mind, and grew. Would she and Peter ever have children? Suppose they had waited too long, like Angie and Frank? Wouldn't houses grow more and more expensive, leaving them always behind? What had there been on the landing?

Footsteps dawdled in the hall. The door opened sluggishly, to admit the faint shrieking. It sounded weaker now, choked. She stood up. She'd had enough of the stained wall and the cries.

"Did you get some of Jim's acid?" someone asked Peter.

Peter glared, but had to say, "Yes."

"Peter." Had she known he meant to score LSD, she would never have driven him.

He didn't look at her, but at someone who remarked, "You don't see much acid these days."

"It's gone out of fashion," someone else joined in, now that the conversation had become interesting.

"It was a 'sixties thing."

"An optimistic drug."

"Not for the 'seventies."

"There's a lot of heroin in London now."

Cathy waited on the pavement. She wouldn't go back, however

long Peter dawdled. Time clung to her. The street looked so intensely present as to seem unreal.

She gazed at the neglected hedge. The stagnant people beyond the reddened curtain filled her mind. Wasn't Peter growing more like them? Wouldn't he withdraw deeper into himself on his trip, and become more inert?

She knew what had made him so passive and uncertain of himself: he'd seemed an unexpected miracle to his parents, late in their lives; they had treasured and spoilt him — but you couldn't use your childhood as an excuse for the rest of your life.

Peter appeared, glancing about like the hero of an inept spy film. How could she argue him out of himself without seeming to want to emasculate him? He hurried to the van, his hands in his pockets guarding his hoard. He wanted to go home, to smoke until he was too stoned to roll another. She would sit in the flat, having nowhere else to go. Oh, why couldn't something happen to change their situation?

CHAPTER XXII

"I want to join out," the little boy said.

"Do you!" Cathy exclaimed. The turn of phrase amused her. She would never have said, "Do you mean you want to cease borrowing books?" as one of her colleagues did.

The miniature face stared up at her, impatiently serious. "You keep your tickets, then," she said. "You might want to borrow books again sometime."

The little boy went out shaking his head: he was too old for fairy tales. "You can go now, Cathy," the librarian said.

She climbed the spiral staircase. She was proud of her sureness on the gallery; she'd conquered that fear, though she avoided looking down through the metal mesh. Would she be capable of walking on the top gallery of the Picton library, which was judged unsafe for the public but not for the staff?

In the staffroom, eggs jostled in a pan of bubbling water atop a cooker small as a gnome's. Coats huddled on the back of the door. She sat; the chair exhaled. On her way to work she'd bought a leftover *Weekend Echo*. She ignored temptingly bizarre headlines — BLESSING OF DEATH FOR SKELETON DOG, SHOCK FOR SAINTS, GROUP TO FIGHT CLINIC'S AXE — and turned to HOMES FOR SALE.

The prices were terrifying. The turning page whispered, as though to dissuade her from searching. She read on, glancing first at the price at the foot of each ad, like a reader making sure of the end of a book before starting. What was this price — a misprint? She read the ad, beginning to dare to hope.

Liverpool 4: Attractive terraced house. 2 bedrooms,
bathroom/w.c., kitchen/dining room, living room.
Useful outhouse to rear. £3250. Callers welcome.

She read the address. It must be near Anfield football ground.
"Useful outhouse to rear"! That sounded like a detail in a murder
story; she giggled.

"Callers welcome." Today was her half-day. She could view the
house this afternoon and then, if it appealed to her, show Peter round.
He mightn't be at home now—and besides, she didn't want an
argument to delay her. Oh, she hoped it would be worth seeing! However often she imagined owning a house, she couldn't fully conceive
what it would feel like.

She clattered down the spiral. "You look pleased with yourself,"
said an old lady who read four romances a day and who always chatted
to her. Her words made Cathy feel more so.

Cathy hurried to the Aigburth Road take-away, whose menu
covered the wall with over six hundred dishes. On Lark Lane, light
caught brass in an antique shop, like a glimpse of a sunset. Her
wrapped plastic tray warmed her frosty hands. She'd walk in Sefton
Park. Its nearness was one thing she still liked about the flat.

She walked, crunching water chestnuts. Her breath steamed and
vanished. Fog diluted the edge of the park, where trees were gray
silhouettes. People drifted vaguely in the distance, like smoke. When
they reached the fog they dissolved.

At last she found a waste-bin, and deposited her tray and wooden
fork. The litter was furry with frost. "Tumsey! Tumsey!" a woman
was shouting. When Cathy realized she was calling her dog, that made
her giggle more.

She walked by the lake, skimming pebbles over the ice. Frozen
ripples wrinkled the surface like frowns. Ducks quacked, a muted
creaking, among bushes. Trees shone pale against the darkly luminous
sky, as though the landscape were printed in negative.

By the bandstand, which was no whiter than the rest of the park,
she left the path and walked beneath the trees. The ground squeaked
underfoot. She gazed at the intricate tapestry of grass and fallen
leaves. Every outline was vivid with frost; every blade of grass,
however small, was separately visible. The dusting of frost on the

dozens of colors only emphasized them. How could anyone need to take LSD?

She stepped over whitened antlers of branches. Frost drifted like stray snowflakes from the trees and touched her face. Birds the colors of the leaves hopped, searching. They glanced at her, but didn't fly.

She headed for the avenue which led to the obelisk. That was the way to Lodge Lane, the 27 bus, Anfield, the attractive terraced house. She didn't fancy driving in this weather. She hurried beside an iced bowling green. Above the café, flags proclaimed Walls Ice Cream.

As she emerged onto the avenue, beside an old metal lamp-post that bore a lantern, she saw a man trudging toward the obelisk, between the trees that paled as they grew distant. She'd race him; it would take her more quickly toward Anfield. She could easily overtake him, for he was limping.

All at once she was convinced that she recognized him.

How could she, when she hadn't seen his face? Good Lord, the world was full of limping men. But there was something about the lopsided figure — If he were who she thought he was, he might help her to be less nervous in the flat. "Excuse me," she called loudly without thinking.

His head turned swiftly as a startled animal's. Then he was limping away, more rapidly. Seen together, his gait and his speed looked grotesque. They made her think of a fleeing injured beast. Was he too frantic to care about appearances?

She'd glimpsed his face. Why was he fleeing? Was he on a job, and anxious not to be questioned? Or had he mistaken her for someone else, in the fog?

She ought to let him go. After all, Fanny wasn't supposed to have told anyone about him. He looked rather pathetic, a parody of a detective, limping quickly into the murk with his right hand buried in his pocket. Hadn't Fanny said that the limp was false?

She must have been wrong. There was no reason why detectives couldn't limp. Abruptly Cathy began to run. She would never forgive herself if she didn't at least ask about the man who'd persecuted Mr. Craig. He needn't answer if he didn't want to. She set herself to catch him before he reached Aigburth Drive, a deserted blur that looked more like a drift of smoke than a road. Why, there was a good reason for this detective to limp: it would help her catch him.

CHAPTER XXIII

On Sunday the children were intolerable. Horridge felt as though he were locked in a zoo. Did the neighbors let them out of their cages in shifts, to make sure there wouldn't be a moment's silence? Cries and squeals surrounded him until long after dark. Clearly their parents weren't anxious to suffer them. A football pounded the wall of the flats, oppressive as a pulse, dismaying in its unpredictability. Just let them break his window— He thought of the razor in his coat pocket. He must control himself.

On Monday he was ready for the park. Besides, he oughtn't to depart from his routine; someone might notice. Just behave normally. He strolled to the bus stop. Fog lay in the concrete valleys, as though ghosts of rivers had returned.

The bus nosed forward, illuminating swirls of watery milk. Massive faceless tower blocks floated by. A few trees grew solid and glistening, then melted again.

The fog drew back from Melwood Drive. The bus quickened down the avenue between the trees. He felt released. A woman sat behind him, singing that she was glad she was Bugs Bunny.

Could he hold on to his freedom? During the night he'd dreamed of Wales. Slate had gleamed silver, expanses of grass had flowed softly; the sky and everything beneath it had shone. Surely that must be where he was meant to go.

Sunlight spilled into the bus, which had climbed the hill out of West Derby, above the fog. Next week's disability benefit would give him the fare to Wales and pounds left over. That would see him through until he found a job. You didn't need brains or qualifications to work on a farm. There must be jobs available: people liked to huddle together in cities — or believed they did, because they'd been told so. There must be jobs that didn't involve climbing or too much walking.

He strolled toward Aigburth Drive. Fog lurked in side streets; distant trees were an abstract gray mass. At the roundabout he glanced toward the house. Its horseshoe of a drive lay beside the unkempt grass. The luck of that horseshoe must have been waiting for him; it hadn't helped Craig or the painter, both of whom had let it become overgrown.

He couldn't resist a peek at the house. He had conquered evil there. He made his way along the edge of the park. The grass of the path was pale and glistening, a slug's track.

He held onto a tree, and peered around the trunk. Nothing moved except the silent sluggish lapping of fog. The cracked wet bark made him think of a reptile's cold hide. He stared harder at the windows, cursing the stealthy veil of fog that made his eyes feel blurred. His fingers gripped cracks in the bark until moisture oozed beneath his nails.

Recoiling, he limped away. His skin stirred uneasily. Nothing had been wrong except the fog and his imagination. He'd stared too long, that was all. There had been no large head in the depths of Craig's flat, no glistening eyes: just a reflected cloud. There had been no shadow of a seated woman on the painter's curtain.

Suppose they'd rigged up a dummy in there, to scare him? They might have found her and be keeping quiet about it: they were sly enough. Should he flee to Wales at once?

He mustn't allow them to confuse him. He flapped his hands at his breath, whose constant drifts interfered with his vision. None of them could know she wasn't on holiday. There could have been no shadow in her flat, for there had been no light within. Had there? When he glanced back, the house was a featureless block of smoke.

His mind wasn't befogged. He knew what he had and hadn't seen. He trudged toward the pool opposite the bandstand. On the avenue, trees were blackened by moisture. Huge cracked boils gleamed on trunks.

The pool was thinly frozen, robbing him of the reflections. On the ice below the bandstand lay a whitish blur. Perhaps that was its reflection — he thought he made out the columns that supported the roof—but it looked more like a great pale spider, trapped in the ice or dormant there.

That was enough. Nobody could say that he hadn't come to the park. His raincoat wasn't equal to this weather; he was shivering. He didn't feel like taking refuge in the library. The girl who'd seemed to know too much might be there.

He crossed the small bridge. A crippled branch reached for him over the railing. He wouldn't have to ignore that for much longer; he might never come here again. He resisted an urge to snap the branch. He wasn't a vandal. Besides, he noticed as he limped along the avenue, someone was approaching the bowling green, and would have seen him. He hurried past, anxious to reach the point at which the end of the avenue would clarify.

"Excuse me," a voice said.

He was turning before he could check himself. Where had he heard that voice before? His gasp sucked fog into his throat. Fog tried to persuade him that his eyes were lying—but they were all he could trust. Behind him was the girl who had done her best to hinder his search for Craig.

Was it fog or sweat that clung to him? It felt thick as mud. This was no coincidence, her finding him. Perhaps she was helping the police, to avenge her precious Craig.

Let her catch him. Let her dare. He felt less courageous than his words; he fled, trying to outdistance the violent crawling of his skin. Had the fog rusted his joints? His bad leg felt like a broken puppet's. Each limping step dragged at him like a dentist's hook, and maddened him.

Behind him was silence. She was trying to make him turn again, was she? He wasn't Dick Whittington, he wasn't a child to be lulled by nursery rhymes. Or was she creeping on the grass, sly as a homosexual? Just let her come near enough— His nails picked the blade ajar.

He heard her running. For a moment he felt as though his entire skin had burst with fear. Then, as the fog revealed Aigburth Drive, he bared his teeth and the blade. She must be a dupe of the police; certainly she was a fool. Didn't she realize that when they reached the road, nobody would see what happened to her?

The obelisk would block her view of him, and give him the advantage of surprise. He hoped she wouldn't take as long as Craig, but so long as he made sure that she couldn't cry out, it wouldn't matter. He remembered how to do that. He ran toward the obelisk, to give himself time to prepare.

As he reached the obelisk, she slipped on the frosty path.

Her flesh slapped the ground loudly. He hoped she'd injured the breasts she flaunted—that she'd burst them. He turned swiftly. She was yards away. Could he reach her before she recovered, and finish her? Fog thickened on the road, offering him its aid.

She still couldn't know where he lived; otherwise the police would have visited him. He must cling to that advantage. He ran across the roundabout, clutching his bad knee with his razor hand to drive himself onward. In his pocket the razor leapt like a trapped bird.

The clank of his heels counted his steps toward Lodge Lane. His limp translated them into dull agony. At Sefton Park Road, cars waited for the smoking traffic lights to change. Fog that stank of petrol helped conceal him; the snarling of engines covered the sound of his limp.

He ran past the lights at the far end. They were mounting their scale to green, to release traffic at him. There was a bus at the stop— a refuge. Ice tried to slip the road from beneath him; cars roared a warning and surged forward. He dodged in front of the bus, daring it to run him down.

Several people were still to board. He edged among them. Only when he'd climbed on board at last and had found a seat did he begin to relax. He had to sit at the back, facing away from the journey. At least he'd be able to see if he was being followed.

The bus juddered away. Discolored figures trudged beside blurred shops. Yellowed headlights probed toward the bus. A van was following. No, that wasn't her face peering through a windscreen the color of ice. His mind refused to unclench; it squeezed his thoughts into a small hard impregnable mass, that felt as though it might explode and sear his head with pain.

Opposite him, someone lit a cigarette. That wasn't allowed downstairs. He mustn't complain, mustn't be conspicuous. The man grinned at his frown; smoke oozed from his face, a defiant mask of black mud pockmarked by rain. Horridge's hand clenched on his pocket. No, no! Seedy shops drifted by, an empty schoolyard, a tower block whose lit windows looked half-melted. Why, he'd almost passed his stop! They wouldn't confuse him so easily. He grabbed the metal pole and swung himself into the aisle.

The girl was sitting between him and the exit doors.

Even if the black cap pulled low on her head hadn't been enough, her profile was turned to him. Was she making sure that she saw him, or trying to dismay him with the sight of her? Either way, the shock paralyzed him.

His hand clung to the pole, dangling him. The bus lurched, jerking him like a drunken puppet. BUS STOPPING, a lighted plaque announced. Would she try and prevent him from reaching the doors? Would she set the mob of passengers on him?

The bus halted, throwing him forward. The doors squeaked open. Let her try to stop him, by God. His hand plunged into his pocket. He'd do for a few of them, and she would be first. The edge of the blade bit into his nail.

Nobody hindered him. As he stepped down he glanced at her. Did she look hastily away? She was so intent on the window and its spectacle of fog that she must be pretending. What was she up to now?

The bus moved off, carrying her face among its framed display. He saw her glance at him before her gaze flinched aside. He waited beneath the dripping inverted L of the bus shelter, in case she stopped the bus and dodged back. The lights and the noise withdrew into the fog, which dulled and engulfed them like sleep.

He waited for the Cantril Farm bus. Buses lumbered toward him, unveiling their lit faces. None was any use to him. The fog seemed to congeal his time. Had he been waiting minutes or hours? When at last his bus arrived he tried to clear the window, to watch for pursuit; but fog or dirt was glued to the glass. As the bus drew away, another took its place.

The engine groaned, low and monotonous. The bus felt insidiously chill, invaded by fog. Queues bobbed up from the murk; he was compelled to search each gray peering face. The single narrow curve of road led the bus into Cantril Farm, deeper into concrete, into nowhere.

Reluctantly he used the pedestrian subway. At least he couldn't lose his way down there. He mustn't get lost. The low dim roof oppressed him; it rumbled as a bus halted. Could the roof support all that weight above his head? Glass ground its teeth underfoot as he limped hastily out. He would stay home until the fog lifted. No more trips to the park—the girl had come too close for comfort. Only a few days to Wales.

Turn left here, and go straight on. Concrete reared vaguely around him. Everything was drowned in anonymity. The branches of a stray tree looked like dusty cobweb. Turn right. Now left, between flats whose lit windows looked waterlogged. Then left again, and then—

A wall rose up before him. Its thick veins of graffiti glistened. There was supposed to be a passage here! He must have missed a turning. Go back to it. He tried to think: since he was returning, the passage would be on the right—but how many turns to the right must he make first? Black specks swarmed over his eyes, distracting him. Wasn't that a symptom of approaching blindness?

He hurried back. Walls seemed to shift and advance. Right here, it must be. Wasn't this passage too short? No, it wasn't a wall that blocked his way, only fog. The fog retreated before him—then at once yielded up a wall. Staggering crimson letters caught in the web of graffiti spelled KILLER.

What was that supposed to mean? He groped for the razor, to hack the letters away. No, he wouldn't be tricked into wasting his time. The wall didn't block his path entirely; he could turn left. Surely that was the way he ought to go.

Shortly another wall proved not to be fog, and forced him left again, through a passage. Beyond was the inner yard of a tenement. Piles of flats walled it in on all four sides. It was one of many. He couldn't judge his direction from it. He was lost.

Gray pressed against his eyes. It felt like blindness, which terrified him. Silence clogged his ears; his nostrils were blocked. The fog was robbing him of all his senses. Everywhere around him, concrete lurked in ambush. Nowhere could he see a name. The yard was lifeless as a place of execution.

His skin felt infested. He ran, but couldn't escape the crawling. He managed not to flee back the way he'd come; that would take him back into the same maze. Instead he made for the next passage out of the yard, on the left. His leg plucked at his mind with pain.

Almost as soon as he emerged from the passage he saw the bus stop's metal flag above the drowned concrete valley. He'd returned to where he'd started. Pain set his mind ablaze; he felt an urgent violent fury which he must release somehow. He tried to calm himself. At least he knew where he was; he could start again, more carefully.

Someone was walking down the valley. Perhaps he could ask the way—though most people seemed unable to give directions here: they were as confused as the planners intended. He gazed over the concrete bank of the side path as she emerged from the obscurity. It was the girl. She was still pursuing him.

His fury grew cold and purposeful. This time she'd gone too far. She hadn't seen him yet. He felt almost detached as he observed her, peering about from beneath her black cap like an executioner's. He grinned as he reached in his pocket. That cap was appropriate, but not in a way she would enjoy.

She passed without noticing him. As she neared the blurred mouth of the subway, he moved, making sure he was audible. He heard her falter, then hurry after him. Although the vicious ache of his leg was stoking his fury, he grinned as he limped as quickly as he could toward the execution yard.

CHAPTER XXIV

Cathy picked herself up. The front of her body throbbed like a single bruise. Her breath, when she managed to catch it, joined in. Beyond the obelisk the limping footsteps faded.

That would teach her to chase people. But her fall had angered her. Was she really going to let a little fall deter her? He could at least have come back to see whether she was all right. She strode past the obelisk, ignoring her bruises. She had to go this way to catch a bus to the house for sale.

She reached the bus just as the doors were closing. The driver winked at her, and waited. The poles of the aisle were cold in her hands. Below her heads were displayed, swaying slightly. Was that the detective, sitting with his back to her? She couldn't speak to him. What on earth could she say among all these people?

Fog flooded by. Beginnings of streets emerged momentarily. The man who sat beside her left the bus; someone else trapped her next to the window. She turned her head gingerly to watch the aisle. If that were the detective, what could she do?

When he stood up, she did nothing. She felt rather childish and silly. Well, the bus would take her to the attractive terraced house; that was why she'd boarded it, not to chase him. God, he was looking! Acutely embarrassed, she turned hastily to the window.

His face floated off into the murk. It had all been fun in a peculiar way, despite her bruises. What would Peter say? "Yeah? What happened then? Jesus, you mean you let him go?" Or perhaps he would say, "Good job you didn't catch him. We don't want to get involved with the law." Abruptly she stood and grabbed the bell-pull.

She hurried back toward West Derby Road. Ahead the traffic lights seemed hardly to inch toward her, as though they and she were drowned in mud. They changed, and released a herd of slow buses. There he was—climbing into a lighted entrance.

Before she could reach the stop the bus closed, and carried his illuminated head away. A second bus was waiting for the space. She jumped aboard, though her bruises complained.

Although she didn't like the smoke, she sat upstairs, the better to observe her quarry. She grabbed the front seat, like a child eager to see everything. Her excitement was almost embarrassing. She'd never done anything like this before.

Every glimpse that the fog doled out was vivid: rugby posts on a playing field, tall thin white letter H's left over from a giant's alphabet; a little railway station which was now the Two Acres Poultry Farm. Crowds of housewives boarded at Tuebrook and West Derby Village, but the detective didn't use them as cover to sneak away.

The bus was full of greetings and chat. All the housewives must be from Cantril Farm, and must prefer to journey to these shopping areas. She enjoyed the slow pursuit, almost laughing; it was like a parody of a car chase. "Follow that bus!" she giggled to herself.

All at once the landscape became grayer. Tower blocks loomed as though embodying the fog. Long featureless walls crammed with windows dawdled by. Even the colors of curtains were obscured by fog. Housewives called goodbye. Gazing about, Cathy didn't wonder they preferred to shop elsewhere.

She sat forward, as though to watch the climax of a film. There couldn't be many stops before the terminus. On the single road, people trudged beside the high curbs, along the paths of yellow lines. Her bus halted, blocked by its leader. Among the women emerging from the bus ahead and descending into the subway, she saw the detective.

She clattered downstairs. Oh, don't let her lose him! "You'll forget your head one of these days," the driver remarked, opening the doors for her. The bus drew away its light; the chill of the fog seized her. When the sounds of the bus had retreated, she found she couldn't hear the limping.

Wasn't this a bit ridiculous? How far was she going to chase the poor man? Was she really going to trudge about this unfamiliar foggy place in search of him? It would be frustrating to have come so far for nothing. She thought of the unpleasantness that was seeping into the house on Aigburth Drive. If he could do something about that, he was worth chasing. Though she felt absurd, she hurried into the subway.

On the far side was silence. The walk climbed into the fog. It looked as likely a direction as any. She hurried past concrete yards and patches of grass soaked with gray. Only fog kept her company.

Within minutes she was lost. High identical walls full of flats surrounded her. A notice she'd hoped was the name of the block, or even a direction, proved to say ALL BALL GAMES PROHIBITED. Otherwise the walls were a mess of painted names. Paths led onto tufted mud in which lurked puddles and glass.

When she heard a bus on the main road, she headed back. There was no point in straying further. What a disappointing end to her adventure! She slithered down toward the subway, looking for steps that would take her to the outward bus stop.

Then she heard the limping. It began abruptly, surprisingly close. She whirled, and saw him in a concrete tributary. Was he lost too? He disappeared at once into the fog, but she could hear him clearly. She hurried in pursuit.

The limping echoed in a passage. She managed to distinguish the entrance, though the gap looked almost as solid as the framing wall, with fog. Beyond it, she found herself in what seemed to be a wide deserted yard within a square of tenements.

Oh, don't say she'd lost him! Entrances gaped in the tenements, revealing stone stairs wet with fog. He could have vanished into any opening. She held her breath, though it tasted of the murk.

She heard something. Footsteps? Yes, though they were faint — shuffling. They were advancing toward her, slowly and unevenly. Unevenly! It must be the detective. How would he react when he saw her? While she pondered that, he might elude her yet again. She ran on tiptoe toward the shuffling.

Fog blanked her vision, and robbed her of any sense of distance. How near was the shuffling now? Surely he ought to be visible. She was certain she would jump when they came face to face — and so would he, no doubt, poor man. The thought made her tense, and distracted her. She almost collided with the dim shapeless figure when it shuffled into view.

Cathy gasped. It was an old woman in bedraggled carpet slippers.

Her bare legs were red and thickly veined. She shrank back as though Cathy were a mugger.

"I'm sorry," Cathy blurted. "I thought—" She couldn't say more for choking on her mirth.

"I should think so." The old woman shuffled past, staring: her vacant gums smoked. "Just about think so too," she muttered.

All at once Cathy heard the limping. It was on the far side of the yard, and retreating rapidly. For a few steps it echoed in a passage. She ran toward the sound. Obstacles seemed to menace her, but they were fog.

She found the passage quickly, and ran through. Footsteps came at her from the obscurity—her own echoes. Outside, a path dissolved into fog. On one side stretched a fence, on the other was a rank of two-storey flats that protruded boxily into tiny concrete yards. The prospect resembled an H with its top legs missing, repeated again and again.

The limping stopped. How far ahead? She ran faster than her doubts. Passages gaped between flats; windows dull as fog stood above them. Fancy having a hole where your ground floor ought to be!

Was he in one of the passages? She dodged toward each, then veered away. She had to go deep in each shadowy blurred gap before she could be sure. Oh, please don't let him have hidden in his flat after all this— There he was, in a passage!

It was a dangling shirt that swung its arms as she ran at it.

When she reached the end of the fence, she gave up. Beyond the fence, another passage led out to wide murk. She stood beside a torn poster. AY NO T A BLACK ITAIN, it said. She stared at the flats opposite. A door which looked hardly colored lurked beneath glistening stone steps.

She was dismally fascinated. Anyone who passed could bang on the windows or the walls: no doubt children did. She couldn't have borne living in such a place. It must be like a cage. She would have gone mad.

CHAPTER XXV

So now she knew where he lived. He spied on her through a crack between the curtains. He ought to have killed the old woman as well, instead of letting her presence deter him. At last the girl slunk into the fog. She must have been making sure that he knew he was trapped.

Would she send the police for him? Let them come — he'd make some cuts in the police force. His joke failed to sustain him. He felt shrunken, a rat in a trap; his mind felt crushed. He would flee, except that there was nowhere to go besides the fog.

He sat in the center of the anonymous room, facing the door, razor in hand. He listened to the radio. It might warn him, or help him some-how; surely his luck hadn't deserted him entirely. The gathering night robbed him of the room. He found himself listening for words, he didn't know which, that would tell him what to do. There must be someone on his side. Blurred stations drifted behind the newsreader's voice. Horridge sat forward; the blade clicked. What was that about conspiracy?

But the blurred voice had gone. Oh yes, he knew about conspiracies; the world was full of them. Even presidents could be involved in them, which showed that anyone might be. Sometimes the plotters were careless enough to be found out, but what of those who weren't? What about those homosexuals and their dupes, conspiring against him?

When he switched on the light the walls didn't retreat far. He shut off the radio, which was trying to distress him. He couldn't bear waiting; the room seemed like a condemned cell. Where could he hide? Where might the police not look for him?

Yes, of course. He never went to the pub — but he could pretend to be one of the herd. Why, that would make him seem normal by their standards; he would be unobtrusive there. He transferred his documents into his raincoat, in case the police broke in, and left.

Men were tramping along the path. Were they going to the pub? They looked brainless enough—too brainless to conspire against him. He followed them, so as not to be alone in the fog.

He'd judged their destination rightly. Already the pub was crowded. Addicts, all of them—but at least the sots would be too befuddled to plot against him. He reached the bar at last and bought himself a lemonade, despite the barmaid's faint amused contempt. She was there to serve, not to have opinions.

On his way to an empty table, he stooped to pat a dog: some animals were trustworthy, unlike human beings. Then he saw it was a blind man's dog. Wasn't its owner watching him? Horridge restrained himself from snatching the dark glasses, and hurried to his table.

He surveyed the enemy. A few people sat alone, drinking morosely. Mightn't they be connected, perhaps communicating by signs? They looked secretive enough. Whenever he caught one of them gazing, the gazer glanced quickly away. Were they homosexuals, or police? He suspected there wasn't much difference.

Whenever he sipped his lemonade or moved in any way, there came a burst of laughter. Of course it was never from the same direction. They wouldn't affect him with such a cheap trick—nor with the remarks he could almost hear. Was someone talking in a foreign language? Was it Russian? The dim light seemed to hold him fast, like amber.

He watched the television perched above the bar. Tobacco smoke befogged its screen. Policemen beat up criminals; an orchestra urged them on. "Step into a dream and leave reality behind," sang an advertisement for a holiday camp. Oh yes, that was what they'd like everyone to do—but they wouldn't cloud *his* mind, not with drugs or anything else.

Behind him a workman was talking about "doing a foreigner." That didn't mean getting rid of an immigrant; it meant sneaking away from your job to do work while your employer wasn't watching. It showed how foreigners weren't to be trusted. Someone sat down opposite Horridge.

He glanced at the man, ready to glare him away. Company would distract and discomfort him. It was Mr. Fearon the key-cutter, gazing curiously at him. "I never knew you came here," the old man said.

"Didn't you?" Horridge managed to speak coolly, though his heart was frantic to escape.

"I don't see the point in coming here, lad, if you're going to drink that stuff."

Did the lemonade make Horridge look effeminate? It might draw attention to him. He rose angrily, and struggled to the bar to demand a pint of beer. On the television screen, a beer glass jerked itself thicker and taller, growing gigantic; its cap of froth bulged. "Big head," a male chorus praised it. "The body that satisfies — it can't be modest no matter how it tries." How could they get away with broadcasting such filth?

Though he would have preferred to avoid the old man, he had to return to his place; no other seat was empty. The drinkers who pretended to be alone were still spying. Mr. Fearon nodded approvingly at the beer. "That's right, lad. That's what you need."

"I don't *need* it at all."

"You're a bit on edge, aren't you?" The old man seemed to lose interest in him, and gazed at the News. The newsreader muttered amid the uproar. At last Mr. Fearon said, "I see they've caught that murderer."

Horridge spoke sharply, to cut through the dizziness that had spread from his mouthful of beer. "Which murderer?"

"Which one?" The old man gazed quizzically at him, as though amused by his sharpness. "Which one do *you* mean?"

Oh no, Horridge wasn't caught so easily. They both knew perfectly well whom they meant. He gulped his beer, for the old man had been staring at it, making out that he intended to hold it untouched all night. "You'd call him a murderer, would you?" Horridge said.

"Wouldn't you?"

He'd had enough of this game of questions. It was time someone had the courage to state a few facts. Deep in the uproar a voice was babbling like a madman's, but that wouldn't make Horridge crack. "I'd call him a guardian of the law," he said. "Someone who stands up for what he knows is right. If the law won't deal with corruption, someone must. A few more like him and the world would be a lot cleaner."

He was saying too much. Shut up, he screamed at himself, shut up! But the old man appeared not to be listening; he was staring past

Horridge at the television. Giddy with suspicion, Horridge turned. The newsreader's face was staring straight at him.

The man looked down, pretending to read his script—too late. They were using the television to watch Horridge. It must be easy, with all these bugging devices. And by God, Mr. Fearon was in league with them—the old man had been pumping him to make him talk! Before he could restrain himself, his hand plunged into his coat pocket.

He gasped. Oh God, his birth certificate had the names written on it. If they caught him now, that would be evidence against him. He lurched to his feet and stumbled away; his head felt sodden with beer. "Too much for you?" Mr. Fearon said.

As Horridge dodged between the stools that barred his way everywhere, as he battled his way through the hubbub that clung to him, he saw his grandfather entering the pub. The old face was strong and calm as a rock. Horridge ran to him, kicking aside a stool. His luck hadn't changed, he was saved. But it was an old drunkard, his cheeks redly laced.

Horridge staggered into the night. His head was unsteady and brimming; fog had seeped into his skull. By an irony which amused him not at all, his drunkenness helped him find his way home; he kept tramping doggedly until he saw the notice, torn now.

When he opened the door he heard them waiting for him in the dark, muttering. It took him minutes to ease the door shut, and to bare the razor blade. It was only the voice of the plumbing, the incoherent voice of a madman locked in darkness. It wouldn't send him mad, they needn't bother trying.

He felt his documents hanging on him. He had nothing with which to rub out the names. Gardner, Peter David. Gardner, Catherine Angela. He snarled at them: no doubt they too would like to see him locked up. He hid the documents in the wardrobe, and felt slightly less endangered.

Before he touched the radio, his hand drooped. Might they be using the radio to listen to him? Could they do so even when it was supposed to be switched off? He stood in the bare cell. His mind felt hollow. The blade snatched at the light, dulled, snatched. He stared at the razor as if it might direct him.

He stared at the razor as if it might direct him.

CHAPTER XXVI

"Where were you?" Peter demanded.

Should she tell him? Her tale would sound absurd. Even if she held his attention, the ending would hardly be worth it. "Looking at houses," she said.

He turned back to *The Incredible Hulk.* "There's one I haven't looked at yet," she said. "Come and see it now."

Might her chase have allowed someone else to beat them to it? Her frustration made her persuasive. "Oh, all right," he grumbled at last.

The fog was lifting intermittently. The van sped through its gaps. People were coming home from work; she watched houses light up. Pavements glistened like tar beneath streetlamps.

As she'd thought, the house was near the football ground. Dead floodlights towered above the tiers of seats. On the corner of the side street, a window was blocked by ripples of tin like a Venetian blind—but on the upper storey, light shone through curtains. She knew how it felt to live over emptiness.

The advertised house didn't look bad. An arch of bricks framed the front door; alternate bricks were painted brightly. The door opened onto the pavement, but she hadn't expected a garden. It looked a snug little house—they could make something of it. Not until she struggled to lift the knocker did she realize how rusty it was.

The echoes of its slow thuds died away. Were more echoes returning, or were those sounds footsteps? The door juddered open, revealing an old man in a suit and dressing gown. His face was shrunken close to the bone, and looked small and timidly hopeful, like a little boy's.

"Are you for the house?" he said eagerly. "It'll be just the job for you, I can tell."

He trotted backward, making way for them. The hall was dim; well, they needn't keep it so. Were all the vague blurs on the walls shadows? Peter touched one and examined moisture on his hand.

"Here's the living room." Within, a small fire coughed thickly. Cathy understood now why he wore so many clothes; she shivered. She would make the house warmer.

"It's been a good little house." The old man rested one hand on a framed photograph of a family; he was the father. The frame and its glass were free of the dust which sprinkled the room. "But it's too big for one person alone," he said.

He turned to Peter; this was man's talk. "The rates are a bit high for me. They're very reasonable. They'd be no trouble if I were your age."

Cathy didn't quite see why that should make a difference. Behind the scenes she thought she heard rodents moving. "Let's see the rest," Peter demanded.

She frowned at his rudeness — or was she less anxious now to view the rest? They followed the old man. The kitchen walls were sweaty; a table hardly wider than a chair stood beside a protruding sink. "You could have a dining table in here," said the old man hopefully.

He led the way upstairs. Peter stepped aside to tread on a board under the staircase; it leapt up, exposing an earthy hollow like a grave. Dust hung swaying from a lampshade above the stairs, and made the flex thick and furry as a caterpillar.

"This is the married bedroom." The old man sounded wistful. Half of the double bed was bare; rust outlined the nuts and bolts of its frame. He leaned on the headboard, smiling like a salesman, as if they must be persuaded by now.

"What's in here?" said Peter on the landing.

"Oh, that's another room. It needs a few things doing." The old man hurried toward him; the floor broke into a chorus of creaks. Peter held open the door for Cathy to see. Beneath a ragged tear that displayed wooden ribs, a heap of plaster lay on paper fallen from the ceiling. The walls streamed.

In the living room, the old man said, "How does it look to you?"

His hopefulness was dismaying, for it seemed to contain no pretense. Peter waited impatiently in the hall. "We'll have to think about it," Cathy said, trying to be gentle. "But—I'm afraid it isn't quite what we're looking for."

"Well, never mind." Was his smile meant to reassure her, or himself? "I understand," he said. "It's a bit small if you're planning to have children."

Peter was hurrying to the van. "So much for that," he said triumphantly. "If that's all we can afford it's not worth looking." She didn't bother keeping up with him. Let him wait. He was only hurrying to roll another joint.

CHAPTER XXVII

At last Horridge managed to sleep, but never for very long. Beer lay uneasily in his head and his stomach. His skull throbbed in time with the beat of the clock, whose ticking chanted nonsense, trying to tempt him to listen. In the darkness the plumbing muttered. Just let them come near. He clutched the razor.

He should have followed Mr. Fearon home. There was no use trying to find him now, in the fog. The old man would be able to look up his address in the voters' list, if he didn't know already. Horridge writhed beneath the imprisoning blankets. He should have killed Mr. Fearon.

Dawn crept into the room. It looked like fog, though the day was clear. Were they waiting for daylight before they arrested him, so that his neighbors could watch and approve? No doubt they would make the arrest appear legal and necessary. People were eager to believe anything.

There was one place where they mightn't look for him. He need hide for only a few days, until his money was due. He'd thought of it during the night. The idea had seemed dreamlike, but now it felt solid and right.

He switched on the radio. That would make them think he was staying. "Scattered showers and good sunny periods," the newsreader said. What was the other voice murmuring—about a man obsessed with the idea that he was being watched, who had attacked a policeman?

Oh no, that wasn't Horridge. They needn't waste their time. No doubt they'd faked the incident to confuse people. Or perhaps they'd driven the man mad. The voice withdrew, having failed to delude Horridge. He turned to another station, and another. He couldn't shake off the feeling that each new voice was the same voice, disguised. Were they aiming special broadcasts at him for some reason? A blare of pop music faded abruptly. "And it's just ten past nine," a disc jockey said. "Ten past eight, I mean."

Horridge scrubbed himself thoroughly. He didn't know when he would next be able to wash. Razor in hand, he squirmed into his raincoat and slipped the weapon into his pocket. He spent minutes easing open the front door, so that the radio wouldn't hear. Let it sit there singing to itself — it was a fool, like its masters. His last glance showed him the wardrobe. He was glad to be leaving that behind. During the night he'd dreamed that blood had burst it open.

Before he reached the bus stop the ground began to hiss, rattle, blanch. Above the concrete desert the gray air was viciously striped with hail. The pelting stung his cheeks; his skin felt slashed. So the newsreader had been lying. He was one of their dupes.

Horridge wouldn't be driven back. He knew where he was going; they wouldn't stop him. Hail melted underfoot, and tricked his bad leg from beneath him; he almost fell. The storm slackened, only to renew itself vindictively. A mass like frozen porridge collected amid the grass, which twitched. Icy dandruff clung to his shoulders.

He stumbled under the bus shelter. It had no wall to ward off the hail — one of the planners' sadistic jokes. Against a stagnant sky the color of dust, tower blocks menaced him. The rushing air cut at his face. Let them do their worst. Did they think he had no stamina? He grasped the razor. If only he could meet Mr. Fearon now!

The bus was full of workmen — at least, presumably that was what they called themselves. No doubt they were off to erect one of their signs: MEN WORKING, as though that were news — which of course it was these days. They mumbled to one another. Didn't they dare own up to what they were saying? Talking about him, were they? Too many of them looked elusively familiar. They'd better not come too close, if they knew what was good for them.

When the bus reached Shiel Road, he stayed on board. That'd surprise a few of them! He rose just before the Boaler Street stop, and tugged peremptorily at the bell. He waited until the bus had carried its mob of spies away.

Opposite was the box from which he'd spoken to Craig. It was appropriate that he'd returned to the scene of his first triumph. He was shivering; his raincoat was glued coldly to him. Could he really take refuge in his old home, where there weren't even windows?

Yes, by God. Someone else had been able to sleep there. It would only be until he collected his train fare. He could drag the mattress into the most sheltered corner. He would survive. They wouldn't get rid of him, oh no.

He limped toward Boaler Street. No time for doubts. He'd have plenty of time to ponder once he was safely hidden. Why did the line of shops look false as a stage set? Why did it seem terrifyingly insubstantial?

Because there was nothing behind it: his street had gone.

He stared at the muddle of bricks and wood that had been his home. He felt as though his innards had been ripped out. He was beaten. They had won. Had someone told them of his plan to hide here? Nearby a bulldozer prowled, a bully making sure that he didn't take refuge anywhere else.

The fallen streets had revealed a large building of orange brick. It squatted on a patch of mud, and looked like a toy lost while still new. Above its door a sign said POLICE. At once it became menacing as a dream grown solid in daylight.

He fled, limping. A car marked POLICE drew away from the orange block, but turned aside from him. Let them arrest him — they wouldn't find much. His birth certificate was shut in the wardrobe; all his documents —

Including his payment book. He wouldn't be able to collect his disability benefit. They'd managed to trick him. They'd robbed him of escape. His limp carried him staggering onward, onward, with nowhere to go. The razor patted his hip. It was his only friend, the only thing he could trust. But where could the two of them hide?

CHAPTER XXVIII

In Peter's head a loud metallic voice said, "We have lift-off."
Symbols were crystallizing rapidly and unstably on the walls. When
he looked in the mirror, his pupils were spectacularly dilated; he had
the eyes of a mummy's mask. Instead of a face he had a set of masks
that played over one another constantly, like shuffled cards. Today he
would find himself beneath them.

Sue lay on his bed; Anne was sunk in the deepest chair. He was
glad he'd decided to take the trip with them. Already he felt closer
to them than he'd felt to Cathy for awhile. He didn't feel criticized, even
implicitly. They accepted him for what he was.

He oughtn't to take acid while Cathy was near. Her anxiety for
him only made him feel threatened by a bad trip. If she had been here,
her obsession with the atmosphere of the house would have infected
all of them.

Like an oracle, Sue announced, "I'm not going to work tomorrow."

"We'll report sick," Anne said.

He nodded sagely. You shouldn't work the day after taking a trip.
Reporting sick was funny, though: acid was ultimate health. Still, work
was a game, and lies were a way to win like any other.

They were sharing visions now. They watched the elaboration of
the trees beyond the window. He couldn't remember when he'd felt
so safe. Was he secure enough to reach down into himself, to the part
of him which he knew was there but which he could never quite
perceive, the part that would solve all his problems?

"We got some nice sounds from the record library," Anne said.
"They'd be good now."

Without her asking aloud, Sue and Peter waited on the landing, so that she didn't feel alone in her flat. Eventually she returned with a record of Mozart's Clarinet Concerto. Mozart made Peter think of Craig: he'd liked that sort of thing. A faint stench drifted out of the dark stairwell. It was all right. Cathy wasn't here to make them apprehensive. He seemed to recall having heard some nice sounds by Mozart.

The music sounded deft and sinuous. Fat Germans danced over fields. Peter saw Mozart performing rapid conjuring tricks, waving his wand which was the baton he used to beat the orchestra, capitalism's club beating the workers, all of whom had to lock themselves into evening dress to look middle-class. Bright caricatures raced through his mind, a speeded-up cartoon film.

In the park a dog was barking. It tried to join in the music, then it began to snap at Mozart's heels. All three of them giggled uncontrollably. Mirth exploded from them like farting.

The second movement of the concerto was slower. The long notes of the clarinet seemed oily. Peter moved uneasily in his chair. A huge worm oozed along. Its moisture clung to his skin. The worm was dying. A corpse was near him.

Fear paralyzed him. It was all right, the images must be coming from the girls, they weren't his. The acid couldn't be as strong as this; they'd split the tab three ways. Just let it slow down, just for a moment, just so he could see what was coming, please stop for a moment, he wouldn't take acid again, ever, he promised — But death had entered the room, and held him immobile. If he opened his eyes they would burst, putrefy.

At last he opened them, to escape the sight of Mozart's face collapsing. The face was there on the record cover, squirming. Mozart was dead, that was all! The acid strobe flashed in his eyes like an unavoidable warning. Trees were bones on which writhed remnants of flesh. In the clouds Craig's face was flaking away beside a woman's face. Death was total disintegration, the core of yourself flying apart into a void. Sue's and Anne's faces were coming away from the bone, pried loose by their terror.

He managed to stand, on legs that felt scrawny and fleshless. The light seemed not to reach him, as though he were unable to perceive it properly — as though his eyes had died. Dimness was advancing.

Beneath the floor, which felt thin as ice, lay an eager grave. For a moment he meant to flee and leave the girls. "Let's go in the park," he blurted.

They stood up gingerly, as if going blind. Their slowness clung to him like the moisture of the worm. A pair of Cathy's tights hung like the skin of a starved child, a terrible sexless absence between its legs. He mustn't scream. He guided them as far as the landing. The stairwell was an enormous dark pit that shifted and crawled like earth.

Sue drew back trembling. "It's too far," she wailed.

"Come on. We've got to try." He sounded like dozens of films. It wasn't how he sounded that mattered, only what he did. He poked the time-switch. Wide bare staircase, stark unsteady bulbs: *Psycho*. "Come on. We're all right. Come on," he repeated all the way downstairs, and led them out of the horror film.

So that was all. It was so simple. He need only act masculine, instead of holding back for fear of failure. He'd led them all to safety. He closed the front door carefully, like a home-owner protecting his house.

They walked in the park. Never before had he seen so many colors. Piercingly vivid ripples passed through the grass. Trees unfolded patterns, mysterious and Oriental. Primitive hieroglyphs appeared on stone. He was an archetypal man, guiding and guarding his women. They sat by the lake and became the movement of light on water.

A dog ran past them. Its red pelt glowed; each hair was separate. They watched the play of its muscles, complex and graceful. "You ought to become vegetarian," Anne said.

"Cathy cooks vegetarian once a week."

He sensed their silent contempt. Was it justified? He felt disloyal to her, and alienated from the girls. Perhaps they could tell, for Sue said, "We're going on."

It didn't sound like an invitation. "I'll stay here," he said.

Climbing the grassy slope, they held hands. It occurred to him that neither of them seemed involved with men. Did they have sex together? That was irrelevant. Though he'd pretended to accept it, he had never really believed lesbianism existed. Now he saw it, it seemed in no way startling. The acceptance made him feel more masculine, less vulnerable.

Eventually he managed to read his watch. Cathy would be home soon. Should he be there when she arrived, to rid himself of the lingering sense of disloyalty? He strolled toward the house, which moved wakefully.

Someone was ahead of him on the stairs: a man, who looked deformed. Strangers often did when you were tripping. The face looked elusively familiar, but its masks were shifting. He must be moving into one of the flats; he was fumbling in his pocket, no doubt for a key. His stare made Peter paranoid — but perhaps it was the trip that made the stare seem odd.

Peter hurried upstairs. The slam of his door calmed him slightly. He sat at the window to watch the mystical gestures of the trees, the temple dancers. He tried to inhale calm. Shit, it was Cathy's fault. She was infecting him. Just now he'd felt as panicky in the middle landing as she had behaved.

. . . death had entered the room. . . .

CHAPTER XXIX

"Shall we eat vegetarian tonight?" Peter asked.

Cathy knew at once that he was tripping. When he embraced her, his smell had changed. That dismayed her. It was as though he'd become someone she didn't know — someone who might not want to know her? "All right," she said dully.

She'd hoped to interest him in homes for sale, and to discuss their budget — some hope, no doubt. Or might the trip have made him more suggestible? It was impossible to tell, for during the meal he insisted on listening to Mozart. He looked relieved, triumphant.

In a lull between movements she said, "Is that Fanny?"

Surely she'd heard a vague noise. Perhaps Fanny had come home early. The music scurried brightly. She made to turn it down, but saw his growing unease. Her question must have made him paranoid for some reason. She'd go down later, and knock.

They were washing up when Sue and Anne called. The girls looked timid, anxious not to tarry. Well, that was a relief. "We're going to stay with some people," Sue said.

"We don't like the house anymore. We nearly had a bad trip today."

Cathy glimpsed Peter's grimace. She didn't especially care that he'd taken his trip with the girls: if he had to take the stuff at all, what did it matter who his companions were? But it depressed her that he didn't want her to know.

When the girls had gone, he turned the record over. All right, she didn't want to talk either — not to him. A flute and a harp played together, blithe as children. She sat and closed her eyes. She felt exhausted. The music faded as she withdrew into herself in search of peace.

His voice woke her: her name, or some word. "What's the matter?" she said irritably.

"You were asleep."

"Yes, I know that." Perhaps he didn't want to be left alone while he was tripping, but he would never let her doze: he was like a spoilt child who couldn't bear a moment's inattention to him.

He gazed at her reproachful stare. "Don't you want to?"

"What?"

"You know." He gestured at his genitals.

In their lovers' language they'd had a word for it. Now he resembled a child begging for a sweet. "Do you love me?" she said.

"Yeah," he said restlessly, and stood up. "Come on."

"No, you don't."

"All right then, I fucking don't. Christ, why do you want to be told all the time? Can't you feel it?"

"No." That was precisely the trouble.

He slumped on the bed. "What the hell. It doesn't matter."

She couldn't talk to him while he was in this condition. Either of them might say something they couldn't take back, and destroy their marriage. "I'm going out," she said.

"Go on then, fuck off."

She tramped downstairs, dizzy with suppressed emotions. Need she go out in order to talk? She knocked on Fanny's door. Was that sound the muffled echo of her knock? She pressed her ear against the door, but the silence seemed total; any sounds were inside her head. Suddenly she realized that the time-switch was about to give out. She would never find it in the dark. She ran toward the switch. Footsteps came behind her — her own, resounding. She jabbed the switch and ran down to the porch.

Glancing back from the van, she saw that only her window was lit. It couldn't have been Fanny, after all. Peter was alone at the top of the emptying house. Well, it was his fault. She drove to the Halliwells'.

Angie read her feelings. "Give Cathy a drink, Frank."

The alcohol released her speech — not that she needed much persuasion to talk. Talking relieved her, even if they couldn't help. "I don't know if it's worth it. I don't know if we have a marriage left anymore. I don't know if I want to keep us together because I love him or just because I can't bear to think of a marriage breaking up."

"What seems to be the problem?"

"Oh, Frank, for heaven's sake," said Angie, as though he were displaying typical male insensitivity.

But Cathy hadn't explained. "All sorts of things," she said. "He's been taking drugs."

Frank tapped his glass. "Well, so are we."

"Illegal ones, I mean."

"It must be a substitute for something," Angie said. "I think children would be good for both of you."

"We can't have children till we have a house."

Frank dawdled over pouring himself a whisky. He kept letting snatches of soda fizz into the glass. Eventually he said, "I can't promise anything."

Had she asked him to? Cathy blinked at him, bemused. "But I know of some houses that may be going cheap," he said. "They're no palaces, mind. They need improvement work. The thing is, there might be a way to get you a loan for the purchase. Someone owes me a favor. Don't count on it just yet. I don't want to build up your hopes."

When she drove home the night seemed mellow. The sodium glow that embraced houses looked like firelight, constant and warm. Was she just heartened by alcohol? Had alcohol made Frank encouraging? No, she was sure he could do what he'd said. He must be able to. She drove slowly, though she was eager to talk to Peter.

She parked. She was more drunk than she'd thought, too much so to have been driving: why, she was seeing a light beyond Fanny's curtains. She couldn't focus on it; it seemed dim and mobile. It must be the light from her window, leaking down to Fanny's. She climbed the emptily reverberating stairs.

CHAPTER XXX

"Frank says he may be able to wangle us a house."

"One we can afford? No chance."

"Yes, he thinks so. Really, Peter, we've got to move while we can. Houses will only get more expensive."

"Yeah? Well, I've been thinking too, and I think we're stuck here."

"That's what you'd like, is it?"

"Jesus, don't blame me for it. It's what has to be. Reality. Didn't you ever hear about that?"

"Maybe we will be stuck here, if you don't settle down to something."

"Like working in the libraries? You stay there if you want to. That's not worth shit."

"It's better than sitting around stoned all day."

"Oh, that's what you're getting at, is it? Did that fuckingfascist tell you what to say?"

"I don't need anyone to tell me what to say. You're so stupid about drugs. Bringing out that joint at your parents' — you only wanted to torment me. You're so stupid."

"Yeah, right."

"And you're sly, as well. You didn't want me to know you'd been taking acid with those bitches."

"Yeah, right."

"Is that all you're going to say?"

"Yeah, right."

"I can't talk to you. I want to go to bed."

"I'll bring myself down with some Librium, if you can stand having me in the same bed."

"Oh, don't be so stupid and self-pitying."

By now he was sure he had heard her voice before. It was the voice of the girl in the library who had been so curious about his search for Craig. If she lived here, that would explain everything: her curiosity, her pursuit in the fog.

It all made perfect sense. She was married to the creature with the long hair, or living with him and pretending to be married: he remembered the names he'd copied down. Their conversation showed how corrupt the creature was. Had Craig maintained a hold on him through drugs? Perhaps he was homosexual too. Would homosexuals wear beards? They might, to confuse people.

Or had the conversation been staged to delude Horridge? Had the creature recognized him on the stairs? Horridge had heard the girl drive away. Pretending they were poor when they owned a car — whom did they think they were kidding?

Perhaps they were trying to distract him while their friends in the police closed in. He should have killed the creature on the stairs and dragged him in here — but before he'd had the chance, the creature had scurried upstairs into his hole. Let them send their friends. There wouldn't be much left of anyone who came through that door.

Through the ceiling he heard the creak of a bed. Filthy animals — at least they would be too busy now to spy on him. Suppose the police were on their way? The prisons were full of homosexuals, as they ought to be. They weren't going to put him in there, in the squirming corruption. He would rather die — but they wouldn't force him to that, oh no. They were the ones he'd be cutting.

The candlelight plucked at his attention. Objects moved on all sides of him, as though the clutter of the painter's flat were closing in. The dim room jerked. No, his eyes weren't twitching nervously. He wished he could switch on the light, but he mustn't risk lighting up the window.

Stop this nervousness. The long-haired creature had looked blind with drugs. If he had recognized Horridge, the police would be here by now. Or were they biding their time until Horridge slept?

No, that wasn't their way. They enjoyed using force; he'd seen that on the television in the pub. There would be a mob of them to overpower him. He would be as helpless as Craig's victims, and perhaps they would do to him what Craig would have.

He hurried to make sure that the catch held the lock closed. His movements disturbed the flame. The wardrobe doors shifted. No, they hadn't opened; nobody had peered out and ducked back. There was nothing in there but an object, unable to threaten — just like his father.

He sat and stared at the flame. At last his gaze held it steady. The police weren't coming, no, no. He was safe here. When he'd realized that he could hide here, he'd realized almost simultaneously that he'd saved himself by leaving his payment book in Cantril Farm. Had he applied for his money the police would have pounced at once.

He couldn't stay here forever. Where could he get the money to take him to Wales? Dim objects tiptoed toward him, and retreated. Surely circumstance would come to his aid. After all, he was in the right.

He felt both chilled and coated with sweat. He crept to the bathroom. The candlelight tried to make him avoid shadows and collide with their objects. He dared to switch on the bathroom light; it couldn't reach the window. Should he stay in here, where it was brighter? But he would feel trapped.

He scrubbed himself, and searched for a towel that he could use. All of them smelled of the painter, a cloying sweetish scent. Eventually he had to use one. The scent clung slyly to him. Outside the bathroom things moved in the dimness, conspiring. When a face appeared, his snarl of fear rasped his throat. He had to stare at the face with its protruding ears before he was convinced that he knew it: his face in the bathroom mirror.

His stomach felt queasy. He had to use the toilet. He left the bathroom door open, so as not to be closed in. In the main room things moved stealthily to watch him. He found to his disgust that the painter had no lid with which to cover the toilet. His face stared up, drowned in filth. Though it risked alerting Craig's spies upstairs, he pulled the chain.

The candlelight fluttered as he emerged. What had disturbed it? Had the wardrobe doors just closed? No, he wasn't deluded so easily. There was a faint unpleasant smell: paint, probably. Why wasn't there any air freshener? Because the painter had scorned cleanliness, of course.

He felt observed. He'd left the lighted bathroom open; now he lit the kitchen. The bright rooms looked as though they were threatening to stage a shock, and they made the outer room more dim.

Should he lie down and try to sleep? No, he needed to keep his wits about him. Besides, there was no bed. She must have slept in Craig's. Horridge wouldn't have touched her bed if she had had one: it would have been infected.

What was observing him? No, it was none of the dim twitching objects; nothing was raising its head to peer at him. But there were hidden eyes in the room. They were hiding from him on the draped canvas. He'd bring them out into the open. That would settle them.

When he uncovered the canvas, the candlelight shook. The face that stared up at him writhed as though ashamed; its eyes gleamed. Was this another mirror? Or was the light deforming the face? When at last he was sure that it was a painting of himself, the tension of his entire body twisted his hands into claws.

So she had been completely in Craig's power. She must have meant to show her painting to the police. Had he killed her before she'd done so? His warped hand dragged out his razor. He began to slash the face. Flakes of its eyes and other features rustled down the canvas. When the face was a scraped blur, he slashed the canvas into streamers.

He sank back on the chair, smiling. So much for the trap she'd tried to set for him. Now she could do nothing: she was lifeless and locked away, as she ought to be. Let her clutter leap about frantically; it didn't impress him. It looked scared of him, as well it might.

The room steadied. That was right, just let it keep still. He nodded approval. The flame moved sleepily, gentle as firelight. He remembered the cottage, mellowed by the glow. The light lulled him. He nodded, and dozed.

The cottage was near, and the quarry. He must stop dawdling. He struggled dreamily to his feet and limped toward the wardrobe. Somehow he managed not to trip up. How had he acquired so much junk? He must have strewn the floor in order to select what to pack.

His eyes were glued half-shut by sleep. The wardrobe looked unfamiliar. Never mind musing — he wanted to be sure that his payment book was safe. The wardrobe doors opened for him, or seemed to, though he had to help them.

His coat had fallen. It lay huddled on the bottom of the wardrobe. Or was it his coat? The light was so dim. He leaned closer. Dear God, it was one of Craig's victims. He must release the sufferer, if it wasn't too late.

Only when he turned to hurry to the light switch did he realize where he was. His movement plucked at the flame of the remaining stub of candle. Oh God, he'd blown it out! He felt darkness surge out of the wardrobe behind him, hands outstretched. But the flame calmed at last, though it sputtered intermittently. He had to close his eyes before he could turn back and slam the wardrobe doors.

He dragged the chair to the patch of brightness from the lighted rooms. Paper tore beneath its legs. He sat staring at the wardrobe, whose doors moved feebly. No, she couldn't get out. She was too weak.

He couldn't spend another night like this. He must escape — to Wales. There was nowhere else in the world that he felt would welcome him. How could he get there? Steal aboard a train? Walk all the way? The thought dragged his lips harshly over his teeth.

Dawn sneaked into the room. The curtains stained it purple, as though to signify the painter's continuing presence. When sunlight reached through the curtains, it seemed not to touch him. He was imprisoned in his skull, trying to see his way to Wales.

Upstairs the bed creaked. Did they indulge their filth in the mornings as well? He heard the pad of footsteps, brief mutters, more creaking. A low conversation began. They didn't want him to hear — they must be talking about him. He strained his ears.

"Will you meet me from work?" the girl was saying. "We haven't walked in the park for ages."

There came a muffled sound that might have been assent. What did the conversation mean? It was obviously false, this friendliness after last night's row. Perhaps they were arranging not to be there when their friends came for Horridge.

Once the girl had passed his door, he tiptoed to the window and parted the curtains narrowly. As she hesitated by the van before walking away, he saw her face. Yes, it was the girl from the library. The confirmation made him feel in control again.

The girl and her creature must have been completely in Craig's power. The entire house must have been. She hadn't wanted Horridge

to know she lived here; that was why she'd followed him by bus —
because he would have recognized the van.

Now only she and the long-haired thing could recognize him. He
ought to finish them: the world would be better off without them. As
an achievement, that seemed unsatisfactory; he would still be trapped
here. If only there were some way of —

His mouth fell open. He didn't care that he must look like a
simpleton. Yes — yes, of course! That was the way! It was so simple.
It solved all his problems.

He gazed about triumphantly. Strips of canvas dangled; the
wardrobe doors were closed and still. Those things he'd conquered.
Now he must plan his final victory. How lucky he was to be alone,
without distractions! It allowed him to think everything through clearly.

How was he to achieve his purpose? He made for the bathroom,
to splash cold water on his face. That would wake up his thoughts.
He hadn't reached the door when he heard rapid footsteps on the drive.

As he ran to the window, the easel seemed to dodge into his path.
His limping tripped it up. Never mind the crash — he must see who
was approaching. It was only the postman, who ducked into the porch
and emerged again quickly.

Horridge let the curtain fall. The easel lay silent, playing dead.
Had anyone heard the crash? Probably only the long-haired creature,
who would be too timid to do anything. Suppose he came down to try
and find out what had happened? Horridge grinned; that would help
his plan.

He began to slash the face.

CHAPTER XXXI

Peter heard Cathy leave the house. Should he have gone with her to Fanny's exhibition? He didn't want to be bored by that stuff. But having been closer to the girls than to Cathy made him feel guilty, irritable. Oh come on, he'd promised to meet her tonight.

He watched her from the window until she disappeared toward Lodge Lane. The park looked calm and vivid; its colors stilled him. He could see so many, thanks to the acid. He hoped the effect would remain.

He ought to do some work today — but you should leave the day after a trip clear for re-entry into normal consciousness. Still, the Librium had made him tranquil, not at all nervous of failure. Should he write? Here came the postman, to delay his decision.

He heard the patter of letters, and went downstairs. Jesus, he was the only person in the house — except for the guy with no name on his bell, who must have made that noise a few minutes ago. He didn't feel in charge of the house — more as though he were abandoned in it. His footsteps rattled in the empty rooms.

All right, he knew he and Cathy ought to move. He was inert, he knew that. He saw himself all too clearly — that was part of his trouble. But it wasn't his fault if they couldn't afford to move. He didn't want charity from that fascist.

He sorted through the post. Nothing for him, except a bill. Wasted journey. He glanced at a card with a Welsh postmark — from Fanny? No, it was addressed to her.

What happened? Wouldn't your fans let you get away?

At least give us a ring so we know you're all right. We
hope you'll still be coming.

Surely she'd gone last Thursday. Cathy had told him so. At least,
she was supposed to have gone. Were her friends right to be anxious?
Might she be lying injured in her flat?

He climbed slowly to the middle landing. Now he reflected, the
fall he'd heard had sounded too loud to have come from the ground
floor. Had it been in her flat? He hesitated outside her door. If she
answered it and proved unharmed, he'd feel ridiculous. He didn't even
like her; that would make it more embarrassing.

At last he knocked, so softly that he might have been pretending
not to. Come on, if that was the best he could do it wasn't worth doing.
He knocked again, and bruised his knuckles.

While he rubbed his knuckles there was silence. Then he heard
a sound beyond the door, brief but definite: an object being dragged?
He strained his ears, but could hear only their own murmur. "Fanny?"
he called.

Silence displayed his voice to him. He called again, and felt ludi-
crous. Here he was, standing in the middle of an almost empty house,
calling, "Fanny, Fanny." If she didn't want to answer, that was up to
her. He trudged upstairs.

Now he was uneasy. He didn't think she was particularly fond of
him — but was that a reason why she wouldn't answer? Could she be
unable to? Cathy had thought she'd heard noises in the flat last night.
Perhaps she hadn't imagined them.

He could at least push the card beneath Fanny's door. Still, there
was another, more adventurous possibility. He went into the kitchen,
and gazed out at the fire escape. He wouldn't be able to work until
he knew whether anything was wrong. Besides, the adventure would
be more exciting than work.

He carried the kitchen chair to the window, and raised the sash.
It rattled loudly, unused to being disturbed. The maneuver proved to
be more difficult than he'd expected: he had to clamber over the sink,
and was forced to sit on it for a moment. Would it give way? It held,
and he struggled over the windowsill.

When his heel struck the iron platform, the entire fire escape vibrated audibly. Jesus, this wasn't so much fun after all. Oh come on, the thing wasn't going to fall down. He wormed himself noisily beneath the sash, and stood on the platform.

He felt victorious. Beneath him the back yards and gardens were ranked, penned in by brick walls. Nobody employed him; he was free. Cathy wouldn't dare stand here. Wasn't that another reason why they ought to move? Suppose there were a fire?

He descended the iron stairs, which quivered. He moved slowly, to steady them and his pulse. Fanny's kitchen window was wide open. Did that mean she was at home? Perhaps — but not that she was unharmed.

He hesitated, peering into the part of the bare kitchen the window revealed. His blurred shadow made it dim. Eventually he leaned in. Metal gleamed sharply at him: a knife on the draining board, beside a rolling pin. The kitchen was deserted. Dare he climb in? He felt bold yet vulnerable, like a child.

Out of the empty kitchen a voice whispered, "Peter."

He recoiled. The guillotine of the sash chopped the back of his neck. He swore; of course, the whisper had come from the main room. It must be Fanny. "What?" he hissed, feeling like a parody of a conspirator.

"Peter, help me."

Clambering through the window was more of a task than emerging from his own had been. At last he succeeded in thrusting his feet past the sink. He grabbed the sink and let himself fall, jarring his ankles.

At once a voice said, "Now close the window, quickly."

It wasn't Fanny's voice. A man had come into the kitchen — the man who had watched him and Craig, and who'd skulked near the house. "What are you doing in here?" Peter demanded. "Where's Fanny?"

The man limped within arm's reach. Peter remembered the figure on the landing, whose stance had been deformed. "Make less noise," the man said with a kind of tight-lipped glee, "or I'll cut you. Close the window."

In his hand a razor glared. Immediately Peter was seized by his nightmare: his body was hacked open like meat, like Craig's. He was paralyzed. Could he shout for help? Could he struggle with the man?

Craig had been stronger, and he'd been no match for a razor. Already Peter could feel his fingers slashed to uselessness.

"The window. I won't tell you again."

Even if Peter shouted, the razor would finish him long before help arrived. He reached out and closed the sash; compulsion rather than thought dragged his hands down. Their trembling dismayed and infuriated him. His stomach felt like the whirlpool of a drain.

"Now then," the man said. "You're going to drive me to Wales."

Despite his panic, Peter felt close to hysterical laughter. It made his words jerky. "No chance, brother. I can't drive."

Before he could move, the razor flicked toward his right eye. The pain was steely cold, but the liquid that spilled down his face was warm. He had to struggle to raise his hand, to discover where the blade had touched him: just below the eye.

"You're going to drive me to Wales."

"Jesus Christ, are you mad?" Peter screamed. "I can't drive!"

"Shall I cut you again? I've told you once to make less noise."

Peter's hands writhed, struggling to signify his truthfulness. "You've got to believe me." Blood trickled into his mouth. "My wife's the one who drives. I can't." This was grotesque; he was chatting reasonably, as though the man were a persistent hitchhiker. "I can't fucking drive," he moaned.

The man shook his head, as though offended. He advanced; the razor lifted. Peter's back thumped the corner beyond the window. He was trapped, with no weapon in reach. "Then you're no use to me at all, are you?" the man said.

CHAPTER XXXII

The library was clear. The last of the old people who converged on the light and warmth like moths had gone. Here was someone, knocking urgently on the doors. He wasn't Peter; he was a plaintive spinsterish man whose books were due for return today. Cathy accepted the books mechanically, and wondered where Peter was.

He must be on his way. She'd phoned the flat to remind him to meet her, but there had been no reply. She waited outside the library. Her colleagues hurried away. Cars whisked by; groups of people passed, chattering and laughing. The pair of telephone boxes shone, glass exhibition cases with nothing to show. A cold wind nagged at her.

Fanny's pictures had been startlingly cheap. A few were still unsold; she'd liked them all. Should she have bought one? Peter bought his comics without consulting her. Where was he?

On his way through the park, no doubt, and smoking a joint: that would rob him of his sense of time, among other things. She might as well meet him; waiting frustrated her. She dawdled along Lark Lane. The shops were dark, but light and a cheerful uproar filled the Masonic pub. A gargoyle leaned out from the old police station.

On Aigburth Drive the occasional lamps looked inadequate as matches stuck in the night. By squinting, she could just distinguish the van parked near the house. There was no sign of Peter. He must be in the park. He knew the route that she always used.

She walked down the path among the trees, avoiding heaps of turf cleared from the lawns. She was sure they could talk more freely away from the house; last night she'd had an irrational suspicion that they were being overheard.

A car droned along Aigburth Drive. When it had passed, silence closed in. The cold wind set trees creaking. Branches were intricately clear against the dim sky, and looked surrounded by an aura. They stirred delicately as ferns.

On her right was a tennis court. Beyond the wire netting, a shape squatted. She almost shouted at it, infuriated by her start of nervousness. But it wasn't Peter lurking to leap out at her. It was a heavy roller.

Now she was wary. It would be just like him to hide in the dark to scare her. Peering out from behind a tree, head wagging — but it was a bush. She hurried down to the lake. The park exhibited her footsteps, its loudest sound.

Above her, Eros stood on one tiptoe atop his pinnacle. In daylight he always looked as though he were waiting impatiently outside the café for someone to bring him an ice cream. Now the hovering life-size figure troubled her. It made her feel that it wasn't the only figure nearby.

She paced beside the lake, toward the bandstand. Violent wings fluttered on the water, which lapped nervously. The dark was crowded with shapes that moved on the edge of her vision, creeping around behind her. "Peter," she cried, enraged.

The silence returned her cry, flattened. For no reason that she could define, the sound made her fear for him. Had he had an LSD flashback? Might he be unable to meet her? She peered anxiously into the shelter near the bandstand, but all the shapes in there were darkness.

No doubt he was home by now, and wondering where she was. And of course he wouldn't understand why she had been worried. She must hurry home. Shapes were waiting for her: a group of bushes tall as men shifted restlessly beside the path. Were they all bushes?

Certainly they were. She knew that as soon as she'd passed them, when none of them had seized her. And those were only litter-bins that crouched on the forecourt of the café. A black stain spread across the sky, dimming the park. Cracked and wrinkled concrete snagged her feet.

Wasn't there one litter-bin too many? Rubbish — she'd never counted them. No, nobody was lurking on the benches by Eros. Nothing was sneaking after her except windblown litter. She hurried onto the avenue, toward the obelisk.

Had any of the bins moved? She glanced back. No, of course not. How stupid! Along the avenue, trees stepped out stealthily from behind one another. Again she looked back. None of the blurred shapes moved before the advancing darkness engulfed them.

Nearly home now. Just let him watch what he said if she found him waiting there. She hoped he was waiting. The obelisk grew nearer. It was wider than a man. Just let him jump out at her! Wasn't that a shadow protruding from behind it? No, only a wet patch on the ground. Nobody was hiding.

As she hurried toward the house she saw that the flat was dark. Oh, where could he be? Getting stoned, no doubt — leaving her to shiver on the dark deserted road. She glanced automatically toward the van, to check that nobody had interfered with it.

A thick strip of darkness outlined the nearside door — too thick. The door was ajar. Peter must have gone into the van for something — but why on earth couldn't he have locked it after him? Not that there was anything in there worth stealing.

She pulled the door back, and poked her head in to glance at the jumble of petrol cans, crumpled stained paperbacks for long journeys, the capacious old armchair for those who wanted to sit in it. Her harsh gasp made her cough. A couple was sitting in the armchair.

Good God, couldn't they find anywhere else? Her shock gave way to amused incredulity. She'd heard of squatters, but this was ridiculous. Why were they so still? The girl's head rested on the man's shoulder; his arm embraced her. Deep in Cathy's mind was bewilderment and worse. Dimly she made out that the long-haired one wasn't a girl at all, for he had a beard. Why, they were both men. She squinted at the face beneath the long hair. Why was it so desperately urgent that she see?

"Ah, there you are," the other man said. "Get in."

He sounded as though he were taking up a previous conversation. Her mind refused to work; all she could do was switch on the dashboard light. It revealed the detective whom Fanny had met, sitting with his arm around Peter. Peter's forehead was darkened by a large bruise, if it was nothing more serious. Dried blood linked the corner of his mouth to his right eye.

"Get in and make no noise," the man said.

Her mind seemed incapable of grasping the situation. She couldn't struggle past the notion that Peter was dead. She had no idea what to do. Who was this man?

As she faltered, his free hand reached toward the hand that dangled negligently beyond Peter's shoulder. She heard a slight click; a blade gleamed. His free hand pulled back Peter's right eyelid, exposing the moist white ball, unconscious or lifeless. She had never felt before how thin the skin of an eyeball was.

"I won't tell you again to get in."

She thought of Mr. Craig, and knew at once what this man had done to him. The police had caught the wrong man. Everything seemed unreal — that wasn't a detective, that wasn't Peter, that wasn't a razor — but nothing was unreal enough. The gear lever punched her leg as she clambered in.

"That's right. Now close the door. Get behind the wheel. Start the engine. Gently. You wouldn't like my hand to jerk, would you?"

Perhaps if she obeyed everything he said, immediately, not questioning, the nightmare which threatened her wouldn't arrive. Surely this must end soon — but she knew it had hardly begun. In the mirror she saw the dull gleam of the blade, hovering before Peter's eye.

"You're going to drive me to Wales," the man said.

"You're going to drive me to Wales," . . .

CHAPTER XXXIII

She could only concentrate on driving, in the hope that that would hold back her panic. She mustn't make a single error. The traffic lights at Sefton Park Road jolted the van slightly; so did those at Lodge Lane. Each time the hovering gleam wavered.

"That's right," the man said. "Just you go slowly. We don't want the police stopping us, do we? You won't be able to stop me now."

He sounded as though he had a personal score to settle with her. The steering wheel's jacket was already damp with her sweat. "Which part of Wales do you want me to drive to?" She was trying to gain some hold on the situation, but her voice was jerky, uneven.

"Oh, don't you know? All right, we'll pretend you don't. You just keep going until I tell you not to."

He was insane. She was beginning to realize that now. If she told him he'd mistaken her for someone else, that might make him worse. Her hands were shaking. When she grasped the wheel, it trembled. She had to slow the van still more as it maneuvered over the potholes of Lodge Lane.

"No need to go to sleep. We can move a bit faster than that. What do you think you're driving, a hearse? Eh, a hearse?"

He was laughing, a dry insect sound. She halted the van beside a block of dark shops; a broken window grinned jaggedly. Perhaps he would attack her, but she couldn't go on like this. "I can't drive if you hold that so close to him," she muttered dully. "I can't concentrate. I won't risk it."

"Don't you tell me what to do!" His voice was thin and vicious.

The blade gestured before Peter's face. "I've got the upper hand now! I'll cut him again!"

Her indifference hardly shocked her; the nightmare had drained her emotions. In any case, Peter might be dead. "That won't do you any good. It won't make me drive."

He stared at her in the mirror. Her face felt slack, too burdened to show concern. At last the blade drooped beside Peter's shoulder. "All right," the man said. "Now get on with what you're here to do. And just remember, I've had enough of all your tricks. I'll have his eye out in no time."

It had begun to rain. She wished she could feel it on her cheeks, to refresh her. The van's cacophony of small noises surrounded her, refusing to be left behind. The smell of petrol had turned cloying; it clung to her nostrils. In the mirror heads swayed, and the gleam.

Rain glittered on splashes of light outside pubs. It slashed headlamp beams obliquely, and made the van sound like a tin can beneath a storm. Vague lights drifted underwater on the roadway. Shops and terraced streets glistened blackly. A few people ran, hiding their heads.

She drove across the lights at Smithdown Road. "Where are you going?" the man demanded.

His voice twitched her hands on the wheel. "To the tunnel," she said almost angrily.

"Is that so. Just make sure you've no idea of heading for Cantril Farm."

A Bingo hall swam up, spreading its carpet of light. Another set of traffic lights stood on the roots of their deformed reflections. She turned left, hurling a puddle aside.

"Where are you going now?"

"To the tunnel. That's the way to Wales."

"I know the way. Don't think I don't. You've underestimated me long enough."

She mustn't answer. His words might drag her into his madness. Whenever she spoke to him she felt her mind unfocusing. She drove. Rain pelted the van; rain rushed incessantly over land bared by demolition. It emphasized her metal cell.

The van rolled downhill, toward the city center. Ahead and to her left was the University clock. Nearly five to ten. Surely the downtown streets would be crowded. Mightn't someone see what was wrong? Mightn't they call the police or even be quick enough to overpower the man before he injured Peter permanently — if he hadn't already done so?

Rain streamed down bright display windows. Streams deepened in the gutters. Rainbow patches of petrol shone on the roadway, amid the riot of neon. London Road was almost deserted. A few couples hurried, or huddled in doorways; somber figures queued in a chemist's. Whenever anyone crossed in front of the van, the gleam lifted in the mirror.

The empty foyer of the Odeon sailed by on its amber glow. Two men were striding away from the cinema. Could she call out, wrench the van off balance, disarm the man? He might go berserk, and even her nightmare failed to show her what would happen then.

She drove toward the Mersey Tunnel. There were few pavements now. Cavernous subways led beneath the roadway, but nobody was walking. The tenements of Gerard Gardens stood close to the road, deafened by incessant traffic.

The tunnel closed overhead. It was bright and pale as a hospital corridor, and seemed as ominous. Rear lights led her along the subterranean trail. She felt the city pressing on the tunnel, and then the weight of the river. She was trapped and helpless as a puppet in a tin box.

Overhead lights flicked by. In the mirror the faces flickered monotonously with shadow; the image in the frame looked like a senile film — unreal, unconvincing. Peter was so still. She hadn't seen or heard him breathing. Mightn't he be dead? If he were, that would end the nightmare; she could jump from the van at the far end of the tunnel, without worrying about him.

Her thoughts — surely they weren't hopes — dismayed her. She mustn't think such things, she must plan how to save him. Somehow, when she halted at the toll booth, she had to alert the man in the booth without letting the madman see.

She passed the halfway sign: LIVERPOOL/BIRKENHEAD. The tunnel was interminable; its vanishing point receded like an optical illusion. Sweat stung her eye. She dabbed the trickle away, blinking and weeping. She must clutch the tollman's hand when she paid him, and show him with her eyes that something was wrong behind her. Suppose he spoke and gave her away?

The string of red lights dawdled uphill. A string of white lights was let down beside them. The vanishing point became a curve in the tunnel, and crept forward. Nearly there. It'll work, she reassured her shaking hands.

An arch of glaring light advanced down the tunnel, dazzling her; a driver had neglected to switch off his headlights. She was groping stealthily in her handbag for the toll, so as not to betray to the man with the razor what was coming, when he spoke.

"Just one thing before we get there. Don't try talking to your friends in the pay box."

Had he known all the time what she was planning? Could he read her mind? The mirror flashed a warning. The gleam looked as though it was touching Peter's unprotected eye.

If the van jerked, if a car in front halted suddenly, if her hands (which felt cramped by panic) twitched on the wheel— Cars nosed between the booths and sped away. Paid, the red signs sprang to green. She mustn't do anything here. Later she could take him off guard, jam on the brakes, attack him with something: not now, not when the razor was so ready.

A green light passed the car ahead. She inched the van into the space, and rolled the window down. It would be all right, the man in the booth couldn't see behind her. She had the correct money, she wouldn't need to wait for change, the madman wouldn't have time to wonder if she was planning to trick him. She tried to stop her hand from trembling as it lifted the coins toward the booth. Her tightness seized her fingers with cramp, which jerked the coins from them. She heard the money fall on the road beside the van.

Oh dear God, please no! She didn't dare glance at the mirror. She wasn't trying to trick him, she wouldn't leave the van, she must slide the door open just a crack and reach down—

"It's all right, love," a man called. "I'll get it for you."

He had been chatting to the man in the next booth. As he strode over, she glimpsed a sharp flash in the mirror. Should she grab the money before the man reached it? But he was bending beside the van; coins clicked, or something did. When he straightened up, she saw he was a policeman.

She was paralyzed. Not until his uniformed arm, beaded with rain-drops, reached into the van could she stretch out her hand for the coins.

How ought she to sound so as not to arouse suspicion? Grateful, casual, cool? "Thank you very much," she said, and sounded like an extra who was unable to make her single line convincing.

He was staring past her. "What's the matter with your friend?"

Her tongue felt poisoned, swollen. Her mouth felt like a rag doll's, sewn. Mustn't she tell him? This might be her only chance of rescue. The taste of petrol churned in her. If she opened her mouth she might be sick.

She was struggling to force words past her panic when behind her the man said, "Too much to drink. He was in a bit of bother. We're taking him home."

Surely the policeman wouldn't believe that. She glanced at the mirror, and saw what he saw: two dim figures sitting in the back, one slumped against the other. Peter's injuries were mitigated by the darkness; the razor hid behind his hair.

After a while the policeman said, "Yes, he looks as if he's had enough. You'd better take care of him."

He stared at Cathy, then reached for her hand. Was he about to give it a secret clasp, to tell her he'd seen what was wrong? No, he'd scrutinized her only to judge whether she was sober, and now he was taking the toll from her hand to pass to the booth. The green light sprang up ringing.

"Good night," the policeman said, and turned away. Cathy's hands clenched on the wheel. Was she about to cry for help? Perhaps, but she subsided miserably. From beside Peter's face the gleam had crept out, ready.

CHAPTER XXXIV

She drove toward Chester. Her mind felt empty as a balloon. Though the rain had slackened, few people were about in Birkenhead. Roads and pavements reflected desertion and bright windows. Other places passed beside the main road: Port Sunlight, Bromborough, Ellesmere Port. None was as present as the watchful face in the mirror. Beside the swaying razor, Peter's eyelids twitched.

So he was alive. Or had only shadows moved? Before she could read his face, which looked like a mask in the sodium glow, the street-lamps swept behind. Night seized him. From the darkness the man's voice murmured, "Just you keep still if you know what's good for you."

Peter was moving, then. She was distressed by how little that heartened her: if anything, it made her more tense. Peter might begin to struggle, inadvertently or otherwise. Oncoming headlights displayed the faces in the mirror. Peter's face was still, perhaps unconscious. The man's eyes flickered warily.

Afterimages of headlights clung to her eyes. She felt insomniac, light-headed. Was her mind trying to comfort her with the cliché that it was all a dream? She knew that it was nothing of the sort, though her emotions had fallen into a doze. She couldn't plan any escape, for she didn't know how Peter might react and couldn't communicate with him. Lights drew the tableau of faces into the mirror and let them collapse into darkness.

Abruptly the man spoke. Were the lights bothering him? He sounded dangerously irritable. "Don't take all night. We've a long way to go."

Petrol stations passed, bright as day. Occasional houses blinked between trees. Her patch of light unrolled the road. Everything outside the van seemed unreal, unattainable as a film on a screen. The van enclosed her with the nightmare, from which everything else was separate.

She bypassed Chester, and headed for North Wales. "That's right," the man said approvingly. Was he becoming amiable? Might he let them go? But he said, "Trying to tell me you didn't know where we were going. You won't see me falling for that, oh no."

She must halt at the next petrol station. She must try to escape instead of avoiding thoughts of how the drive might end. The next petrol station was dark. Her light gleamed in the extinguished faces of the pumps.

When she hesitated at a signpost he said impatiently, "Go on, don't be pretending you don't know the way." In the mirror his hand pointed irritably, and she turned the van in that direction. They were heading for Corwen in North Wales, it seemed.

Now there were few headlights other than hers. The blur of her light fled incessantly over the monotonous road. Hedges paled and vanished, grass blades sprouted light. Around her the huge night was empty.

How could he tell in the darkness that she was driving where he wanted to go? She dared not speak, in case he began to tell her of his plans. Apart from the creaks and jangling of the van, silence lurked behind her. Once she turned and stared into the dark, afraid of what might be happening there. His voice exulted: "No, I'm not asleep. You needn't think I am."

The patch of light went on, and on. The night was featureless. His voice clung to her ears. She stared dully at a glow ahead, above the hill that she was climbing. A wind blundered against the van, unnerving her.

The glow resembled the ghost of a dawn. Was it a fire? No, it was steady. As the van clambered uphill, she felt hope struggling to rise. Oh, please say that the light was — please let it be — The van plunged down the slope. The light blazed from a petrol station.

The forecourt looked deserted. Only when she was almost there did she see that one upright shape was a man, for his sleeves flapped in the wind. He stood beside a pump, which he was repairing. The petrol station wasn't open, after all. That didn't matter! He was someone, he was help! "I've got to get some petrol," she said.

The click came at once; the razor brandished light. "Oh no you haven't. Do you think I can't see all these cans? You've got plenty here."

"They're empty," she pleaded, almost weeping.

"They better hadn't be, for your sake and his."

But they were. As the van slowed, the man beside the pump waved her away. *Closed*, his lips pronounced soundlessly. Couldn't she drive at him, infuriate him, make him board the van, enraged? The blade was still now, and looked to be touching its victim.

She drove miserably. It was impossible to tell whether she had enough petrol, since she had no idea where they were bound. Perhaps he would only strand them when the petrol ran out, so that they couldn't call the police.

The smells of the van grew stronger, more sickening. The metallic clamor tormented her nerves. Was any of those sounds the click of the blade? Her patch of light seemed hindered by the night, and hardly moving.

The sky glowed ahead. It couldn't be dawn yet, though she felt she'd been driving forever. Whatever the glow was, it couldn't help her. If only she had grabbed the policeman!

The glow hovered over Corwen. She drove across a bridge. Beneath it, unseen, the River Dee rushed darkly. Slate houses surrounded her with the color of fog. Inns passed, striped like zebras. A clock showed that it was nearly midnight. The long street was deserted. If just one person appeared— What? What could she do?

"My father brought me here once, in a proper van." The man's conversational tone was more than grotesque; it was frightening, for he sounded sure of himself, of his plan. "You thought I'd forget the way, did you? Oh no. My mind isn't so easily snapped."

The van echoed beneath a railway bridge. The long street led her through a market square. From the street, alleys of slate houses climbed a looming mountain. It was a small unspoilt town—the kind of place she would have liked to visit with Peter. At the back of her mind was a notion, heavy and immovable as a rock, that she would never see this place again.

She was still praying for someone to appear when Corwen and its light retreated and faded. The night led her into itself. Mouths of side roads glimmered briefly; beyond them all was darkness. She was hardly aware now of driving.

"Oh no," the man was muttering. "You all think you're so clever. You didn't think I had this place to come to, did you? You aren't so infallible as you'd like to think."

Something was wrong. He sounded nervous and threatening. Wind tugged at the van, almost snatching the wheel from her slippery hands. Abruptly he demanded, "Where do you think you're going?"

Panic rose in her throat, harsh and thick. He had lost his way in the dark. She swallowed, choking. At last she managed to calm her voice enough to say, "Where you want to go."

"Oh, this is where I want to go, is it?" Sibilants hissed viciously. "Don't try that on with me, you bitch. Just don't try."

The van edged forward; she seemed hardly in control of her limbs. Her voice shook. "Well, you tell me where you want to go."

"Don't try that, either. You won't confuse me, don't bother trying. Shall I make him scream? Will that help your driving?"

The van advanced, inexorable as her nightmare. What could she say that he wouldn't distort, that wouldn't madden him further? All at once he shouted, "Stop here."

He was going to finish them. The night was on his side; there was nothing but dark for miles. "Stop here," he snarled again before, dully, she could do so.

The headlights made a milestone blaze. She felt him leaning forward. The razor was approaching. Sickened, she lowered her head to hide her throat beneath her chin. But he was staring beyond her. "There it is," he said.

He was gloating again. What hallucination was he seeing, out there in the dark? "You thought you'd pass it when I wasn't looking," he muttered. "Very clever of you. But you didn't succeed, did you? Left past the milestone. That's where we're going."

At last she had to move the van. Reluctance weighted her limbs. If he had mistaken the landmark, what would he do then? If not, they were approaching the end of the journey. What had he in store?

To the left of the milestone was a road of sorts. It wound uphill. The van lurched and swayed, almost beyond her control. Where was the razor? She fought the wheel as the van plunged splashing into a flooded dip.

The road writhed unpredictably. Her surroundings were included in her nightmare now, a maze of stone and blinding darkness. Infrequent slate walls blazed spikily. Trees glinted with raindrops, as though the branches were crowded with watching birds. For a moment she saw their bodies, black and still.

She felt as though she were struggling with fever. She was suffocated by the churning of the van, its monotonous frustrated roaring, the vindictive antics of the road, the stench of petrol, the ominous silence behind her. How long was it before a gray shape loomed ahead—a slate box, a building, a cottage? "Here we are," the man said.

Exhausted and almost resigned, her shoulders began to slump. Could this really be the destination he'd taken so much trouble to reach? Was he unable to see that the windows were empty, the door askew? Shadows peered out at the van. The cottage could not have seen a light at night for years.

She heard his indrawn breath. Oh God, he'd seen! Would he turn on her now, or force her to drive until the petrol gave out? But he sounded as though he'd had a sudden inspiration. "Just keep going until you're told otherwise."

The van ground uphill. The road climbed tortuously. The wheels slipped on fragments of slate, screaming. Objects plodded out of the night—a dead tree split down its middle; a small cairn, half collapsed. Now there was a notice board, lying on its face beside the track. What did it say? Her light had scarcely touched it when he said, "That's right. Stop here. We're going to stretch our legs."

She tried to grasp her frantic thoughts. Once they were out of the van, could she knock him down and drive away with Peter? His limp would help her outrun him—but she must be able to make a quick getaway. "Shall I turn the van?" she said, praying that it didn't sound like a plea.

"Oh yes, you do that." He sounded indifferent or secretly amused.

She had turned it only halfway—it was facing across the track, illuminating a waste of surfaces of slate—when he said, "All right, stop now. Leave the key in the lock, or whatever you call it. Now get out."

She would be leaving Peter alone in the van with him. The jagged slate was harsh underfoot. The headlamps spotlighted the bare gray stage. She stood gripping the door, unable to move away. "Go on, Catherine Angela Gardner," the man said.

How could he know her name? His voice sounded like the sentence of a judge in a nightmare. The blade stirred restlessly. Bewildered, unable to hold onto her thoughts, she backed away slowly.

"Keep going. Get away from the van. Right away. Now stay, you bitch."

She could see nothing within the van. The headlamps blazed at her; above them the windscreen was opaque as thick ice. The silence isolated sounds of muted scuffling. Please let him decide that he wouldn't drag Peter, please let him come out alone. She would win somehow. Every loose chunk of rock was a potential ally.

When he emerged at last, Peter was with him. They staggered out like a seaside postcard's parody of drunkenness. The lump on Peter's forehead was larger, and shone purple. The line of dried blood still marked his face, like ink from an untidy child's pen. He looked drowsy, hardly aware of his situation, perhaps concussed — and absolutely helpless. A yearning to protect him, a refusal to believe that he was going to die, seized her. She felt nauseous and dizzy.

The man propped him against the radiator grill, where he slumped a little. "Go on," the man said to Cathy. "Walk until you're told to stop."

Desperation, or her distance from him, gave her the courage to say, "No, I won't. I'm not leaving him with you."

"Oh yes you are." The razor flicked up. "Or I'll take his face off."

His threats were growing wilder. Mightn't they be mere words? But the blade flashed; blood started from beside Peter's eye. She felt like screaming or sobbing, or both: anything to express her powerlessness. Her feet did that for her, as she trudged stumbling backwards, away from the light.

"That's right. Keep going. No need to look. I'll tell you when you've gone far enough."

She glanced behind her. At the dim edge of the light, the ground dipped. Was that her chance? Once she reached the dip, perhaps she could stay below the light and circle round behind him — if the cold didn't make her too clumsy: her limbs felt embedded in ice. If she could take him off guard, she would do whatever was necessary to rescue Peter.

She was almost there. Oh, please let the slope beyond the light be steep enough! Please let her be able to dodge behind him quickly, without making a noise! There mustn't be any loose stone to trip her. She must be careful yet swift.

She glanced back toward the lights, to pretend she had no plan. Peter was sagging against the radiator. The man was gazing intently at her; perhaps he would gaze for a while, to make sure she didn't disappear. Please make him gaze. She backed to the blurred edge of the light, and stepped off.

She felt her foot plunge into nothingness.

It threw her off balance, and she fell. Her other knee crashed down on the slate. The explosion of pain dulled her thoughts. For a moment she believed there was only a slight drop beneath her, exaggerated by the return of her old phobia. It was only a dip in the ground, just a short slope— Then she heard how long it took a dislodged piece of slate to fall.

Her knee slid down the slope, scraping over rock. Both her legs dangled into the quarry. Her frozen hands scrabbled at the edge, and managed to drag her to a kneeling position. She struggled panting to her feet. The night and the headlamps shook with her pulse. She had scarcely risen when the wind seized her and flung her back.

This time her legs cleared the edge completely. There was no chance of dragging herself to her knees. There was no hold for her clutching fingers. Her nails were no match for the edges of slate, which broke them. She was sliding into the bottomless dark. She knew it had an end, which would be jagged.

Ahead of her, distant as infinity, the figures stood between the lamps. She heard the man say "ah" in appreciation of her fall. He stepped forward. Behind him Peter, no longer supported, slumped toward the ground.

The man was coming to help her fall. He was impatient to be finished. She dragged at the stone with her hands, using her palms now instead of her useless nails. Her feet, whose weight tugged her down, struggled to fasten on something, anything, to help her clamber. Below her the unseen slate was unhelpful as ice. She stared numbly at the stone on which her hands were pressing. They were paralyzed there; if anything, her slippery palms were inching toward the edge.

She heard a scrape of rock, and then a blow. The thump sounded like the fall of a heavy stone—but it wasn't earth that it had struck. Her mind was too possessed by fear to admit hope. Nevertheless she stared toward the light.

Peter hadn't overcome the man, who was still limping toward her.

He must have struck Peter, who stood swaying in front of the van. She had been right not to hope.

A last surge of effort, instinctive as the clawing of a trapped animal, made her drag at the stone with both bruised palms and try to heave herself back onto the rim. Her body had never seemed so clumsy, or so heavy. Her hipbone struck the very edge of the quarry, and began at once to slide back into space.

She shoved frantically with both hands, and managed to roll over on her back. Her foot caught in a gash in the slate. She was no more than her own width away from the edge, and sliding toward it. She pushed again, and reached stone too rough to allow her to slide.

The man limped straight at her. His unsteady leg rose; he was going to kick her over the edge. She managed to crawl out of his path, but he turned at once and followed her. The light caught his face. His mouth was huge with blood like inexpertly applied lipstick. "You haven't done for me yet," he was muttering, muffled by blood.

She crawled backward, terrified. Her retreat seemed intolerably slow, but to clamber to her feet would delay her still more. The wind threw itself against her, trying to force her to the edge. Though he was limping, he was quicker now than she.

As he reached her and drew back his good leg to kick, his injured leg betrayed him. His foot slithered toward the rim. "You bitch," he screamed as he fell. She saw the edge of the quarry bite into his face. A long clamor of bumping and scraping fell into the dark. Nothing else came up from the quarry except, for a few seconds, a faint bony rattling of stone.

Peter stumbled toward her, still holding a fist-sized rock. It was brightly stained. He passed her and flung it into the darkness. After its thud, the scuttling of stone seemed unnervingly prolonged.

He stood at the edge, his whole body shaking. "Jesus, I did it," he mumbled to himself. "I did it." At last she succeeded in standing up, and went to hold him. She felt as though she might never again be able to speak. When she turned his face to her, she found he was shaking with laughter.

"You bitch," he screamed. . . .

EPILOGUE

Peter plodded along the street. The pavement blazed like chalk; the paint of all the houses shone as though fresh. Above Anfield the floodlights gleamed, though they were extinguished for the summer. He stepped off the pavement, into the house.

The silence was abrupt and violent. He closed his eyes to clear them of the street's glare, which clung to them and dimmed the stubby hall. Often the house was invaded by chanting from the football ground. Was that why the silence seemed unnatural?

No, it was only that Cathy was holding her breath, nervously waiting for him to announce himself. He dropped the carrier bag of vegetables. "Me," he called.

The ritual annoyed him. Why was she still nervous of any noise that entered the house? Why wasn't she answering? "Me," he roared.

At last he heard her gasping, "Yes." She was upstairs, and sounded short of breath. Was anything wrong? He climbed the stairs irritably; the treads reverberated, muffled by the close walls. On the walls hung two of Fanny Adamson's paintings. After he'd told the police to check her flat he'd impulsively visited her exhibition. He'd found that he enjoyed her work more since taking his trip. Cathy liked her paintings, and they might be an investment. As soon as the news of her murder was published, interest in her work had grown spectacularly.

He glanced proudly at the paintings. They hung well. He found he enjoyed using the drill for jobs around the house. There were still jobs to be done; some of the cheap improvements had been shoddy. Why wasn't Cathy speaking?

She lay naked on the bed. Sunlight through the curtains made her glow orange. Her exercises had tired her into silence. She lay smiling at something within herself. Was it hidden in her head, or was she experiencing the child in her large belly?

When he sat on the bed she opened her eyes. "How are you?" he said.

She seemed to debate whether to be honest. Her smile faded. "I'm depressed — I don't know why. I suppose depression is part of it. I expect it'll pass."

"We'll go and see the Halliwells if you like."

"Not if you don't want to."

At times he resented having to be grateful while repaying Frank's loan; it made their relationship uncomfortable. But he'd been grateful for the chance to take Cathy away from Aigburth Drive. "Oh, I don't mind," he said. "I can smoke a joint first."

She looked away, her face limp with resignation. "Maybe we'll just walk up to Stanley Park."

Perhaps he wouldn't smoke a joint; he could get pissed at Frank's instead. Not that he intended to stop smoking — Christ, he needed some relaxation. He took her hand. Was he displaying the razor scar on the back of his hand, to remind her that he wasn't weak?

She kissed the scar. What was she remembering? On the stage of glaring light he'd pretended to be still stunned, waiting to be sure the slasher was preoccupied with Cathy before he seized the chunk of rock: hard, heavy, jagged, satisfying. He'd felt the man's mouth cave in, but the razor had snapped at his hand like a bird of prey. He'd thought the blow had finished the slasher. The bruise on his forehead had sent him wandering dizzily, until he'd glimpsed the man advancing on Cathy. For a moment he'd thought the man had won.

Her lips moved on the scar. Was she avoiding speech? By smashing the man, Peter had revealed to her what he was capable of. He wasn't sure that they had come to terms with that revelation. Once, when he'd tried to talk about that drive to Wales, she had changed the subject. She had seemed guilty — he hadn't asked why.

All at once she clasped his hand. "I love our house. Don't you?"

"Yeah." She seemed more and more unpredictable. He'd had to grow used to her shifts in mood: her sobs at Fanny's paintings, her locked-in silences, sudden fits of weeping, starts of panic at no sound he could hear. For months she had been too tense for sex. Eventually she'd begun to relax, though sometimes crockery in her hands broke into a spasm of chattering, as though she were trying to hold still a poltergeist. Now, like the limp which her fall had given her, her apprehension was fading. Or was her calm the product of brittle control?

She took his pondering for suppressed impatience. "I'll make dinner in a minute," she said.

"No hurry. Nobody's coming to visit. You rest a bit if you like."

They were gentle with each other now, perhaps warily. They hadn't had a row since the identikit picture. The police had shown them a book of eyes, noses, mouths, from which to compose the face. They hadn't agreed on a single feature. "For Christ's sake, let me do it," Peter had snarled at last. "You're no use at all." But the sketch the artist produced to his instructions looked stiff and unconvincing. Neither he nor Cathy had been satisfied.

Her clasp was softer; its meaning had changed. Did she want to make love? Dimness flooded the room, then the orange blaze rushed back as the stray cloud moved on. He couldn't work up any desire; the positions her pregnancy forced them to adopt seemed too absurd.

A noise in the hall saved him from seeming aloof. Her grip tightened spasmodically. "That's the postman, isn't it?" she demanded.

"Right. I'll go and see."

She let go reluctantly. Again her nervousness annoyed him. She ought to be happy now, with the house and the promise of the baby. Was he trying to shift his own unease by blaming Cathy for hers?

He had been lolling against a shoulder in the dark. Cold metal had caressed his face: a razor-blade. That had held him still while he gathered memories, blurred and incomplete: being supported half-conscious to the van, as though he'd been stoned out of his head on cake; Horridge in the kitchen, glancing at a rolling pin, seizing it and thumping Peter's skull. That had enraged Peter—but he'd slumped in the dark of the van, paralyzed by images of the razor. Only the sheer dullness of the drive had allowed his fear to drift away and enabled him to plot revenge.

Yes, it had been the postman. Envelopes overlapped in the hall. He was glad he'd smashed Horridge; pity he'd struck him only once. And he was still protecting Cathy. No need for either of them to be nervous.

He faltered on the landing. He felt odd; his forehead was tight with undefined apprehension. The landing was oppressively small and hot. He found the house less spacious than the large main room of their flat. He hadn't a room to himself, after all; the spare room was full of books, comics, furniture that they couldn't bring themselves to throw away. Soon they'd need the room for the child. He might sell his comics then, before the child ruined them. He didn't read them now.

Halfway down he was forced to halt. The light twitched, plucking at his vision. Outlines trembled; walls and stairs moved uneasily. He closed his eyes and waited for the flashback to recede. Christ, he'd thought he was over the flashbacks. He hadn't taken acid since before that night in Wales.

At last he was able to go downstairs, though the envelopes shifted a little over one another, like cards eager for a deal. All of them looked official. Was someone offering him a job? He hoped he'd be working before the birth. That gave him three months.

One letter was an advertising circular, forwarded from Aigburth Drive. He dropped it angrily. Eighteen months and they were still addressing stuff there. The other letters were from newspapers. Two invited him to be interviewed, one said there were no vacancies for trainee reporters.

Maybe one of the interviews would lead somewhere. Those he'd had so far had been dispiriting. One editor had sounded like a senile comedian. "When did you stop beating your wife? That's the way we have to phrase our questions. That's the secret of reporting." How could Peter work for someone as plastic as that?

"Nothing much," he called to Cathy, and stooped to pick up the circular.

The envelope had fallen on its face. For the first time he saw what was scribbled on the back, by whoever was now living in the flat on Aigburth Drive. The noose of apprehension tightened round his skull.

SOMEONE PHONED

He was reading too much into the words. They could mean a dozen things. Maybe someone had wanted to get in touch with him in search of dope.

SOMEONE PHONED AND WANTED YOUR ADDRESS

When at last Cathy had felt capable of driving away from the quarry, they'd gone in search of the police. By the time the police reached the quarry there had been no sign of Horridge. Peter had been secretly glad: they might have detained him over the killing, searched his flat, found his dope. Horridge had never been seen again, as far as the police could ascertain. They'd concluded that he must have crawled away somewhere to die.

SO WE GAVE IT TO HIM. WE HOPE THAT'S ALL RIGHT!

Upstairs the bed creaked. Cathy was preparing to come down. For a moment he glared at the envelope. Then he hurried to the kitchen, tearing the envelope as he went. ALL RIGHT! said the largest fragment before he tore it in half.

He strode into the back yard. The door to the alley drooped on its hinges. He must attend to that, before it fell. He scattered the envelope into the bin. Clouds were massing; shadows stepped forward within the gaping outhouse, into which his dazzled eyes could hardly see.

Thank Christ Cathy hadn't read it. What effect might her panic have had on the child? There would have been no need for panic. He dumped the contents of the kitchen bin on top of the fragments.

When he grabbed the bag of vegetables from the hall floor, Cathy was standing at the top of the stairs. "Wasn't there anything important?" she said wistfully.

"Not today." He glanced back as he returned to the kitchen. A shadow loomed on the front-door pane; the hall plunged into dimness. "Nothing worth bothering about," he called.

* * * * *

Printing and Binding for this Edition
by R.R. Donnelley & Sons Company, Harrisonburg, Virginia.

Typesetting and Production Services by The Typesetters,
Santa Cruz, California.
Half-tones by Grade-A Graphics, Santa Cruz, California.

*A 100-copy, boxed edition has been produced of this work,
signed and numbered by the author and artist.*

Book Design by Jeff Conner
Jacket Design by Mya Kramer
Proofreading by Merry Bilgere
Special Thanks to: Nancy Tracy, Dennis Etchison, and
Kirby McCauley for their help and support.